Hopes and Fears

By

T. A. Belshaw

For Rosy

For all of my wonderful readers.

Wishing you a very Merry Christmas.

Merry Christmas!

Christmas Book Hub prize

The characters and events portrayed in this book are fictitious. Any similarity to real persons, living or dead, is coincidental and not intended by the author.

Edited by Maureen Vincent-Northam

Cover design by: J. D. Smith Design

http://www.jdsmith-design.com

ISBN: 978-1-8383202-5-6

Books by T. A. Belshaw

Tracy's Hot Mail
Tracy's Celebrity Hot Mail
Out of Control
Unspoken
The Legacy
The Reckoning
Murder at the Mill

www.trevorbelshaw.com

Hopes and Fears

Chapter 1

Alice
Sunday 8th December 1940

The phone rang just as Miriam and I were clearing the dinner plates from my big, oak kitchen table to make way for what was sure to be a noisy and robust game of Animal Grab, a game similar in nature to snap, but instead of using normal playing cards the pack was made up from pictures of animals, and rather than yelling 'snap' when two cards with the same picture was placed on top of one another, the player had to shout out the noise the animal makes. Our evacuee children, Harriet and Stephen were very competitive and were much more eagle eyed and quicker to call out than Miriam and me.

I strolled through to the lounge at the front of the house and picked up the handset wondering who would call at that time in the evening. Most calls to the farm were made during the daylight hours.

'Hello, Alice, it's Godfrey.'

He didn't need to introduce himself; I'd have known his voice on the buzziest of connections. Godfrey was my gangster lawyer, so called because of the wide-lapelled, pin striped suits and the black fedora hat he wore, he also drove a car that wouldn't have been out of place in a James Cagney movie. He had just turned forty and although he was married, we had been lovers for over two years. As he was working at the War Office in London, I didn't get to see much of him. Apart from a fleeting visit on my 21st birthday, we hadn't been together since the weekend of September 7th when I had spent two unforgettable nights with him, sleeping under the stairs of a guest house and on the platform of an underground station as the German bombs obliterated the streets around us.

'Hello, Godfrey, how are you? I hope the bombing isn't too bad. They never tell us how awful it really is on the news reports.'

'It never changes much, Alice,' he replied sadly. 'We lost Jeremy Dart last week, he was working late over at Paddington, the office took a direct hit.'

'Oh, Godfrey, I'm so sorry. I know he was a good friend of yours.'

'My drinking partner,' Godfrey replied. 'The funeral is on Wednesday. I went to see his wife and kids last night.'

'That must have been awful.'

'They were quite stoic, Alice. People are beginning to accept sudden death as something they're just going to have to get used to and I don't think they were particularly close to be honest. I often wondered why he spent so much time at work, or stayed overnight at his club when he only lived a couple of miles away.'

'Still, his children will have to grow up without a father. That's so sad.'

'I know, I thought about my own kids and how they would feel when I got home.'

'Now I'm beginning to feel guilty again, Godfrey.'

'Please don't, Alice. You have no desire to break up my family. We share something special, something beautiful, but I'll grow old with my wife, we both know that.'

I decided to let the subject drop. I did love Godfrey, but he was right, we both knew our relationship couldn't go on forever.

'So, you've given me the sad news, I hope there's something a little happier coming next.'

'Oh, yes, of course, that's why I rang wasn't it.'

'Well, out with it, man,' I scolded.

'You remember in September, I promised I'd get home for Christmas? Well, I've sorted it. I'm only there for a few days though. I'll be coming home on Christmas Eve and going back on the twenty-ninth so I'm hoping we can meet up at some stage.'

'I'd love to, Godfrey, but shouldn't you be spending that precious time with your kids?'

'They're only there until Boxing Day morning. They're going to stay with Virginia's mother until the New Year. She organised it months ago when it didn't look like I could get back.'

'Well, in that case, I think I might be able to find a couple of hours. I'll check my diary.'

Godfrey laughed.

'It won't be Christmas Eve or Christmas Day, obviously, and I understand that you'll probably want to spend Boxing Day with your daughter and the evacuee kids, but how does the Friday sound? That would be the day after Boxing Day. We could spend the afternoon together and go for a meal or a drink in the evening.'

'That sounds perfect, Godfrey.'

'Great. I'll drop by on my way home to wish you a Happy Christmas. I should be in Spinton by seven-ish on Christmas Eve. I've got the use of a staff car so I won't have to bother with the trains.'

'I'll look forward to it. Take care, Godfrey, keep well away from those bombs.'

'I'll do my best, my darling. You take care too. I hope the weather is kind to you on the farm.'

I put the phone back on its cradle and walked back into the kitchen just as the deep, rumbling hum of German aeroplanes appeared overhead. London would cop it again tonight. I crossed my fingers and hoped Godfrey found somewhere safe to shelter.

Stephen and Harriet looked upwards as the low groan of the bombers passed over. Harriet reached out and took her brother's hand. 'Please let Mum and Dad be safe,' she said in a shaky voice.

My heart went out to them. We were sheltered from the worst of the war on our little farm in Northern Kent. Gillingham, a town less than ten miles away was bombed now and then but the closest we had come to disaster was when a huge unexploded bomb was found in a field on the farm that backs onto ours. The bomb disposal team had been called out one murky, Sunday morning when a farm worker found about twenty of the local kids hurling rocks at it trying to make the bloody thing explode. We still have no idea how it got there, the best guess is that the crew of a Heinkel bomber discovered there was one left over on the way home and needed to get rid of it before they landed.

I walked around the table, crouched between the frightened children and put my arms around their shoulders.

'Mum and Dad will be all right, don't worry about that. The bombers didn't get them last night and they won't get them tonight either.'

'They nearly got us though. Our house blew up.' Stephen turned towards me; his eyes wide.

'Ah, but they didn't hit your house, Stephen. They hit the gas main, that's what caused the explosion.'

Stephen was mollified.

'Yeah, they can't aim well enough to get Mum and Dad, can they, Aunty Alice?'

I straightened and pulled them to my bosom.

'They aren't that clever,' I said. 'Oh, that reminds me. Your mum said she'd telephone on Tuesday evening. I marked the date on the calendar. That will be exciting, won't it?'

As the children yelled 'YES!' I looked across the table towards Miriam who was wiping her leaky eyes on her apron, then I looked up at the ceiling as the seemingly endless drone of planes continued.

'Just go home and leave us alone,' I whispered.

Chapter 2

The card game was less boisterous than usual, the children's hearts weren't really in it. Every so often one, or both of them would raise their eyes heavenward as a new wave of aircraft flew over.

Martha, my two-year-old, on the other hand, took an almost obsessive interest in the game. Perched in her high chair between Miriam and myself, she watched the cards turn carefully, waiting for the pig to appear. As soon as she spotted it, she threw her arms in the air and let out a continuous series of grunts and oinks until a new card was placed on the table. Martha loved our pigs and spent a lot of time in the covered pen with the youngest of the piglets.

At eight, Martha was put to bed and the rest of us sat in front of the fire sipping at mugs of milky Ovaltine while Miriam and I told stories about what life was like in Spinton before the war. Because the next day was a school day, the kids went to bed at eight forty-five. As I tucked them in, I gave them each two small balls of cotton wool to stuff into their ears to (hopefully) keep the noise of the planes at bay as they drifted off to sleep.

Back in the kitchen, I sat in my comfortable armchair at the side of the fire, picked up Agatha Christie's Hercule Poirot's Christmas and wracked my brains in a futile attempt to work out who murdered Simeon Lee before the great detective could out the killer. At ten-thirty I put the book down and headed up to bed. Ten-thirty was quite late for me as I was usually up at five to clean out the pigs. During the winter months, I had the luxury of a half hour lie in.

As I lay in bed going over the events of the day, I had a brainwave. I decided to invite Stephen and Harriet's mum, Rose and her husband Terry to stay with us for Christmas. I had invited them to visit in the summer but they both had important jobs and couldn't get the time off. Terry had just started work as firefighter, which meant he didn't have to join the forces and Rose worked in a munitions factory in the East End.

Rose had promised her kids that she would ring them this coming Tuesday. I suddenly felt an overwhelming sense of excitement. What better Christmas present could they be given?

I woke the next morning still full of the joys of spring, I was bursting to share my idea with the kids but I held back just in case Rose and Terry's war work made it impossible for them to accept. So, I did my best to keep out of their way in case the excitement built up to such a degree that the secret just burst out of me.

It was a cold day with a brisk northerly wind that sent the fluffy white clouds racing across the sky. In the distance, thicker, more organised clouds were forming. With the temperature as low as it was, it would be a toss-up whether the clouds would yield rain or snow. I crossed my fingers and hoped it would be rain. We still had a lot of maintenance to do around the farm and snow would bring that work to a grinding halt.

After I had finished cleaning out the pigs, I got Martha dressed in her red wool coat and hat and carried her over to the pens so that she could say hello to Hector and Horace, my prize boars, I knew she wouldn't settle down for her lunchtime nap unless she had seen them. They shoved their noses out between the bars as we approached and Martha shrieked with joy as they nuzzled their sloppy, wet snouts into her tiny outstretched hands.

After lunch I made my way down to the paddock to find Barney. I felt an urgent need to share my secret idea with someone and my foreman was the best secret keeper I knew.

Barney had just finished mucking out the stable as I lifted the plaited rope loop off the gate post and let myself into the paddock.

'Hello, Missis,' he greeted me in his usual, jovial manner. Not a lot got to Barney, his demeanour could make you feel warm on the coldest of days.

'Hello, Barney, I've got a secret and if I don't share it with someone, I think I'm going to explode.'

'Share away, Missis.' Barney stood by the gate and placed one of his huge, calloused hands on the top rail.

I looked over my shoulder conspiratorially.

'Well, it's like this. I thought I'd try to organise an extra special Christmas present for Stephen and Harriet this year. I'm going to ask Rose and Terry if they'd like to stay with us over the holiday.'

Barney beamed. 'That's a wonderful idea. The kids haven't seen their mum and dad since they arrived and that's over a year ago now, isn't it?'

'Thirteen months, it's a long time for kids to be away from their parents.'

'Too long,' Barney muttered. 'When are you going to let them in on the secret?'

'Tea time tomorrow, I hope. Rose has promised to give them a ring on her way home from work. I'll invite her to come and stay with us before I pass the phone to the kids. I won't tell Stephen and Harriet until I know the plan is a goer. I don't want to get their hopes up only to have them dashed.'

'Do you think you can keep the secret that long or will you be able to store it safely away now you've shared it?'

I pulled a face. 'I'm hopeless with secrets. I get too excited; I've been the same since I was little. I'll tell Miriam if I feel the urge to share.'

Barney laughed. 'She's as bad as you with secrets. Watch she doesn't let the cat out of the bag.'

'Oh dear, you're right of course. I'll tell Amy then. She wouldn't give anything away, even if she was being tortured.'

'Now, that's a good call.' Barney lifted the rope loop and opened the gate to let me out.

'I'm trying to think of something we can all do together tonight so I don't keep dwelling on it.'

'Card games? Monopoly?' Barney suggested.

'We played Animal Grab last night. No, it has to be something different tonight. I want to find a way to distract them from the bombers as they go over.'

'Musical chairs? Use that gramophone of yours, crank the volume right up.'

'That's a good idea, Barney, or I could teach them to dance.'

'Me and the missis are going to help decorate the church hall tonight. You could all join us if you feel the need to get out of the house. Bring the kids, I'm sure they'll be welcome.'

'Decorations... That's it, you've nailed it, Barney!'

'Have I?' Barney looked puzzled.

'We're going to make our own Christmas decorations. I've got the baubles and tinsel for the tree in a box upstairs, but we haven't hung garlands and what have you since Mum was alive.'

'That sounds like fun, Missis, but where are you going to get the coloured paper from? There'll be none in the shops.'

I blew out my cheeks. I hadn't thought of that.

'You could do what we used to do when we were kids,' Barney said with a wistful look in his eye.

'Well? Come on, Barney don't keep me in suspense. I need to get this activity organised for tonight.'

'We used to paint old newspapers, and when they were dry, we'd cut them into long strips, then into smaller pieces and make paper chains. It was—'

'Barney, you are a genius.' I got onto my tiptoes and planted a kiss on his cheek.

My big, burly foreman, blushed.

'Right,' I said aloud. 'I need newspapers and paint... Ah, Miriam will have a stash of old papers she uses to light the fire... now, have we got any paint?'

'There's tins of it in the blue shed,' Barney said. 'Some of it has probably been there since the King was a lad, but a lot of it should be all right. I know there's red, white and blue, because, if you remember we used it to paint the timber rails on the back of the truck to celebrate the coronation of King George VI in nineteen thirty-seven.'

'Oh, course we did, Barney you're a genius... oh, I already told you that...' I paused for a moment... 'and what could be more patriotic than using the colours of the national flag... Barney... Oh, you know what I think.'

Barney smiled as he let himself out of the gate and dropped the thick, rope loop over the big post to hold it shut.

‘I’ll fish out the tins of paint this afternoon. I’ll give the contents a stir and leave them at the back door before I go home.’

We walked together in silence for a few moments as I imagined the gaily coloured garlands hanging from the ceiling in the kitchen. When we reached the yard, I stepped towards the back door and Barney made for the barn. He turned back as our flock of chickens squawked and flapped their way out of his path.

‘Oh, talking of Christmas decorations. When would you like to pick a tree?’

‘Blimey, I hadn’t even thought about it, Barney. Would Saturday be all right? I’d like the kids to choose it this year.’

‘Saturday will be fine. I’ll make sure they don’t pick the one we dug up and replanted last year. There are plenty of saplings to choose from.’

‘Just give us a shout when you can spare half an hour,’ I said with a smile. ‘Right, I’m off on a newspaper hunt.’

Barney stuck up a thumb. ‘If you can’t find enough, let me know. The missis has a pile of them in the shed. I’m sure some go back to the Victorian era.’

‘Thank you, Barney,’ I replied with a smile. ‘What would I do without you?’

Chapter 3

After dinner, armed with a stack of old newspapers, three tins of paint and four, two-inch badger hair paint brushes we set about making our own Christmas decorations. I covered my precious old kitchen table with an old oilskin tarp to protect it from the energetically applied sloshes of paint, then made sure the blackout curtains were in place before handing out the brushes and easing the lids from the paint tins.

When one side of a newspaper sheet had been covered, I picked it up and carefully hung it over one of the string lines that I had rigged up a few feet back from the fireplace to allow it to dry. It didn't take too long. Our fire threw out so much heat that we sometimes had to open a window, even in winter. Miriam spent a lot of the time mopping up paint drips from the floorboards beneath the drying paper.

It took us almost three hours to cover and dry off our painted sheets. By the time I took the last of them off the lines it was time for the kids to go to bed.

After a quick flannel wash in the bathroom, the children squeezed Colgate dental cream onto their toothbrushes and under the watchful eye of Miriam, proceeded to clean their teeth for the specified two minutes.

By the time they arrived back at the table I had rigged up a string line across the kitchen and was just hanging the last sheet across it so that the paint could dry completely, away from the hazard of the fire.

'Don't cut the chains until we are home from school, Auntie Alice,' Harriet begged.

I assured them I wouldn't touch the gaily painted paper until we were all sat around the table together again, and turning the wireless down to its normal volume (I had turned it up in an attempt to muffle the sound of the bombers) and humming along to the BBC orchestra as they played their version of Judy Garland's hit, Somewhere Over The Rainbow, I followed the kids upstairs and after giving them both a hug and fresh lumps of cotton wool to use as ear plugs, I turned off their bedroom light and walked through to my own room.

Shivering in the cold air, I stripped to my underwear and pulled on a pair of my father's old pyjamas and his favourite, check-patterned dressing gown. After pulling on a pair of thick socks and my red slippers, I went back downstairs and once again, sat in my comfortable fireside chair and picked up my half read, Agatha Christie novel.

A few minutes later, Miriam passed me a cup of tea and then sat down in the armchair opposite and pulled her knitting needles from the padded box at the side of the hearth. Holding the foot long length of knitting up towards the light, she nodded to herself and hummed along to the radio as she followed the knitting pattern that she had spread out on her lap.

I blew into my favourite blue striped mug and then took a sip of the hot liquid. As I sat back to savour the moment, my eyes rested on the mantelpiece where a photograph of Harriet and Stephen with their parents took pride of place. The children had given me the framed picture for my twenty-first birthday a couple of months before. It was one of my most prized possessions as it was the only item they had from their former lives. My eyes misted over as I remembered the night they had given me such a precious gift. I smiled as I looked down at my book. I would make sure the kids saw their parents this Christmas if I had to drive down in my old farm truck and bring them back myself.

'You look like the cat that got the cream, Alice,' Miriam said, looking across the fireplace at me. 'Have you solved the murder before Poirot or something?'

I shook my head. 'That's hardly likely is it, Miriam? No, this is a surprise I'm hoping to spring myself but I'm still at the plotting stage.'

'Keep it to yourself until you're ready to share then, lovely.' Miriam winked at me, then went back to her knitting.

For the next hour we sat with the sound of clicking needles and the ticking of the clock in almost perfect symmetry, oblivious to the world outside of our kitchen.

Tuesday passed slowly.

Even cleaning out and feeding the pigs seemed to be a chore although it was something I always enjoyed. Martha had fallen asleep in her playpen and I didn't want a grumpy toddler on my hands, so I left her dozing, grabbed four large apples from the parlour and went down to see Bessie my shire horse and her best friend, the grey-haired donkey, Bray. The pair ambled across the moment they saw me approach the paddock and I spent a pleasant fifteen minutes ruffling their manes and stroking their ears as they munched away happily.

After leaving the paddock, I walked back up to the milking parlour come cow shed, but the only occupants were our small herd of Friesian cows. I checked the barn and the other outbuildings before remembering that all the lads were working at the top end, shoring up the hedgerows after half our flock of sheep had been found munching the grass on the side of the lane.

Frustrated, but unwilling to trudge my way across the fields to find them, I returned to the kitchen and found Miriam rewrapping the Christmas cake that she had baked in early October with a brandy-soaked cheesecloth.

'That smells absolutely divine,' I told her.

'This is the last wrap, it's pretty much matured now. There'll be no crumbly cake in this house on Christmas day. It will be as moist as the day I took it out of the oven.'

'Have you made one for the Christmas party too?'

Miriam sniffed. 'Of course I have, it wouldn't be a Christmas party without a brandy soaked fruitcake, would it?' She flicked her head backwards towards the parlour as she folded the cheesecloth carefully over the underside of the cake, then expertly flipped it over and placed it back onto the wooden tray that sat on the draining board at the side of our big, white Belfast sink. 'The other one is in there... I'll know if you've been picking at it.'

'Miriam, I'm shocked that you think I would pick bits off your cake,' I said, trying to avoid her eye.

'It would be the first time if you didn't,' Miriam replied, wagging a finger at me.

She picked up the tray and carried it to the parlour where, using a footstool as a step, she slid the bundle onto the top shelf before stepping down and turning back to face me. 'I'll know,' she scolded.

'Let's have an early lunch,' I said, changing the subject.

'What do you fancy on your sandwiches, ham or cheese and pickle?' she asked, pulling a couple of plates from the drying rack above the gas cooker.

'Ooh, cheese and pickle. Your chutney always gets me in the Christmas mood.'

'I've made piccalilli too, if you'd like that instead.'

'Decisions, decisions...' I mused. 'You choose, Miriam, I'm happy with either. Surprise me.'

As Miriam began to cut big doorsteps of bread from a fresh loaf, I busied myself making tea. By the time I had put the patterned china teapot on the table, Martha had woken up.

'Piggots,' she said, looking me sternly in the eye.

'Let's have lunch first, darling,' I suggested, already knowing what the response would be.

'Piggots!' this time it was a demand.

'All right, all right,' I slipped the tea cosy over the pot and got Martha into her red coat and hat before taking her out to the pens to see the piglets. First, we had to call in on Hector and Horace, my prize boars who stuck their head through the bars as soon as they saw us approach. After five minutes of sloppy snout nuzzling, I carried her to the far end of the yard where the piglets were housed. Leaving Martha in the outer pen, I selected two piglets at random and carried them out to her. After ten minutes or so I began to try to persuade Martha to let the piglets go back to their brothers and sisters but she was having none of it. My daughter had a built-in clock and would accept nothing less than her usual twenty-five minutes.

Back in the kitchen I washed my hands in the sink, then washed Martha's. It was always something she was reluctant to do after playing with the piglets. It was as though the water was washing away their intimacy.

'I've made a fresh pot of tea, lovely,' Miriam said as I slid Martha into her high chair. She placed the pot in the centre of the table, then uncovered the plate of thick, cheese and chutney sandwiches.

'Martha's got a jam sandwich,' Miriam said, producing a small plate with a thin cut, sticky sandwich and placing it in front of the infant.

'Jam, yum yum,' Martha grabbed the sandwich before Miriam could place it on the clipped-on wooden tray.

'She'll get more of that jam on her face than goes into her stomach,' I laughed.

Miriam nodded. 'And that's just how it should be.'

After lunch, Martha was cleaned up and put back into her playpen with her thick, cardboard picture books and her favourite stuffed monkey toy. I picked up my own book but I couldn't concentrate on it. I seemed to be looking my watch or the big clock on the wall every five minutes.

Miriam had noticed.

'Are you waiting for something important, Alice? You'll wear that clock out if you keep staring at it.'

I shrugged. 'No, not really. It's just... well, I can't wait for the kids to get home from school that's all.'

'Ah, you want to get on with those decorations.' Miriam laughed. 'I was always the same when the kids were young. There was always such excitement when I got the box of decorations down. They knew it meant Christmas wasn't far away.'

I smiled, remembering sitting at the big table with my own parents as we sorted through a big box of Christmas stuff to see what would last another year and what would need replacing. There wasn't a shortage of paper back then and there wasn't a war on, so getting hold of the materials to make new paper chains wasn't a problem.

I checked the clock again, then looked away quickly as Miriam tutted.

'Stop wishing your life away, lovely.'

'You're right, as usual, Miriam,' I said, and grabbing my big coat from the hook on the back of the door, I let myself out into the farmyard, opened the five barred gate and stepped off the gravel path onto the lane.

Chapter 4

Amy
Tuesday 10th December

Amy Rowlings lifted the finished, khaki battledress jacket and snipped the cotton thread that still tied it to her machine, then after giving the tunic a quick once over she dropped it into the finished garment's bin on her right. Taking a quick glance over her shoulder at the huge clock set high on the wall at the back of the shop floor, she switched off her machine, stretched, then tried to look busy as Mr Bartholomew, the foreman, stepped into the doorway of his office. Checking his watch against the big clock, he took a quick look across the factory floor where the seventy-five machinists tried, like Amy, to avoid his steely gaze. Rolling his eyes to let the workforce know that he was aware of their malingering, he stepped back inside his office and pressed the green button on the wall that sounded the bell to announce that the day's shift was over.

Getting to her feet, Amy stretched again, then slipped into the aisle between the lines of industrial sewing machines and made her way quickly to the front where her friend Carole Sims was waiting.

'Well, that's the British army kitted out for another battle,' she said as she fell into step.

'Those battledress tops get heavier as the day goes on,' Amy replied. 'I'm sick of the sight of them now. I wish we could go back to stitching the little lightweight summer dresses we used to make.'

'Shush,' Carole replied. 'We make a much better bonus on these things.'

'We do, but I've got muscles like Popeye the sailor man after he's scoffed a huge tin of spinach.' Amy flexed her biceps. 'I struggle to get them through the sleeves of my favourite dress these days.'

As they reached the changing room door, they were stopped from entering by Mr Bartholomew.

'Miss Rowlings, Mrs Sims, your presence is requested.' He flicked his head towards the mezzanine floor where the company offices were situated. 'Miss Handsley wants a word.'

Amy and Carole exchanged glances and turned to make their way up the steel steps that led to the offices.

'Are we getting our cards for Christmas?' Carole whispered as they climbed the stairs.

'I doubt it,' Amy replied with a shake of her scarf covered head. 'We're up to our ears in orders, and it's all well-paid government work too.' She grinned at her friend as they reached the first-floor level. 'Maybe they're giving us a pay rise. Stranger things have happened.'

'Not in the blooming Mill they haven't,' Carole snorted.

The Mill was the nickname the town's population used for the Handsley Garments factory as it had once, in its dark distant past, actually been a cotton mill, driven by a huge, long since removed, water wheel.

Georgina Handsley looked up as Amy rattled on the half pane door. 'Come in, ladies,' she said getting to her feet.

She was a tweed-clad, dumpy woman of about sixty with thin, steel-grey hair tied back in an old-fashioned bun. She had narrow, green eyes and wore an almost permanent frown.

At the other side of the office, a broad-shouldered, navy-suited man looked up from a set of plans that had been spread over a long table. Amy recognised him immediately.

Anton Grayling was the black-haired owner of a rival factory on the other side of town. The garments he produced were meant for the bottom end of the fashion market. The working conditions and wages at his factory were poor compared to Handsley's who prided themselves in the quality items they produced.

'I believe you know Mr Grayling,' Georgine said quietly.

Amy and Carole nodded towards the factory owner.

'You must be wondering why you have been summoned,' the Mill owner continued.

'We're hoping we aren't going to get the sack,' said Carole with a forced smile.

'On the contrary, Mrs Sims,' said Georgina. When she smiled her frown vanished, only to reappear as she stepped across the office towards Anton. 'You two ladies have been selected for a special task precisely because you are the best two machinists in the factory. Your work is exemplary, your attitude is first class and I am sure you will do your best to ensure that the project is a huge success.'

'Project?' Amy looked from Georgina to Anton and back again.

'Mr Grayling and I are about to embark on a joint venture. I must warn you that it may only be a temporary project... it depends on how well the finished goods turn out. There can be no room for error, people's lives may depend on how well you deploy your skills.'

Amy flashed a glance at Carole, then tried to peer around Anton towards the plans that were laid out on the table. Mr Grayling's lips curled in a faint smile below his pencil moustache.

'We want you to make us some parachutes,' he beamed.

Amy's mouth dropped open.

'Parachutes?'

Anton nodded vigorously. 'Our plan is to use the old warehouse area at the far end of the shop floor as a test bed for the project. Because of the delicacy of the fabric, we will have to install some new machinery but you will be given full training, so don't worry about that.'

'And there's only two of us?' Amy frowned. 'Mr Churchill won't be planning an invasion on the back of that, will he?'

Mr Grayling shrugged. 'As I said, Miss Rowlings, we are only setting up a test bed. When you become proficient at turning out a first-class product, we'll get the government bods in to test the things, if they like what we offer them we could end up mass producing them. There may be problems in the supply of top-quality silk as the war goes on and we may have to switch to using Rayon, or even that new-fangled material the Americans have invented... Nylon. It's not just used to make ladies stockings; it has many uses.'

'Erm, what happens if the government bods don't like what we make, or they won't give you the licence needed to buy the silk?'

'Then you'll return to your machines and go back to making army uniforms,' Georgina said bluntly.

'What about our hours, wages...?' Amy looked at her feet as she finished the sentence.

'You'll get the same money, the same hours, nothing will change initially. However, should the government decide that they like what we do, there may be a possibility of a pay rise, certainly a bonus on each parachute produced.'

'That sounds great,' said Carole, nodding eagerly towards Amy. 'When do we start?'

'The machines will arrive by the end of next week. They'll be fitted and tested over Christmas.' Georgina looked towards Anton, then back at the two machinists. 'Now, here's the part you might not like so much. You will need to be trained on the machines but we don't want word getting out about what's happening in the old warehouse, so we will require you to come in for training when the factory is closed.'

'Not over Christmas?' Amy's face was a mask of despair.

'No, not Christmas Day, nor Boxing Day. We'll be using those two days for testing. No, we thought the best idea was that you come in at the weekend after Christmas, both Saturday and Sunday.'

Carole frowned, as she opened her mouth to complain, Georgina held up her hand to silence her.

'Those days work best for us as the factory will be mainly idle. There will be no Saturday morning overtime that week as it's still Christmas and we understand that people need to spend time with their families. You will have a choice in the matter though. Spend the weekend in training at time and a quarter wage and you can take the time off prior to Christmas Day or maybe take Christmas Eve and the Friday after Boxing Day. Of course, you can always work your usual shifts and have the overtime as an extra, it's entirely up to you.'

'I think I'd prefer the time off to be honest. I've got family staying over for the whole week.' Carole thought hard for a few moments. 'If we were to take the time off, would we still be paid time and a quarter for the weekend we work?'

Georgina looked at Anton who nodded back at her.

'Fair enough. Are we agreed then?'

'When would you need to know which days we want off in lieu?' Amy asked. 'I'll need to check what plans Mum and Dad have. They spend a lot of time in church at this time of year.'

'Let me know by next Monday,' Mrs Handsley replied.

Anton suddenly straightened up to his full six-foot two-inch height. 'Now, ladies, I have to stress this is a top-secret project. You must not discuss it with anyone, either inside or outside of the Mill, do I make myself clear? We could become a target for the German bombers if word gets out.'

Amy looked puzzled. 'How can it possibly be kept a secret? Over a hundred people work here, aren't they going to be curious as to what we're up to? And, that back storeroom has been empty since I've been here, the doors are hanging off their hinges and there's a row of windows all along the side. Anyone can look in from the factory floor.'

'Leave that to us, Miss Rowlings. Security will be paramount. You will enter and leave the storeroom from the door at the rear of the factory. The windows will be covered over and the doors, fixed and bolted. The room will be lit from the skylights and powerful overhead lamps. There will be a security guard on duty at all times. No one will get as much as a peep of what we're up to in there.' Anton looked at his watch. 'I have a meeting with the machinery suppliers in an hour, I'd better go. Is there anything else you'd like to ask?'

Amy looked at Carole and both women shook their heads.

'Good. Now, please don't forget, this is war work, therefore top secret. I'm counting on you to see it stays that way.'

Back in the changing room, Amy took off her home-made turban and let her flaxen hair fall around her shoulders. She fastened up her winter coat as she looked into the full-length mirror that hung on the wall at the side of the door.

'Well, that's a turn up for the books.'

'Isn't it just.' Carole put her finger to her lips as she heard a rustle from the cleaning cupboard behind the partition wall. Stepping quickly around the corner she threw the door open to find Beryl Hargreaves, aka Big Nosed Beryl, standing with her ear stuck to the partition wall. Beryl didn't have a particularly big nose; she acquired the nickname for continually sticking it into other people's business.

'Heard enough, Beryl?' Carole asked.

'I wasn't listening, I was just...' Beryl paused for inspiration, 'tidying up the cleaning stuff,' she added lamely.

'Out,' Carole pushed her thumb towards the changing room. Beryl stepped through the open door and walked red-faced around the corner towards where Amy was standing.

'So, what was the big meeting about?' she asked, narrowing her eyes at Amy.

Amy pointed to the big government poster on the wall.

WALLS HAVE EARS!

'I don't know about walls, but it seems broom cupboards do,' she said, turning an accusing eye on Beryl.

'Oh, come on, you can tell me, you know I can keep a secret.'

Carole snorted.

'We may as well send a telegram to old Adolph himself,' she said with a note of incredulity in her voice.

'Ah, top secret, is it?'

Amy leaned forwards and beckoned to Beryl to move closer.

'There's a new order coming in, but it's pretty hush hush, no one is allowed to talk about it.'

Beryl nodded eagerly. 'And...?'

Amy winked at Carole, then put her mouth next to Beryl's ear.

'We're going to start making baggy bloomers for the Women's Land Army,' she whispered.

'Really? Oh, you're having me on.'

The two friends burst into laughter. Carole pulled open the door and arm in arm, still chuckling away, they walked out of the changing rooms and made their way to the time clocks.

Chapter 5

Alice
Tuesday 10th December

At three forty-five on Tuesday afternoon, I pulled on my coat and walked up Long Lane to meet Harriet and Stephen from the school bus. They waved as they spotted me through the steamy window.

'What are you doing here, Aunty Alice? You don't usually meet us from the bus,' Harriet asked, slipping an arm through mine before Stephen had even climbed down from the bottom step.

'I just thought it would be a nice surprise,' I replied.

Stephen jumped from the bus and grinned at me as he ran past. He stopped a few yards further on to examine the dead body of some poor creature that had died in the gutter overnight.

'Leave it, Stephen,' I said as he bent to get a closer look.

'It's a mouse,' he said, straightening up.

'I'm surprised the crows haven't had it by now,' I replied.

Stephen dragged his foot along the gutter exposing the mouse's body from beneath the rotting leaves. 'There,' he said. 'They'll spot it now.' He tipped his head to one side as his sister glared at him. 'The crows have to eat too, it's hard for them in winter.'

Harriet pulled a face and gripped my arm tighter.

'Can we finish the decorations tonight, Aunty Alice?'

'We can,' I replied. 'And we might even have time to hang the garlands we finished last night. The glue will have set by now.'

Stephen dragged his foot along the pile of dead leaves that lined the grass verge, obviously hoping to find more carcasses for the crows. 'What time is Mum ringing?'

'She told me it would be after she's finished work, so that should be sometime between five-thirty and six, depending on whether she calls from the phone box near the factory or the one on the road near her house,' I replied. 'Though she sometimes rings from the corner shop, she's very friendly with the lady that owns it.'

'We've never seen her new house,' said Harriet. 'Mum and Dad moved in after we came to live up here.'

I put my arm around her shoulder and pulled her closer as we walked. 'I'm sure you'll get to see it one day. When things have quietened down a bit.'

'If the blooming Luftwaffe doesn't bomb it first,' said Stephen. He picked up a long, thin branch from the grass verge and began to poke about in the rotting foliage beneath the Blackthorn hedge. 'Ow,' he yelled suddenly and began to suck at his thumb.

I stifled a laugh and looked away as he glanced up at me. 'Stupid thorns,' he said as he threw the branch into the hedge bottom.

Miriam had already laid the table for tea as we stepped into the kitchen and removed our coats.

'I thought we'd have an early one tonight, seeing as some little people have an exciting phone call to look forward to this evening,' she said, stretching her arms out wide to administer a welcome home hug.

Stephen eased himself out of her clutches and pushed his hand towards a plate of egg sandwiches.

Miriam slapped it lightly. 'Not until you've washed those inky fingers and we're all sat down together.' She smiled and ruffled his hair. 'Go on, into the bathroom, the pair of you.'

When the kids were at their ablutions, she handed me a mug of steaming hot tea, then picked up her own blue-striped mug and took a sip.

'What's it like out?'

'A bit nippy. There's not a lot of cloud. I think we might be in for a sharp frost.'

'Right, I'll shut the hens in the barn a bit earlier tonight. Mr Fox will be looking for an easy meal.'

Miriam always called the foxes Mr, even though we saw more vixens at this time of year.

I looked out of the window onto the empty farmyard, the night was already drawing in.

'They're inside already, Miriam. You see to the kids, I'll shut the barn up.'

I shivered as I stepped out of the back door and hurried across the yard to close the big barn doors. The chickens would be safe enough in there for the night. The lads had patched up the many gaps that had appeared since last winter, replacing rotten wood with fresh sawn planks. We stored a lot of hay and bags of seed in the barn and we did our best to keep the weather off them. Keeping the chickens out of the seed bags was another thing altogether.

I wrapped my arms around my chest as I stepped back into the yard and scurried across to the kitchen door. My breath hung in the air as I looked up into the cold night. Venus, the so-called Evening Star, was already out and about on her business, sitting low in the south western sky. Some of the early stars were just beginning to twinkle. I shivered as I thought once again how blessed we were living in the countryside without all of the light pollution the town dwellers suffered.

By five-thirty, we had finished our meal, the table had been cleared and the children were busy gluing the six-inch strips of painted newspaper together to form their paper chains.

I went into the front room to retrieve the three, ten-foot lengths they had made the previous evening and returned with my arms full of colourful garlands.

'Where to hang them, that's the thing,' I said aloud.

'Across the ceiling, from corner to corner,' suggested Harriet.

'I don't think they're long enough for that,' I said as I dropped the garlands onto the floor and stretched them out to their full length.

'Pin them from the corner to the light in the middle of the ceiling,' Stephen suggested. 'They'll fit then.'

'Have you just read my mind?' I asked. I was just thinking that myself.

I picked up the box of brass headed drawing pins from the table and shook two into my hand. Putting one of them between my lips, I grabbed one end of a garland and dragged it over to the corner of the room before looking around for something to stand on.

Miriam spotted my dilemma immediately and pulled one of the old oak chairs from beneath the table. 'Watch you don't swallow that pin,' she said as she pushed the chair into the corner.

Fifteen minutes later, all three of the shiny, colourful garlands had been pinned into place and I dragged the chair around the kitchen pushing in extra pins so that they didn't sag below head height in the middle. I had just got down from my chair when the phone rang. Stephen and Harriet were off their seats in an instant.

'MUM!' they cried in unison.

'Steady now. You'll have me off my feet,' I laughed as they sped by. 'I'll pick up,' I called as they hared into the front room. 'It might be someone for me.'

I lifted the phone and spoke into the mouthpiece. 'Alice speaking. How may I help you?'

'Hello, Alice, it's Rose, Rose Wakelin?'

'Hello, Rose,' I replied smiling like the Cheshire Cat at the kids. 'I'll put Stephen on first as Harriet is more patient. I'd like a word with you in private after you've spoken to them if you don't mind. Don't worry, it's nothing serious, it's just an idea I've had.' I was about to pass the phone to Stephen when I had a thought. 'Rose, are you calling from a public phone box? it will cost a fortune.'

'No, It's all right, Alice. I'm calling from Mrs Pettigrew's corner shop. Lois will just add threepence onto my tab to cover the call.'

'Ah, that's all right, I was going to say, I'll ring you back. Here's Stephen now.'

Stephen almost snatched the phone from my hand and was speaking before he had lifted it to his mouth. He went into minute detail of everything he had done since they had last spoken, including finding the dead mouse on the lane. Eventually he ran out of things to say and with a swift, 'love you too,' he handed the phone to Harriet and stepped smartly back into the kitchen to resume his labours.

Harriet had a completely different telephone manner. She asked how her mother was, how her dad was, whether she'd seen gran, and then listened patiently as her mother replied. She seemed more concerned about her mother being out on her own in the dark with the bombers on their way than anything else. After telling Rose about her latest school report, she wished her mother a safe journey home, then handed the phone to me.

When Harriet was out of the room, I asked Rose how bad things were in London. On hearing that it was no worse than usual, I decided it was time to spring the surprise.

'Rose, do you think you could make it up to the farm for Christmas? The kids are really missing you, and Terry. You're welcome to stay for a few days.'

'Don't mention that louse to me,' Rose spat.

'Oh dear, I'm sorry, I wasn't aware that...'

'You weren't to know, Alice. The thing is, we've split up. He cheated on me one time too many... with a so-called friend of mine too.'

'Oh, Rose, I'm so sorry to hear that. It must have been awful for you.'

'It wasn't the first time, Alice. His trousers spend more time around his ankles than they ever do around his waist. There is too much temptation and he has plenty of opportunities with the job he does now.'

'What is it he does?'

'He's a fire fighter... allegedly, though I've heard the fires are almost always out by the time he gets there. He only joined to keep himself out of the forces, the coward. He works with the ARP and his commanding officer is his long-time drinking partner, so he gets away with murder. He picks up survivors, the ones who are still in shock, he comforts them, takes them to their relatives, then nips around to see how they are. They all think he's a knight in shining armour but he's only ever after one thing. He seduced a blind woman one night;

can you imagine that? He even had some of them in my bed when I was out at work.'

'Oh, Rose.'

'Please don't tell the kids, they'd be devastated, they think he's a hero.'

'I won't say anything to them, don't worry,' I replied softly. 'Now, about this visit. It sounds like you could do with a few days away.'

'It's very kind of you, Alice. I'd love to take you up on it. It would be wonderful to spend some time with Harriet and Stephen.' She paused for a moment, cleared her throat, then continued in a croaky voice. 'It's so kind of you... I was going to post Christmas cards with a bit of money for them, but I'll be able to buy them something and bring it up myself now.'

'How long do you think you'll be able to stay away from your job, Rose? I know you work with munitions.'

'Oh, we've got three days off this year. Part of the roof was taken off in an air raid so we can't use that section of the factory and they can't fix it while we're working underneath, so they're doing it over Christmas. I'm off from lunchtime on Christmas Eve until the following Monday.'

'Wonderful,' I gushed. 'So, you'll come up on the afternoon of Christmas Eve? That's the Tuesday.'

'Yes, I think so. I could stay until Friday if that's all right? I'll get the train back home on Friday evening, possibly the Saturday morning.'

A little bell suddenly rang in my head.

'Rose... Don't go buying train tickets just yet. I have a friend, Godfrey Wilson, he's a lawyer who works at the War Office, in Whitehall. I sat waiting for him once on a bench outside... Oh, sorry, I was wittering on a bit there. Anyway, the thing is, he's coming back to Spinton on

Christmas Eve after work. He's driving back to London on the Saturday. He's got a staff car booked. I'm sure he wouldn't mind giving you a lift. He's a lovely man.'

'I wouldn't want to impose, Alice.'

'Oh, it wouldn't be an imposition, I'm sure he'd be glad of the company, it's quite a long drive.'

'Well, if you're sure he won't mind. It would save me a bit on train fares. Where would I meet him?'

'I think he could pick you up at home, or at your workplace... even outside the War Office. Leave it with me, Rose, I'll get in touch with him tomorrow and report back. Could you give me a call? Or be at Mrs Pettigrew's shop at a set date and time and I'll ring you to confirm it.'

'It's a bit tricky. None of the phone boxes are working around here, they've either been blown up or the lines to the exchange are down, even Mrs Pettigrew's phone only works occasionally. The thing is, I could ask my foreman, Mike, if I could use his office phone. He's a widower, he lost his wife in an isolated bombing raid on the East End last January. He's far too young to be in that position. His kids have been evacuated too, somewhere in Devon; I think. Anyway, he's sweet on me, I don't think anything will ever come of it, but, well, he does let me get away with a bit more than others, he never docks me pay if I'm late. I'll ask him if I can ring you from work at Friday lunchtime, do you think you'll have... Godfrey was it? Do you think you'll have his answer by then?'

'I'm sure I will, Rose. Look, I'd better let you get home. The bombers are passing over now, I can hear them, they'll be with you soon.'

'Yes, I'd better get to the shelter before they arrive. Good night, Alice, thanks so much. Give the kids a kiss from me at bedtime.'

'I will, Rose. Stay safe, love.'

I put the phone down and walked slowly back to the kitchen to find the kids had just finished the last of the garlands. I crouched down between the pair of them and gave them each a kiss on their glue covered cheeks.

'That's from your mum,' I said.

Chapter 6

On Wednesday morning I had to take an early tea break to clean up after one of the piglets squirted poo all over my clean overalls. Martha, who was safely in the arms of Miriam on the other side of the safety gate, thought it was hilarious and chanted 'again, again' over and over until I finally came out of the pen to get changed. After hosing the front of my overalls down in the yard, I went into the house, stripped to my underwear, then, sniffing at myself suspiciously, decided it would be safer to have a strip wash before putting on some fresh work clothes.

Fortunately, my spare pair of overalls was hanging on the clothes horse in front of the fire and had been drying all morning so they were ready to pull on. As we sat sipping our steaming hot drinks, I suddenly remembered I had promised Rose that I'd ring Godfrey. Carrying my mug carefully into the front room I picked up the phone and dialled his office number. Fortunately, he wasn't in a meeting and his secretary put me straight through.

'Hello, Alice, this is a lovely surprise. I trust all is well.'

'Yes, thank you, Godfrey, everything is fine here. I was wondering if you could do me a favour?'

'If I can.'

'Well, it's like this. I've invited Stephen and Harriet's mum, Rose, to stay for a few days at Christmas. The kids don't know anything about it.'

'Excellent, that will be fantastic surprise.'

'Oh, they'll love it, it will make their year, let alone their Christmas.'

'Indeed, so, how may I help?'

'The thing is, she's coming up on Christmas Eve and going back home on the Saturday. Does that ring a bell with you?'

'Ah, I see. You're asking me if I'll give her a lift in the staff car.'

'Oh, Godfrey, would you? It would save her the train fare for a start and as it's quite a long journey, I thought that you might enjoy the company of an attractive woman.'

Godfrey laughed. 'Attractive hey? Well then, how can I possibly refuse.'

'You keep your hands to yourself, Godfrey, you're already spoken for twice over.'

Godfrey laughed again.

'Of course she can travel with me, it's not a problem. I can't refuse you anything, Alice, you know that.'

'You're a Godsend... Godfrey Godsend... it's got a ring to it, hasn't it?'

'That would look good on the nameplate on my office door,' he mused.

'She's ringing me on Friday to confirm everything. Where should she meet you? She finishes work at one o'clock on Christmas Eve.'

Godfrey was silent for a moment. 'I can't finish that early, Alice. It will be three at the earliest. I'll have meetings until after lunch, that's a certainty.'

'Oh, right, so...'

'Do you have her address?'

'I do, the kids have been writing to her all year. She lives in Lambeth now... 37 Drews Avenue, just off the Lambeth Road. She works in a munitions factory in the East End.'

'Lambeth? That's convenient. It's only on the other side of the river from Westminster.'

'Is it?' I had no idea. I'd only ever been to London twice, once on a school trip, the other had been a couple of months before when Godfrey and I had spent a very unusual weekend together sleeping in the London underground as the bombs fell around us.

'Excuse me for a moment, Alice.' Godfrey broke off as I heard his secretary mumbling something in the background. A few seconds later he spoke again. 'I'm sorry, Alice but something's come up, I've jotted her address down. Tell her that I'll be leaving the office at about three-fifteen. I should be with her by three-thirty, it's only a mile or so. I'll run over there the day before so I know where I'm going.'

'Bless you, Godfrey, you're such a kind man.' My voice dropped to a husky tone. 'I'll make sure you're well rewarded.'

'Save that Rita Hayworth impression until I get back to Spinton,' he replied. 'My God, Alice, it will take every ounce of my willpower to stop me driving up this afternoon, you minx.'

I laughed. My resemblance to the Hollywood starlet was always being mentioned. The owner of the town's cinema had even asked me to stand outside to entice in the punters when one of her movies was being shown.

'I'd better let you get on with trying to put Mr Hitler back in his box then, Godfrey, thanks again. I'll let Rose know to expect you.'

'Goodbye, Alice my darling. See you at Christmas.'

'Stay safe and watch out for those bombs, Godfrey.' I blew a kiss into the mouthpiece and waited on the line until I heard the click that told me he'd hung up.

The week passed quickly. Miriam spent a lot of it preparing for the Christmas party we held for the family of the farm workers every year while I spent Thursday afternoon at the bank, drawing out the extra money that would be needed when I added the year-end bonus to the lads' pay packets that I always presented to them on Christmas Eve. From there I went to the sweet shop where I asked Mary Caramelly to make up a couple of dozen packs of mixed sweets for the children of my workforce. Mary was one of those lucky people who had the perfect surname for the job she did. She told me that she'd have the treats ready for the following week and handed me a striped, minty gobstopper, which I stuck straight into my mouth and sucked on with relish.

On the way home I stopped off at the Old Bull at the end of Long Lane and ordered a half barrel of beer and assorted bottles of gin, sherry and port. There was always some beer left over at the end of the night but I saved whatever was in the barrel to dish out before the lads went home on New Year's Eve. Strangely, there were never any spirits left over, the wives always went home singing.

After my farm duties on the Friday, I took the call from Rose, who had to shout to make herself heard above the noise of the factory. The call was very short as the factory owner was on the premises and the foreman didn't want to get either himself, or Rose, into trouble. I passed on what Godfrey had told me and crossed my fingers that she'd managed to hear me over the din.

That evening I asked my already excited wards if they would like me to escort them to town on Saturday to spend their pocket money. Stephen insisted that we visit Stan's Bargain Emporium, words which he always struggled to get out. Empty, was the closest he ever got.

'Well, I hope Stan's shop isn't empty or there will be little point in going,' I said with a smile.

'I hope my fort's still there,' he said, dreamily.

Stephen had had his eye on an American cavalry fort since he had first seen it in the shop back in August. The price on the ticket was eleven shillings and sixpence and he had been saving since then in the hope of buying it. While Harriet spent her pocket money, birthday money and anything she was given for helping out around the farm on sweets, books and doll's clothes, Stephen put ninety percent of his income into his piggy bank and rationed himself to a penny's worth of Blackjack and Fruit Salad chews every Saturday morning. Fortunately for them, sweets hadn't yet been added to the government's official rationing list so he could get eight of the small, square chews for his penny.

'How much do you have saved up now, Stephen?' Miriam asked as she poured cream over a bowl of homemade apple crumble.

'Eight shillings and fourpence,' he replied attempting to stick his spoon into the bowl before Miriam had fully let go of the dish.

'Eight shillings? My goodness, you have done well.'

'Eight shillings and fourpence,' he mumbled through the crumble.

'Don't speak with your mouth full,' Miriam chided.

'You did ask,' Stephen looked affronted.

Harriet put her hand in front of her mouth to stifle the giggle that was building up.

'Didn't you see something in there too, Harriet?' Miriam asked to take the conversation away from Stephen's bad manners.

'She likes the doll's house,' said Stephen before Harriet could speak. 'But she'll never be able to afford it, she spends all her money on silly books.'

'They aren't silly,' Harriet stuck out her tongue at her brother.

'That's right,' I said as I stuck up my thumb towards her. 'Books are exciting and educational. I had books for every birthday when I was young and I used to do what Harriet does and spend all my pocket money on them.'

Stephen moved his head from side to side and screwed up his face as he thought.

'Maybe silly was the wrong word to use. I like books too, but you can get them for free from the library, you don't have to buy them. I was going to get the Just William book out but someone beat me to it. They won't have it back in until after Christmas now.'

'You have to give books back to the library though,' Harriet argued. 'I can keep mine and read them again if I want to.'

'Well... you can just borrow them again from the library,' Stephen was in one of his argumentative moods when he'd become like a dog with a stick and just wouldn't let it go.

'Ah, but what if someone else has taken the book out... like Just William?' Harriet nodded a 'so there' at him.

'Well...' Stephen wracked his brains for a swift repost but when nothing came, he picked up his bowl and began to scrape the last remnants of the cream from the bottom. 'What time are we going in the morning?'

'Late morning,' I replied. 'We can get lunch in the café on High Street and we're going to meet Barney to choose the Christmas tree before that.' I took the bowl away from Stephen before he could begin to explore it with his tongue and placed it in the sink with my own. 'Now, I'd like you two to think about what you'd like to buy your mum and dad for a Christmas present. It will have to be posted on Monday if it's going to have any chance of getting there.'

Stephen's brow furrowed as he thought. Harriet put her fingers on her chin and narrowed her eyes.

'We could get her a tea cosy, she's always moaning about the tea going cold,' said Stephen after a full minute's thought.

'That would be a nice gift, but as they haven't seen you for a long time, I was thinking of something more personal... a photograph of the two of you, for instance.'

'YES!' Harriet shouted. 'We could put it in a nice frame. I bet they have forgotten what we look like by now.'

'I'm sure they haven't,' I said quickly, 'but you have both grown a lot since you got here, it must be the country air. I think your mum and dad would love to see a picture of you. They can put it on the mantlepiece like I did with the one you gave me and look at it whenever they like.'

Stephen nodded sagely.

'That sounds like a plan,' he said.

Chapter 7

Amy
Friday 13th December

At lunchtime on Friday, Amy and Carole were stopped at the door of the canteen by Mr Bartholomew, the foreman.

'Right, you pair. As soon as you've had your lunch, you're to go around the back of the factory and present yourself at the door of the old storeroom. I think you know why you've been asked to enter from that direction.'

Amy nodded.

'Have the machines arrive—'

Mr Bartholomew slapped his clipboard against the wall.

'Miss Rowlings, I believe you assured Miss Handsley that you could keep a secret, yet here you are blurting out top secret news in front of the entire workforce. Anyone could be listening in. Don't you know there's a war on?'

'Yes, of course I do, I'm sorry, Mr Bartholomew. It won't happen again.'

The overseer sniffed. 'I should think not... Now, get your lunches down you ASAP. Someone is waiting to show you around.'

Amy drank her tea quickly and only ate one half of the cheese and pickle sandwich her mother had packed up for her that morning. Waving away the offer of a second cup, she winked across the table at Carole and together they stood up and walked slowly out of the canteen with the eyes of fellow machinist following them as they went.

'I wonder what this is all about?' said Carole. 'I thought they said the machines were being installed over Christmas.'

'Search me.' Amy shrugged as they approached the grey painted metal door.

As if he had been watching their approach through a peephole, the door was opened by a good-looking man wearing a white shirt, black tie and a long, khaki warehouse coat. He ushered them inside, then checked behind to make sure they hadn't been followed.

'Hello, ladies,' he beamed as he closed and bolted the security door behind them. 'I'm Douglas Barrie... and you are Miss Rowlings and Mrs Sims. Is that correct?'

He opened a brown file and studied the papers for a moment.

'Yes, that's right, I'm Amy, this is Carole.'

'Good, well, now we know each other, let's get started.'

Douglas led them to the nearer end of the long room where a woman was standing at a table rolling out a bale of shiny white silk.

'This is Janet. She's cutting some sample panels so that you'll have something to practice on when your training begins.'

Janet looked up from her work and nodded to the women.

'Good, that's the introductions over.' Douglas took Amy's arm and led her to the corner of the room where two metal legged objects were three parts covered by a thick green tarpaulin.

'These are your new machines. They were smuggled in last night after the factory closed. They won't be installed until Christmas, but we thought we'd better get them into place, early.'

Across the wall at the back of the room lay a dozen bales of silk wrapped in hessian. 'This should keep you going for a couple of weeks,' he said with a smile. 'It costs a blooming fortune so be careful with it. We don't want too many seconds, even when you're training.'

'We don't do seconds,' said Carole smugly.

'I'm delighted to hear it,' Douglas said, seriously, 'because if an airman leaps out of his burning plane and his chute collapses, or tears, it will be solely down to you.'

He turned as Carole and Amy looked at each other with wide eyes. Stepping smartly away, he led them across the empty warehouse towards a young man wearing blue overalls who was laying lengths of rope out on the floor.

'This is Jimmy, he's the man who'll be attaching the ropes and pulleys to the finished chutes. You'll hear him more than you'll see him because there'll be a partition wall between the two sides of the storeroom. You'll hear him because he can't stop talking, even when he's on his own. When he isn't talking, he's singing. Isn't that right, Jimmy?'

Jimmy was an oval faced young man with a mop of thick dark brown hair that was combed over from a sharp side parting and held in place with Brilliantine. His bright blue eyes twinkled as he smiled impishly.

'I get lonely, that's why I talk so much,' he said with a wink.

Douglas looked at his watch and tutted to himself.

'Right, I'd better report in.' He lifted his clenched fist to his ear to indicate a phone call. 'I'll see you two in a couple of weeks. Oh, don't even think about sneaking the odd length of silk out of the factory, every length, even the waste will have to be accounted for.'

Jimmy was silent as his superior walked away, but once Barrie had left the building he hurried quickly across the storeroom, past Janet, and stopped by a small white sink. Picking up the kettle, he shook it at them. 'Who fancies a cuppa? There's no milk or sugar though.'

Amy and Carole both shook their heads, but Janet nodded. 'I don't mind,' she said.

Carole walked to Janet's side and watched her closely as she carefully plotted measurements onto a long, wide length of silk.

'I bet you have to be exact on those panels,' she said.

'They have to be cut incredibly accurately, otherwise they end up in there.' Janet nodded to the side where three or four cut lengths of silk lay crumpled up in the bottom of a large metal bin.

'Sometimes the scissors snag,' she said with a shrug. 'There's nothing you can do about it.'

While Carole was talking to the cutter, Jimmy strolled across to where Amy was looking along the long length of a series of metal tables that had been fastened together.

'Where do you live, have you been in Spinton long? I haven't seen you around town. I'm sure I would have noticed you if I had,' he said.

'I've lived here all of my life,' Amy replied. 'I live at Honeysuckle Cottage on Long Lane, just down from the Old Bull.'

‘Ah, I live out of town, I’m in that big ugly block of flats on the Gillingham Road.’

Jimmy pulled a face. ‘They’re damper inside than they are out when it rains. Still, it’s better than some have I suppose. Are you looking forward to the new job?’

‘I am, there’s a lot of responsibility but I’m keen to get started,’ she replied.

Jimmy looked her squarely in the face, then tipped his head to one side and looked at her again.

‘You really are incredibly pretty,’ he said.

Amy shook her head and sighed. ‘And you’re incredibly cheeky,’ she replied.

‘Do you fancy coming to the pictures with me one night?’

‘You aren’t backwards in coming forwards, are you?’ Amy said, shaking her head again.

‘If you don’t ask, you don’t get,’ Jimmy replied, grinning his cheeky grin.

‘Well, on this occasion you’re not going to get. I’m here to learn about the new job,’ said Amy, looking into the waste bin at the side of the cutting table. ‘Do they really throw all this silk away?’

‘They send it off somewhere. Nothing is wasted these days. There’s always a buyer.’

‘Ah, I was thinking, it would be such a shame to just dump it, I could find a use for that stuff.’

‘Are you getting married then?’

Amy laughed. ‘No, I wasn’t thinking of making a wedding dress, I was thinking of something a little more personal.’

‘Cami knickers? Now you’re talking.’ Jimmy’s eyes lit up. ‘You can model those for me any time you like.’

Amy glared at him. 'Not even if I was lying dead on a slab,' she replied with a snarl. She turned away and looked up the full length of the room tapping her foot as she tried to control her temper.

Jimmy placed his hand on her sleeve, but Amy angrily shook it off.

'Look, I'm sorry, I didn't mean to offend you.'

Amy turned and stared at him, open mouthed. 'You failed on that score,' she said.

'I honestly didn't. It's just, well... I work on the shop floor at Grayson's alongside a couple of hundred women. If you think I was being a bit coarse, you should hear what I have to put up with. They don't just use words either, my backside is black and blue when I get home. I'm just used to the mucky banter and innuendo when I'm at work. I really am sorry.'

Amy nodded. 'All right, I accept your apology. I know what it's like working with women. They can be cruder than men at times.'

Jimmy rubbed his bottom. 'Tell me about it,' he said, quietly.

Amy checked her watch. 'I suppose we'd better get back. It's a shame about that waste silk. I was already working with it in my mind. I've got an old Singer machine at home.'

Whistling a cheery tune, Jimmy walked Amy and Carole to the heavy metal door and with a grunt, pushed it open.

'Nice to meet you both. I'll see you in a couple of weeks, hopefully.' He touched Amy on the wrist. 'I really am sorry,' he said.

Amy smiled. 'Forget it, Jimmy, I've heard worse.'

After clocking out at five-thirty, Amy and Carole walked up the hill towards the Old Bull where Amy crossed the road onto Long Lane and Carole walked straight on towards Middle Street.

'See you on Monday, Carole,' Amy waved and turned away.

'Have a good weekend,' Carole replied. 'I might see you in the Bull for the last couple on Saturday night if you're in.'

Amy walked the short distance to Honeysuckle Cottage and pushed the gate open. Her mother opened the door as she walked up the path.

'You've got a parcel,' she said with a wink.

'A parcel?' Amy stepped inside to find a large hessian bag sitting on the floor in the hall.

'A nice young man dropped it off about fifteen minutes ago. He said something about making up for his rudeness today.'

Amy slipped off her coat, hung it on a peg, then pulled at the string tie at the top of the sack. Inside were six silk panels cut into the shape of an isosceles triangle. There was a sheet of folded, lined notepaper sitting on top. Amy unfolded it and scanned the neat handwriting.

'Am I forgiven?'

Amy pulled one of the panels from the bag and held it to her chest.

'For this, I'd forgive you almost anything, Jimmy,' she whispered.

Chapter 8

Alice
Saturday 14th December

At eight o'clock on Saturday morning, I got changed out of my overalls and had a strip wash at the sink in the bathroom. Pulling on a woolly jumper and a thick pair of trousers, I fiddled with my hair and then deciding there was no point in glamming myself up just to trudge through the fields, I returned to the kitchen and pulled on my wellies.

'Okay, it's time to pick a tree, Barney will be waiting for us, get a move on.'

The kids dropped their books on the table and leapt to their feet. Inside a minute they had pulled on their own boots and were fastening their coats.

'Is it a real tree?' Harriet asked.

'We only ever have a live tree,' I replied.

'But won't it die when we dig it up, Aunty Alice?'

'No, because we're going to plant it in soil in the kitchen and we won't let it dry out. One of you will have to give it some water every couple of days.'

'Me, me!' Harriet shouted.

I led the kids into the yard where Barney had already retrieved the cut down barrel from the shed and half-filled it with soil.

'Barney will need a hand to carry that in,' I said, 'it will be really heavy.'

'I'll help, I'm strong,' Stephen said, flexing his muscles.

'I think I'll get George to give him a hand, I don't want you straining something.' I felt his boyish bicep. 'Mind you, I'm impressed with your muscles.'

We began to walk past the stables and over towards the wood at the side of Middle Field.

'They've got bigger since I've been here,' Stephen boasted. 'I've got taller too.'

'I've got taller as well,' Harriet said, looking up at me as we walked through the muddy bit at the edge of the bottom acre.

'It must be the good, wholesome food and the country air,' I said, smiling.

'We never used to eat food like we have now at home,' Stephen said thoughtfully. 'We had lots of chips though.' He was silent for a moment. 'I miss chips.'

'We might get some from the chip shop in the week,' I replied, stepping over a thick branch that had fallen out of the hedge. 'Remind me to ask Miriam what's on the menu this week.'

As he had promised, Barney was waiting for us in Badger Wood, so called for its numerous badger sets. Barney loved the badgers and would sometimes arrive at work ridiculously early just so he could watch them for a while before starting his day.

'Now then,' he said, leaning on his shovel as we approached. 'Which one do you fancy? I've tied a bit of string around the trunks of the likely candidates.'

'This one,' Harriet said immediately, spotting a sapling with a bit of tatty, faded ribbon tied around it.

'That was last year's tree,' Barney said. 'Can't you remember? We tied a ribbon around it so we wouldn't pick the same one this year.'

'Ah, I remember now,' Harriet said, patting the tree's branches. 'It's grown a bit.'

After much arguing and after listening to Barney's expert advice, the kids settled on an eight-foot tree. I nodded my approval. The sapling was the perfect shape, bushy at the bottom, with a spindly top, ideal for our Christmas tree angel.

It took Barney almost half an hour to get the tree out of the ground using a fork, the spade and a thick iron bar as a lever. When it was out, Barney picked it up and threw it over his shoulder while, Stephen, Harriet and I, carried his tools.

Back at the farm, Barney laid the tree carefully in the yard and called to George Foulkes who was working in the cow shed. Together and with many a grunt, they lifted the heavy barrel and carried it into the kitchen.

'Same spot as usual, Missis?' Barney asked when they were inside.

I nodded and the two farm hands slid the barrel into place in the corner of the kitchen. Returning to the yard, Barney picked up the sapling while George went to the shed to find some hand tools.

Fifteen minutes later, the tree had been planted, loosened, turned, replanted and straightened, three times over. The tip of the tree was about a foot short of the ceiling. Barney looked at it and nodded with satisfaction.

'It's a bit taller than last year. You'll need the step ladder to get the angel on top. Give me a shout if you're struggling with it.'

Miriam handed me a mug of steaming hot tea and smiled as she studied our new tree.

'It's a lovely shape, Alice. Are we decorating it now, or when you come back from town?'

'NOW!' yelled Stephen and Harriet together.

I shrugged and took a sip of my tea. 'We've got plenty of time,' I said.

Ninety minutes later, the tree was dressed. We had only lost one or two of the glass baubles since last year, which was a bonus as they were now impossible to find in the shops. We finished it off by laying long strips of silver, aluminium tinsel across the branches. Standing back, I nodded in satisfaction. 'Right,' I said, 'who's got the angel?'

Harriet picked it up from the bottom of the box and held it out with a sad look on her face. 'It's a bit tatty, Aunty Alice. Her wings have fallen off.'

'Oh dear,' I said, as I examined the distressed angel.

'I think it's on its last legs,' said Stephen.

'You're right, we need a new one,' I said, dropping the angel back into the empty box.

'What are we going to do? The tree needs an angel,' Harriet said.

'We'll make one,' I replied.

Walking to my desk, I tore off the thin, green cardboard cover from the back of my accounts book and carried it back through to the kitchen. Forming the cover into a cone shape, I cut off a couple of strips from my precious roll of Sellotape and stuck the angled edge of the cone to the main body. Tidying it up with a pair of sharp scissors, I held up the angel's body for inspection.

'She needs a head,' said Stephen.

'Ah, I've got just the thing,' I said and began to rummage around in the bits and bobs drawer. 'There,' I said, holding up the white ping pong ball that had been hidden in the corner.

'She needs a face,' Harriet said, excitedly.

Picking up a thick pencil, I drew round eyes, eyebrows and a smiling mouth onto the ping pong ball.

'You can hardly see it,' Stephen complained.

'I have an idea,' Miriam said, hurrying to the stairs. When she returned, she carried her box of cake mascara and a tiny brush. Scooping a tiny bit of the black powder from the box, she dropped it onto a saucer and added two drops of water. Mixing it into a paste with the brush, she straightened and pointed to the pencil. 'Dip it in and go over the lines,' she said.

It worked a treat, a couple of minutes later we had a happy smiling face drawn onto the ping pong ball. Snipping off another strip of tape, I stuck the head to the angel's body then sat her down on the table while I fashioned a pair of wings from the remaining bits of cardboard.

'How's that?' I said, holding her in the air like a trophy.

'Let's put her on the tree,' Stephen called, hurrying across the kitchen

I opened the cupboard under the stairs and dragged out a short pair of stepladders. Climbing up to the third step, I stood, unsteadily as I reached out to try to hook the angel over the top of the tree. I got nowhere near.

'I think you'd better call for Barney,' I said, gingerly stepping down.

Stephen rushed out of the back door and returned with Barney in tow. My foreman was over six foot tall and as wide as a tallboy.

'Having trouble?' he asked, stating the obvious.

'You know what I'm like with heights, Barney,' I laughed nervously.

Barney took the angel from me, put one foot on the stepladder, then turning away he walked across the kitchen to where Martha was watching proceedings from her playpen.

'Come on, little one, you can do the honours,' he said, lifting her into the air.

He carried Martha to the tree and then, with the confidence that only men seem to have when holding small children, he climbed to the second step, and after putting the angel in Martha's tiny hands, he held her out towards the apex of the tree. 'Put it on the top spike,' he said.

Miriam held a hand over her mouth, Harriet looked on wide eyed as Stephen laughed and clapped.

'Careful, Barney,' I said, my heart in my mouth.

Martha acted as though she had been hanging angels all her life and reached across the six-inch gap to drop it over the spike at the top of the tree. We all applauded as Barney stepped down from the ladder. He handed Martha to me and I pointed to the angel and bounced her in my arms.

'Clever girl,' I said.

'Angel,' Martha said, then turned her head towards the back door.

'Piggies now,' she said.

Chapter 9

Alice
Saturday 14th December

At twelve o'clock we sat in the tea shop in town looking out of the fogged-up window as we sipped our hot drinks and nibbled at the dry cake that tasted as though it had spent a day too long under the glass counter. Stephen, bored as usual, began to draw with his finger in the condensation on the shop window. After twenty minutes I put him out of his misery and we got to our feet and made for the door, moving aside to allow a pair of elderly ladies to enter.

'Thank you, dears,' the first of the pensioners smiled at the children. 'I'm ready for a cuppa, I'm parched.'

'I wouldn't bother with the sponge cake,' Stephen advised. 'You'll be even parchder.' He looked at me quizzically as I tried to usher him out of the café before he got us into trouble. 'Is parchder a word?' he asked.

Outside, the Saturday lunchtime streets were full of shoppers. Jam-packed buses trundled along the narrow town roads as the half day Saturday workers made their way home from the factories. The bustling market place echoed with the shouts of, 'Plums, get your lovely plums, they're big, they're beautiful just like your... mums,' and 'sprouts and cabbage, fresher than your lodger, put it on a plate for him, girls, he'll love you for it.'

We visited the wool shop where I bought a few ounces of navy wool for Miriam's latest project, then we dropped in at Woolworths to top Harriet up with sweets. Stephen got his usual penny's worth which amazingly used to last him all through the weekend. He unwrapped a Blackjack liquorice chew and popped it into his mouth as he studied the toy shelves.

'We're not shopping for toys today,' I reminded him. 'We don't know what Santa has got in his sack for you.'

'I was only looking,' he said as he put the balsa wood bi plane model back on the shelf. 'I'm saving up for the fort, remember?'

'I'm very impressed with your new found determination, Stephen,' I said as we left the shop and stepped out onto the pavement.

'Can we go to Stan's now, Aunty Alice?' Stephen asked as he tugged impatiently at my sleeve.

'All right then,' I replied. 'Let's go and have a look at your fort.'

Stan's Bargain Emporium was a big store, three shop units wide and laid out over two floors. We made our way past the battered, upright piano, a sofa that had seen many a better day and a dining table with more scratches than an old Al Jolson record and headed for the stairs. On the first floor behind the bed frames, mattresses and wardrobes, was the small, toy section.

The shelves were stuffed with battered board game boxes and die cast cars that looked rustier than their real counterparts out on the street. Sat on upturned fruit crates in front of the shelves was a line of dolls and teddy bears, some in very good condition but others missing an eye or a clump of hair. On the floor, in front of the dolls and bears was a large cardboard box stuffed with doll's clothes. Harriet hung her nose over it for a few seconds but turned away when she heard Stephen's horrified wail.

'They've sold, it. They've sold it, Aunty Alice.'

My eyes followed Stephen's pointed finger. There, beneath the window, was the object of his dreams, a wooden cowboy fort with model cavalry soldiers pointing their rifles from the ramparts at a dozen or so Indian figures, resplendent in their feathered headdresses. Pinned to the front of the fort was a piece of card with the word, *SOLD* written across it in black crayon.

Stephen was distraught.

'Aunty Alice...'

I crouched down beside him and put my arm around his shoulder.

'Never mind, Stephen, there'll get another one in before long.'

Stephen's eyes filled with disappointed tears. 'It won't be that one though.'

'Aunty Alice, the doll's house has gone.'

This time my eyes followed Harriet's pointed finger. The last time we had been in the store there had been a beautiful, white fronted, doll's house. Three foot in height, it was crammed with elegant Edwardian furniture. There was even a real porcelain sink in the kitchen and an upstairs bath. It had a price tag of eighteen shillings.

'You'd never have saved up enough to buy it anyway,' sniffed Stephen.

'I might have, I was going to start saving after Christmas, but there's no point now.'

'You wouldn't have saved up for it; you spend it all on books and sweets.'

'I can save, can't I, Aunty Alice?'

I took my arm from around Stephen's shoulder and looked at him sadly.

'Is there anything else you'd like to buy, Stephen? I can lend you the money until you open your piggy bank.'

'No, the rest of it is all junk.' There was to be no appeasing him.

'I'd like some doll's clothes,' Harriet piped up as she rummaged through the box.

'You've got no money left,' said Stephen. 'You can't borrow any because you can't pay it back.'

Harriet shrugged. She was ever the pragmatist.

'I'll get some next time then.'

'Come on, you two,' I said putting my hands on their backs and guiding them towards the stairs. Stephen took one last, lingering look over his shoulder before his head slumped forward.

'It's not fair,' he said.

'Life isn't fair all the time, Stephen,' I said softly. 'Now... I've been thinking. You need to get that present for your mum organised. Come on! The photographer's is only around the corner.'

Jenkinson's Photography (Weddings and Christenings a speciality) was a red-brick shop on the corner of High Street and Cooper's Gate. It had a large, plate-glass window that displayed numerous aspects of his work. As we entered, a small bell tinkled and a few seconds later, the photographer came in from a room at the back. He was a tall, wiry man with thinning hair and a pencil line moustache. He took off his horn-rimmed spectacles and polished them on his tie.

'Hello,' he said cheerfully. 'How may I assist you?'

'We'd like a portrait of Stephen and Harriet, please,' I said with a smile. 'It's a Christmas present for their mum and dad, they're still in London.'

'Excellent.' Mr Jenkinson clapped his hands together and crouched down to study the children.

'Very photogenic,' he said after a few moments. 'Would you like the picture taken now or would you rather I book a session for you in the week?'

'Now, if possible,' I said. 'It might be difficult in the week, they're at school you see.'

'Well, I'm open until six, if ever you need anything else.' The photographer opened the door at the back of the shop and led us into his studio. Looking around as if it was the first time he had stepped into the place, he clapped his hands again. 'Okay, are we going for a plain background or would you like to have it taken in front of a backdrop?'

I looked at the kids, 'What do you think?'

Stephen looked at his sister, they both shrugged.

'Would you like to dress up for the picture? That would be fun?'

The kids were suddenly full of interest. 'What can we dress up as? Can I be a soldier?' asked Stephen.

'I don't want to be a soldier, can I be a fairy?' Harriet asked.

'You can't have a picture of a soldier with a fairy,' Stephen complained. 'It would look silly.'

'How about a cowboy and Indian picture?' Mr Jenkinson suggested. 'Or, maybe a pair of pirates?'

'PIRATES!' Stephen and Harriet looked at each other and nodded eagerly.

Mr Jenkinson led us to the far end of the room where he pointed to an overflowing box of clothing.

'See if you can find something that fits. There are hats in the other box over there.'

As the kids rummaged through the boxes, the photographer set up his lighting and hung up a sheet with the picture of an old sailing ship printed on it. Walking to his camera tripod, he looked through the lens before asking me to sit in front of the backdrop while he set the picture up.

A few minutes later, Stephen and Harriet came in from the changing room. Stephen was dressed in knee length, black shorts with a white shirt and a red spotted handkerchief tied around his neck. His tricorn hat was a couple of sizes too big and hung over his eyes, one of which was already covered with a black eye patch.

Harriet wore similar trousers with a red and white, horizontal striped shirt with a navy spotted handkerchief around her hair. 'Can you help me with it, Aunty Alice? I can't get it tied up properly.'

When she was satisfied with the way she looked, the children climbed onto the staging and struck what they obviously thought was a pirate pose.

Mr Jenkinson leaned forwards, looked through the lens and then straightened up again.

'There's something missing,' he said thoughtfully. 'Ah I know what it is.' He turned and rushed to the back of the shop. When he returned, he was holding a stuffed, blue and yellow parrot.

'Now, who's going to have this on their shoulder.'

'ME!' shouted Stephen.

Harriet looked at the tatty bird with distaste.

'I don't want it,' she shuddered. 'Is it a real one?'

'It was once,' said the photographer. He placed the dusty old bird on Stephen's shoulder and held it in place with a safety pin. 'Don't move around too much, young man, I'm not sure how well it's fixed.'

Fifteen minutes later, the job was done, the kids had put their own clothes back on and we were in the shop choosing a frame.

'I like the gold one,' said Harriet.

'No, the silver one is best.' Stephen was adamant.

'Let's let Mr Jenkinson decide what looks best when he's developed the picture, shall we?' I suggested before a full-blown argument could ensue.

The children nodded reluctantly.

'How much do we owe you, Mr Jenkinson?' I asked pulling my purse from my bag.

As Stephen and Harriet looked around the pet's picture corner, the photographer wrote out a receipt.

'It will be eight and six for the standard six by four photograph, or eleven shillings for a twelve by eight-inch enlargement, including the gold frame.'

'We'll take the enlargement,' I said handing him the money. 'When do you think it will be ready to collect? Their mum is coming up for Christmas and they haven't seen her for over a year now. This picture will mean so much to her.'

'I'll get it done for mid-week,' he promised. 'Pick it up any time after Wednesday.'

'I'll call in again next Saturday if that's all right?' I said, stuffing the receipt into my bag.

'How would you like your portrait done?'

'Me?' I stuttered, wide eyed. 'Oh, no thanks, I don't do photographs.'

'That's a shame,' he replied. 'With the right lighting, you'd look exactly like that film star, Rita Haywood.'

'Worth,' I corrected him, 'it's Hayworth.'

'Well, however you say it, you do bear a remarkable resemblance to her.'

I smiled. 'It has been noted, Mr Jenkinson.' I turned towards the door to collect the waiting children.

'I'll do it half price,' he offered. 'It would look fabulous in my window.'

'I'll think about it,' I said as Stephen opened the shop door.

Chapter 10

When we got home from town, Stephen hurried to his room and came back down carrying his piggy bank.

'What have you brought that down for?' I asked as I hung up my coat.

'We have to pay you for the photo, Aunty Alice. It's our present so we can't let you buy it.' He took the rubber stopper from the bottom of the porcelain pig and shook it until a few coins came out. 'How much was it?' he asked.

My heart swelled. 'Oh, it was sixpence, I think.'

Stephen narrowed his eyes as he looked at me. 'It was more than that, Aunty Alice. The frame had a tag on it that said three and six.'

'Ah, but that was without the discount,' I replied quickly.

'What's a discount?'

'It's a bargain, when you buy something cheaper than it should have been. Mr Jenkinson thinks he might get some more work from us, so he's knocked some money off the bill. He gave us the frame for free.'

'But it was still more than sixpence,' Stephen said, looking at me closely.

My eyes darted to Miriam; I couldn't tell him the photo cost more than he had in his piggy bank.

Miriam mouthed, 'two shillings' at me and winked.

'All right, there's no fooling you is there? It was two shillings for the photograph.'

Stephen nodded and began to count out the coins. When he had twelve pennies, a sixpence and two threepenny bits in his hand, he held it out and tipped it into mine.

'Harriet can pay me back later,' he said.

'But that means I'll have no pocket money for two weeks,' she said.

I gave them sixpence a week and another sixpence if they helped out with the washing up or feeding the chickens.

'Hmmm,' Stephen thought about it for a few moments. 'All right, you can buy my pennyworth of sweets every week for the next twelve weeks. That way I'll save extra and you'll still have plenty of money.'

Harriet threw her hands around his neck and hugged him and my eyes began to leak.

'That really is very generous of you, Stephen,' I said croakily. I walked quickly to the sink and made out I was looking out of the window as I dabbed my eyes on the tea towel. 'Who's for a cuppa?' I said eventually.

Miriam, for once, was made of sterner stuff. 'What about your fort?' she asked.

'It's been sold,' Stephen replied. 'I don't know what I'm going to save up for next. I think I'll wait to see what Santa brings before I decide.'

'I think that's very wise,' Miriam said softly. 'I'm so sorry to hear about your fort.'

'That's all right,' said Stephen stoically. 'Life is full of ups and downs, isn't it?' He looked at Harriet and smiled. 'That's what Mum always says.'

'And she's right,' I said. 'Always listen to mums. They give the best advice.'

I had just returned from taking my Saturday evening bath when Amy opened the back door. 'It's tipping down,' she said, shaking the rain from her flaxen hair.

Miriam had just taken the children through for their own bath and I was standing in front of the fire, swathed in towels as she stepped in.

'This is a pleasant surprise,' I said as she shook her coat on the top step before closing the door and hanging it up on the hook on the back of it. 'I thought we were meeting at yours.'

'I'm full of surprises,' she said. 'You're going to need a brolly tonight.'

I nodded. 'It might ease off before we go.'

Amy and I always spent Saturday night at the picture house in town, we usually followed up with a few drinks at the Old Bull at the end of Long Lane. This week it was Laurence Olivier and Greer Garson in Jane Austen's Pride and Prejudice. Both Amy and I had read the book countless times and couldn't wait to see what Hollywood had made of it.

She smoothed down her green dress and sat at our big oak table. 'Does my hair look frightful? It was only spitting when I left the house.'

Amy couldn't look frightful if she dressed up as a Halloween witch, complete with facial warts and chin hairs. She was the most beautiful woman I had ever seen, both inside and out. She seemed oblivious to her own beauty, even though she had to constantly spurn the advances of the eligible and not so eligible men of the town.

'It might need a bit of work before we go, but then it will only get soaked again on the way to the bus stop.'

'Hence my request for a brolly, dear heart. Weren't you listening?'

I took my towel turban from my own hair and began to rub at it gently, leaning over the fireguard in front of blazing log fire.

'I've got news, but it's very hush hush,' she announced.

I stopped rubbing at my hair and looked across to the table where she sat, fiddling with her necklace.

'I'm all ears,' I said.

'This can't go anywhere outside of this room, Alice. I could be shot.'

'Shot?' I replied. 'I know there's a war on, my darling, but shot?'

'It's a big secret,' Amy said looking over her shoulder towards the back door in case anyone was listening.

'That's good. You know I can keep a secret.'

Amy's mouth gaped. 'Alice! You are the absolutely worst secret keeper I've ever known... apart from Miriam that is. Look how you were with your own secret last week?'

I was puzzled. 'My own secret?'

Amy looked towards the parlour to make sure the kids couldn't overhear.

'Rose's visit,' she hissed. 'It was your own secret but you were bursting to tell anyone who would listen. You're a terrible secret keeper.'

'That was different,' I replied. 'Anyway, come on, out with it. You can't leave it at that.'

Amy looked over her shoulder again. 'Parachutes,' she said.

'Parachutes? What about parachutes?'

'I'm going to be making them at the Mill, but it's top secret. They don't want it to get out in case the German's bomb us.'

I laughed. 'Do they really think there's a German spy in the factory?'

'Not just in the factory, out and about... you never know, really.'

'No, I suppose not,' I replied. 'I hope they've kept the news away from Big Nose Beryl, or old Adolph will be pointing out Spinton on the map as we speak.'

'She doesn't know. Not yet anyway, though I have a feeling she'll find out soon enough. You know what she's like.'

'She's bound to find out if the entire workforce is going to be producing them,' I said.

'It's not the whole factory, dear heart. It's just me and Carole at the minute. We've got to go in the weekend after Christmas for training. I've been given the Monday and Tuesday before Christmas off to make up for it.'

'The two of you won't keep the RAF going,' I said.

'No, they're just using us as guinea pigs. They needed the best machinists. The government have to inspect the parachutes we make and pass the workmanship before the company gets an order.'

'Ah, I see. Well, that's going to be interesting for you.'

'It's not the best bit.' She clenched her fists, held them to her chest and gave me a wide-eyed, excited grin. 'Jimmy, the rope man... he tried to chat me up... anyway he's given me a load of waste silk. He's supposed to bale it all up and send it back, but he gave me SIX lengths of it.'

'WOW!'

'I know, and it's top-quality silk. You couldn't buy better in Harrods.'

'Ooh, I'm excited for you. What are you going to knock up with it?'

'You mean which high class garments am I going to produce with my excellent sewing skills?'

'Yes,' I nodded seriously. 'Of course, that's what I meant.'

'I'm not telling you,' Amy replied. 'I'll show you when I've finished.'

'Oh, come on? You've told me the important bit.'

'You've had enough secrets for one night,' Amy replied, giving me one of her looks. 'Now, come on, get yourself dressed. Laurence Oliver won't wait for us.'

As I was about to go upstairs to get ready, Miriam and the kids came in from the bathroom.

'Come on, you two, upstairs, get your jim-jams on,' she urged. 'And be quick about it, you'll catch your deaths of cold.'

I smiled at them fondly as they hurried by and took the stairs two at a time.

'Amy's making parachutes,' I said, turning towards Miriam.

'Parachutes?'

'Yes, and Jimmy the rope man who fancies her has given her a ton of top-quality silk to do with as she pleases.'

'Oh, my goodness. Silk? Oh, Amy, you lucky girl. What are you going to make?'

Amy blew out her cheeks then let the air out slowly. 'It was supposed to be a secret,' she said, looking hard at me. 'No one is supposed to know.'

'Oh, come on, it's only Miriam.'

'Can you make me a parachute, Aunty Amy?' said Stephen as he stepped back into the room.

Amy blew out her cheeks again and put her head in her hands. 'If the Mill gets bombed,' she said, looking hard at me again. 'I'll know who to blame.'

By the time we left the picture house the rain had pretty much stopped and we walked along Middle Street arm in arm, stepping around the deepest of the puddles. Over the road, the chip shop was already doing a brisk trade. We crossed over and joined a short queue to buy our portions of fish and chips before sitting on the low wall opposite the bus stop, to eat them.

'Wasn't Greer Garson fabulous as Lizzie Bennet?' I said. 'I believed in her right from the start.'

'She was wonderful, so was Laurence Olivier as Mr Darcy. My goodness, he was everything I ever hoped he would be... and Mary Boland... Mrs Bennet, she was straight out of the book, wasn't she? So funny.'

'I didn't get the archery bit though,' I said, blowing onto a hot chip before biting into it.

'No, one or two things were a bit different,' Amy replied. 'I think it's because the script was based on the stage play, not the book.'

'Really?'

Amy nodded and cut into her fish with her wooden fork. 'I read about it in my Photoplay magazine. My uncle imports it with the records he buys in from America. You can't buy it in the shops over here. I'm so lucky.'

Amy was the biggest movie buff I knew. She could remember not only the plot and the cast but many of the lines from most of the movies we'd seen. We never got to see them when they were brand new. Our little back water movie theatre was always a few months behind the big cities.

The rain was just starting up again as we spotted the bus trundling down the hill. Dropping our fish and chip wrappings into the bin, we hurried across the puddle strewn street and took our place at the back of the queue. Fortunately, the rain storm sputtered out almost as quickly as it had begun and my umbrella was only needed for a few moments.

The Old Bull lounge was jam-packed as I took my place at the counter and looked across to the public bar as the men of the town elbowed each other out of the way to get the landlord's attention. I waited patiently for Stan to spot me, when he did, he waved away the noisy protests from the barflies, and smiling, came into our side of the pub.

'What's she got that we haven't?' yelled Arnold Calderwood, a metal worker from the local foundry.

'If you can't see that for yourself, you'd better get some new glasses.' Stan called back over his shoulder. He smiled at me again. 'Now, Alice, two port and lemons, is it?'

The snug, or lounge bar was mostly occupied by women. Stan put an extra ha'penny on a pint for anyone drinking in that side of the pub. We were pleased about that, it kept most of the riff raff out.

We joined a crowd of Mill girls and listened to the local gossip for a while before Amy heard the unmistakeable whiny voice of Big Nose Beryl. She turned to see her standing at the end of the bar with two of her cronies. She hadn't noticed Amy, who stepped quietly across the room to stand behind her.

'She's up to no good with that new fellah we spotted in the canteen last week, I'm sure of it.' Beryl paused to sip her drink and missing the warning looks from her two friends, she continued the character assassination.

'She was locked in the old warehouse with him. They were in there together on their own for ages. I don't know what's going on in there, she's saying nothing about it, but when she came out, she was straightening her skirt.' Beryl touched her nose. 'Now, I'm not one to gossip as you know, but... well, you have to believe the evidence of your own eyes.'

I nudged Mary Kelly and nodded towards Beryl. 'Wait for it,' I whispered.

Beryl took another gulp of her drink and was about to expand on the topic when she felt Amy's hand on her shoulder.

'So, Beryl. You saw me and Mr Barrie, the government procurement officer lock ourselves in the warehouse and I came out with dishevelled clothing. Is that correct?'

Beryl visibly deflated.

'Not you, nooooo, not you, Amy. I was talking about...' Beryl tailed off as she looked into Amy's angry face.

'Not me? So, who was this... floozy who was up to no good at the same time as I was in the warehouse with the aforementioned Mr Barrie, Carole Sims, a Grayson's engineer and one of their female cutters? Because I didn't see anyone else in there at all. I think we might have noticed if anything like that had been going on.'

Amy smiled sweetly at Beryl. 'Come on, Beryl, spill the beans, we're all desperate to know who this flighty piece is.'

'I don't know her name, I think she's from Grayson's.'

'Ah, well that would be Janet then? She was the only other woman there at the time. I'll ask her all about it when I see her next.' Amy sipped her drink. 'She was a big woman, Beryl. I don't think I'd like to get on the wrong side of her.'

Beryl, who had had one gin too many, scowled at Amy.

'You think you're so clever, don't you? But you'll get what's coming one of these days.'

'Perhaps so.' Amy looked into Beryl's face with steely eyes. 'But whatever I have coming, won't be delivered by you. Now, I've told you before. Be very careful what you say about me or any one of my friends or you'll wish you had never been born.'

She glared at Beryl's friends, then turned her attention to the town's biggest gossip once more.

'Never forget that I know everything there is to know about you, Beryl. I know about the things you steal from the Mill; I know about the lies you told about Mr Bartholomew when he first took the foreman's job on.' Amy took a slow sip of her drink. 'And I know all about your fancy man. The one you see on Wednesdays when your Leonard is on nights.'

Beryl turned three shades of purple in as many seconds. Her two friends stared at her goggle-eyed.

'So, Beryl. If you'd like me to keep the news of your sordid little affair to myself. You had better stop spreading malicious gossip about me and the other Mill girls. I wonder what your Leonard would make of it? I've seen you sporting the odd black eye. I think you'd get more than that from him if he ever found out. He doesn't have the calmest of tempers, does he?'

'You wouldn't... You... Look, that was a one off, I was a bit worse for wear... I—'

'You were at it at his house last Wednesday night, Beryl. You and... do I have to name him here?'

'It's a lie. A dirty lie. I was at home all night.'

'You were seen coming out of his back door at half past ten, Beryl. But the thing is, the rest of the Mill girls don't think it's any of our business, so we keep it pretty much to ourselves. We don't go around telling the world about things that don't concern us. You should try it. You never know, you might earn a tiny bit of respect.'

Beryl took a deep breath, then still red faced, she turned, placed her half-drunk glass of cider on the bar and walked quietly out of the pub leaving her friends looking at each other with pursed lips.

Chapter 11

Alice
Sunday 15th December

The rain was still coming down on Sunday morning as I made my way around the pens, cleaning, feeding and scratching the backs of my big boars Hector and Horace. Because the weather was so bad, I decided to take two of the latest batch of piglets into the house to play with Martha in her pen instead of bringing her outside. She squealed louder than the piglets when she spotted them in my arms and began to jump up and down in her playpen. My border collie pup, Tess, was just as excited at seeing the miniature porkers and as soon as I had put them in the pen with Martha, she circled it repeatedly, yapping and whimpering as her sheepdog instincts came to the fore.

Amy arrived at eleven-thirty. She had attended church with her parents and was still wearing what her mother called 'her Sunday best dress' under her thick winter coat.

I shook the kettle at her, then when she nodded, I filled it up and placed it on the gas hob to boil.

'How was the Reverend Villiers?' I asked as she pulled off her coat.

'Insufferable as usual,' she replied with a sigh. 'The man is a drinker, a big one, but every Sunday he castigates the townsfolk who partake in the devil's brew after a hard week's work. He really is a hypocrite. He hits the booze most evenings. He was almost arrested one night when the police were called out. They found him in the churchyard shouting insults at the moon, dressed only in his underpants.'

I shuddered. 'I heard about that. It's not something you can easily get out of you mind when you picture the scene. Perhaps he's just feeling guilty about his own failings and the sermon is aimed at himself.'

'I doubt it,' Amy replied. 'He's far too self-centred to see any personal faults. Dad has seen him in some proper states when he's been up to the vicarage to help him write his sermons, and when he comes to ours, it's only a matter of minutes before Dad's whisky bottle is out.'

'Your dad likes a drop though; I remember that time—'

'All right, all right,' Amy cut in. 'Don't remind me about that. I've only just been able to look our next-door neighbour in the face, poor woman.' She shook her head slowly, then changed the subject.

'I meant to ask yesterday, did you get the kid's present sorted?'

'Yep, it's done if not quite dusted. I've got to pick it up in the week. Mr Jenkinson offered to do a portrait of me at a discount. He wants to put it in the shop window apparently.'

'What did you say? He asked me if he could do my portrait too, he wanted to enter it into a competition in London. There's a big cash prize for the model and the photographer by all accounts.'

'And you said no? Amy, you might have won.'

Amy shrugged. 'I did think about it.'

'You should let him take one. it could be fun. Do you get to go to London yourself if you're one of the models?'

Amy nodded. 'If his picture is selected for the long list, and to be fair to him one of his entries has made it every year for the last three years. He's a brilliant photographer, but he's never won it.'

I lifted the big pot and poured tea into Amy's mug. 'Is there milk in the jug?'

Amy nodded and tipped a splash into her tea. 'I'm not sure I'm cut out to be a model, even for a one-off competition.'

'You'd be perfect,' I said. 'Go on, Amy. It's only a picture.'

Amy considered it, placing her fingers on her lips as she thought.

'I'll do it if you will,' she said after a few moments.

'What? He doesn't want me for his competition.'

'No, but he wants you for his shop window. Come on, Alice. Fair's fair. I'm in if you are?'

It was my turn to think hard about it. 'I could give a copy to Godfrey for Christmas, did I tell you he's coming up on Christmas Eve, we're going out for dinner on the Friday.'

'That's a great idea, Alice,' Amy enthused. 'He's only got that grainy old picture I took of you. A proper professional one would look much better on his bedside table.'

'How do you know he's got my picture on the bedside table? You've never been to his London flat.'

'You told me when you got back from London in September. He kisses it every night.' Amy pursed her lips and blew a series of kisses at me. 'Isn't that sweet?'

I blushed and looked away as she fired off a dozen more kisses.

'I was wondering what to get him if I'm honest. All right, if we're going to do it, when should we get it done? He's open until six most nights but you don't finish work until five-thirty.'

'I'm off the Monday and Christmas Eve,' she said brightly. 'We could do it then.'

'No, that's no good, I want to give it to him on Christmas Eve. Godfrey is dropping in on the way home.'

'Give him a ring, see if he'll open late for us.'

'Will he answer on a Sunday?'

'You won't know until you try,' she replied.

'Hello?'

'Hello, Mr Jenkinson. It's Alice Mollison. I'm sorry to bother you on a Sunday but I just hoped for a quick word.'

'That's quite all right, Alice... may I call you Alice?'

'Of course. Now, the thing is, I was thinking about your offer yesterday and I've decided to take you up on it if it's still on the table, but I'd like to have it before Christmas. It's going to be a present, you see.'

'Wonderful. You'd look perfect in my window... then again I could put you on my feature wall, a bit of discreet lighting and no one would be able to take their eyes off you.'

I felt myself blushing.

'Do I have to get dressed up for it then?'

'It would be nice; I see you as the Hollywood starlet. You know, the dreamy sort of picture you see in the magazines. Soft lighting, curls around the shoulders, sparking eyes.'

'Ah, I see, you don't want me to dress up as a pirate then?'

Mr Jenkinson laughed. 'Only if you insist.'

'I'll find something to throw on,' I replied. 'Now, I have another bit of news for you.'

'News, for me?'

'You remember Amy Rowlings? She came in with Detective Bodkin a while back. He had some photographic evidence that needed developing.'

'I remember her well, a stunning young lady.'

'Are you still interested in using her as a model for the London photographic competition?'

'I'd give my eye teeth for the chance to enter her into the competition. She's a sure-fire winner, I'm sure of it. I only got a fourth place this year.'

'Well, I think I can persuade her to sit for you. Would it be all right if we came in together?'

'It would be... Oh, Mrs... Alice, this has made my day.'

I smiled across the room at Amy and nodded. 'When do you think you could fit us in? Amy works until five-thirty every night and I'm busy on the farm in the mornings.'

'How would... could you get in this afternoon? I've almost caught up with the developing and enlargements. I'd be free after two o'clock.'

I put my hand over the mouthpiece and grinned at Amy. 'He can do us this afternoon,' I said. 'After two. What do you think?'

'It's a bit short notice,' she replied. 'I was hoping to have time to build up to it. Shall we have them done after Christmas instead?'

I shook my head. I wanted that photograph for Godfrey.

'All right then. But I'll have to go home to get changed. I'm not having my picture taken wearing my frumpy Sunday dress. What sort of thing is he expecting me to wear anyway?'

'This afternoon will be fine, Mr Jenkinson. I'll make sure Amy is dressed suitably.'

'I see her in a summer dress,' the photographer replied thoughtfully. 'A print dress, not too busy a pattern though. We don't want anything to distract from that wonderful face.'

'What about me?'

'As glam as you can make it,' he replied. 'We're doing Hollywood after all.'

'Glam,' I said, looking despairing into my wardrobe. 'I can't do glam, I have nothing to do glam, in.'

Amy pulled out my best polka dot dress. 'I see what you mean, it's nice, but it's not exactly Hollywood.' She thought for a moment, pulled out my little black dress, held it up against me, then hung it back in the wardrobe.

'You could have a look through my stuff.' She looked at me with a critical eye. 'Though your body has changed shape a bit since you last borrowed one of my dresses.' She turned me around and studied me from the back. 'You've become quite matronly,' she said, as she slapped my backside.

'MATRONLY!'

Amy bit her lip but the laugh burst out of her anyway.

'I still fit into my clothes,' I said defensively. 'They're a tiny bit tighter across the hips, but they still hang nicely.'

'I think you're a better shape, actually. Motherhood suits you,' Amy turned me around again. 'Yep, definitely. You're a full-grown woman now, not a young slip of a girl.'

'I'm only twenty-one.' I replied. 'You make it sound like I'm thirty or something.'

'I was paying you a compliment,' Amy said, looking forlornly into my wardrobe. 'Is this the lot?'

'Well, there's my mum's stuff. It's in the back bedroom.'

'Now you're talking!' Amy sped out of the room. 'Your mum could do glam with the best of them. Didn't she once meet the Royal Family at a garden party at the palace?'

I furrowed my brow as I thought. 'No, though she did meet them in the Royal enclosure at the Epsom Derby. She was with her sister from Knightsbridge, she married very well.'

Amy rushed along the landing and flung open the spare bedroom door. We had used the room for extra storage since Bodkin, my short-term lodger had moved out.

Amy stepped inside and threw open the double wardrobe doors.

'WOW!' she said. 'Some of this stuff belongs on a cat walk.'

She pulled out a black dress covered in glittery sequins. 'Oh my God, this is beautiful... for the right occasion of course.' She hung it back on the rail and pulled out three or four more, holding them up for scrutiny before laying them out on the single bed. When she got to the green mermaid's dress, her eyes popped open. 'THIS ONE! Oh, my goodness, it has to be this one.'

I frowned. 'It's a bit figure hugging, isn't it?'

'It's perfect for those hips of yours.'

'OI!'

'I mean it, come on, try it on, Alice.' She bobbed up and down in excitement. 'Come on, get those rags off.'

I sighed and stripped to my underwear. Amy studied me critically. 'You're amazing, you know that? There's hardly an ounce of fat on you.'

'It's the pigs,' I said, 'they keep me fit.'

Amy held the dress in front of me and grinned. 'The underwear will have to go... It's going to be a tight squeeze.

'No!'

'Well, the brassiere will have to come off regardless. It's a bare shouldered number. You can't look glam with your bra straps in full view.'

I blew out my cheeks and unhooked my bra.

'Right, arms up, let's pull it over your head.'

'I think you have to step into this one,' I replied. 'I'm sure that's how Mum got into it.'

'That makes sense.'

I stepped into the dress and began to tug it up over my thighs wriggling as I pulled.

'Those bloomers have to go, Alice. They're crumpling up. You'll look like you've got flabby hips.'

I sighed, stepped out of the dress, pulled my thick winter bloomers down, then tried again. This time I managed to get the dress all the way up.

'WOW! Alice, I could fancy you myself.'

I looked down at the vast amount of exposed flesh.

'It's a bit revealing, isn't it?'

'It's perfect, Alice, though I doubt Godfrey will get any sleep at all after kissing your new photo.'

'I want to see myself in the big mirror,' I said, walking to the door with tiny steps because of the tightness of the dress around my knees.

Amy rushed along in front. Urging me to make haste.

Back in my bedroom, I studied my reflection in the dressing table mirror, tugging at the front of the dress, then trying to stuff my breasts further into the material.

'It's too revealing. I said it was. Mum wasn't quite as big in the bosom department.'

'Dear heart, trust me, it's perfect. Do I ever lie when fashion is concerned? I always want us both to look our best, and my goodness, you look absolutely, drop-dead, gorgeous, Alice. Seriously.'

I stepped back and looked again at my bare shoulders and the swell of my breasts as they tried to burst out of the dress. Pulling the clip from the back of my hair, I let my curls fall around my shoulders before striking a pose and pouting.

Amy clapped and danced an excited jig.

'Rita Hayworth is in the building,' she said with a grin.

I looked down at the fish tail part of the dress which dragged slightly on the floor as I stepped back a bit further to get a view of the whole dress.

'Don't you think it makes me look shorter?'

'Heels, darling,' Amy responded. 'Your high Oxfords will be just the job.'

And, she was right. They were.

After applying a green eye shadow, I rubbed in a thin layer of vanishing cream onto my cheeks and topped it off with a delicate dusting of ivory tinted powder. Pursing my lips, I pulled the top from my favourite red lipstick and smoothed it over my lips. Amy stuck up her thumb and whistled when I turned around to show her the finished effect.

'Remind me not to invite you to my wedding. I want to be belle of the ball, that day.'

It took me a while to get down the stairs in the super tight dress. Miriam's mouth dropped open as I stepped into the kitchen.

'My goodness, Alice. I thought your mum had come ba... never mind... you look beautiful.'

Stephen and Harriet danced around me as I wriggled my way across the floor towards the table.

'I've just had a thought,' Amy said, slapping her head with the palm of her hand. 'How are we going to get there? You can hardly walk in that dress. It will take us hours.'

'We'll go in the truck,' I said.

'Will you be able to drive it wearing that?'

'I'll give it a go,' I replied. 'I might need some help getting in and out though.'

Miriam, practical as ever, took a clean sheet from the laundry pile and laid it across the double seat in the cab of my ancient truck. 'That'll keep the oil and muck off your clothes,' she said.

After three attempts to get into the driver's seat and three spectacular failures, Amy got out of the passenger seat, came around the back of the truck and together with Miriam, stuck their hands on my backside and part lifted, part pushed me up into the cab.

'The things I do for love,' I said, as Amy slammed the door behind me and clambered up into the passenger seat.

'I don't know how I'm going to get back in after the photo,' I said.

'Hang on.' Amy jumped down again and hurried into the house. When she came back, she was carrying a brown paper bag stuffed with clothes.

'The stuff you just took off,' she said, smiling. 'You can get changed after the photo shoot; we don't want to embarrass Mr Jenkinson by asking him to grab hold of your bum and hoist you into the truck.'

'Drat! I could have got changed into this at the shop, what an idiot, I am.'

'It's too late now, Missis,' Amy replied. 'Come on, I've got to get changed yet. You'll have to sit in the truck while I get ready, I'll never get you back inside again on my own, and I'm not asking my dad to help.'

Driving was difficult to say the least, but I managed to kangaroo hop the truck first to Amy's house (where I waited patiently for her to get dressed into her strawberry and cream polka dot dress) and then along Gillingham Road to the High Street, where I pulled up and parked partly on the kerb opposite the photographer's shop.

To get out, I had to slide across the seat, shuffle about to get both feet together on the running board, then jump backwards, hoping desperately that Amy was in the right place to catch me. Fortunately, she was.

We spent over two and a half hours in the studio, though my own shoot only lasted for about forty minutes. Mr Jenkinson tried me in a dozen different poses in front of two or three backdrops before adding a fine lace curtain to the mix and starting up a small fan to blow a gentle breeze across the set. In the end, the shot he decided on, meant that Godfrey would never get to see me in the full-length mermaid dress. He settled on a head shot, with my curls falling around my shoulders as I showed off my 'wonderful' bosom.

'Classic Hollywood,' he said as he clicked away.

While the photographer was setting Amy up for her shoot, I went into the back room where Harriet and Stephen had got changed into their pirate costumes, and pushing an angled chair under the door handle in case Mr Jenkinson inadvertently caught me getting changed, I struggled out of the dress and pulled on my wool skirt and thin jumper. Amy had forgotten to pack my blouse and underwear. My coat was still hanging on the back of the kitchen door.

Folding the mermaid's dress carefully, I slipped it into the bag, then after putting the chair back in place, I walked through to the studio.

'We're going to be a good while yet, Alice. Would you like to go up for a cuppa? The kitchen is on the left at the top of the stairs.'

And so, for the next hour and a half, I sipped tea and flicked through a few of Mr Jenkinson's photography magazines whilst listening to the big band sound on the radio. On the hour, a grim sounding newsreader tried his best to put a gloss on more bad news.

Eventually, I heard Mr Jenkinson call my name and I grabbed my brown paper bag and hurried down the stairs to where Amy was perusing the photographs on the shop's feature wall.

'He is very good, isn't he?' Amy whispered flicking her head towards the display.

'That's where you're going, Alice.' Mr Jenkinson switched off the spotlights in the studio and stepped out into the shop. 'Right in the centre.' He pointed to a rail of spotlights hanging from the ceiling. 'You'll be highlighted by a couple of those. I can't wait to develop the film. I've never had two such beauties in front of my camera on the same day.'

'Or, indeed, ever,' said Amy with a wicked grin.

Mr Jenkinson laughed.

'Or, indeed, ever,' he agreed. He turned to me and offered his hand. 'Thank you for persuading Amy to model for me, Alice, and thank you for posing as well. The photographs will be ready for Saturday, I'll make sure of it.'

I smiled. 'Thank you, Mr Jenkinson. I'm really looking forward to seeing how they all come out.'

Amy put her hand in front of her mouth and hurried out of the door. She was still giggling like a schoolgirl as we walked towards the truck. She pointed to my bouncing bosom.

'Talking about things coming out. It was a close-run thing at times. My heart was in my mouth when you stretched to scratch the back of your head.'

'Shush,' I said, laying my arm underneath my breasts to stop them jiggling as two old men nudged and winked at each other. 'Fancy not packing my underwear.'

Chapter 12

Alice
Monday 16th December

On Monday evenings we would all sit around the radio with a pencil and paper as we tried to pit our wits against the great detective, Inspector Hornleigh of the Yard, on the Monday Night at Seven radio show.

Inspector Hornleigh would spend fifteen minutes interrogating witnesses to a crime. Then the audience was encouraged to try to pick out the mistakes made by the suspects and guess who the perpetrator of the crime was. Miriam hardly every picked the culprit and I wasn't that much better despite all of the Agatha Christie books I read. Amy (if she was with us) had a one hundred percent record and we all watched her face closely as the clues piled up to see if she would give anything away.

Stephen didn't jot down any clues but used to shout out, 'It was him,' or 'it was her,' every time a new character was introduced. Once, he insisted it was the vicar, although the vicar was the actual murder victim. He would then claim to have got it right when the perpetrator was eventually revealed.

Harriet would always sit next to me and peep over my arm as I was jotting down clues, so, she always got it right, or wrong, depending who I chose. This week was a particularly tricky one and I got it spectacularly wrong. Amy, who was sitting at the big oak table opposite Stephen, shook her head at me when I revealed my suspect.

'How could it have been her? She only spoke three languages, English, German and French, the murderer left a note in Latin. It was obviously the golf club captain.'

'But he was brought up in Coventry, how did he learn to speak Latin?'

Amy rolled her eyes. 'When he was first introduced, Hornleigh mentioned that there was a picture of a rugby team on the study wall and, as the detective described his appearance, he mentioned that he was wearing a Rugby School tie, which meant that he was educated at public school and all public schools have Latin on the curriculum, he would definitely have learned it.'

I frowned as I tried to follow her train of thought.

'Then there was the sixteenth century, Catholic prayer book on his desk. Didn't that ring any bells?'

I shook my head. 'Should it have?'

'Bibles and prayer books were all printed in Latin, my dear. Until Tyndale had a go at an English one and he was branded a heretic for doing it.'

'I give up. How are we supposed to know these things? How do you know these things? I went to the same school as you, remember?'

'Ah, but I listened in the history lessons,' Amy patted Stephen on the head. 'Take heed, young man.'

I got to my feet, tore up my notes and threw them angrily into the fire. 'I thought, because she was good at languages...'

'She may well have spoken Latin, dear heart,' Amy looked up at me as I walked past to make us all a cup of milky Ovaltine, 'but there wasn't a single clue that pointed to the fact that she could.'

Miriam looked up from her knitting.

'Well, I think you ought to be a detective yourself, Amy. You always solve the mysteries.'

'They don't like women in the police force,' Amy replied bitterly. 'The men don't want showing up.'

Harriet put up her hand to speak, as though she was in the classroom.

'What's the matter, darling,' Amy said softly. 'You don't have to put up your hand at home.'

'I didn't want to interrupt,' she replied.

'What is it you want to say, sweetie?'

'When I grow up, I want to be a doctor.'

'Good for you,' said Amy with a smile.

'You can't be a doctor, there aren't any women doctors are there?' asked Stephen.

'I think there are a few,' I said, 'but it is very difficult for women to get into medical school.'

'You could be a nurse,' suggested Stephen.

'I don't want to be a nurse; I want to be a doctor.'

Stephen thought for a moment.

'I'd let you be a doctor in my hospital if I owned one.'

I smiled. 'That's very kind of you, Stephen. We need more people like you in society.'

I walked slowly across the kitchen, handed Harriet her drink and put my arm around her shoulder.

'You can be anything you want to be, my lovely. Don't ever let anyone tell you anything different.'

I crouched down and looked into her face.

'Times are changing, Harriet, and they're changing fast. By the time you grow up there will be opportunities for all women to realise their dreams. It might be harder for us than it is for men, but we're just as good, just as capable, more so in a lot of ways. Some men think we're only put on this earth to cook, clean and have babies, but they're wrong. We can do so much more than that.'

Stephen tipped his head to the side and looked across at me.

'Are there any famous women though, Aunty Alice? I can't think of any.'

'Well, you aren't thinking hard enough, Stephen,' I said as I began to tick a list off on my fingers.

'What about Marie Curie, the famous scientist? What about Catherine the Great? She ruled Russia. Cleopatra was queen of Egypt, then there was Elizabeth the first, Queen Victoria, she ruled over the biggest empire the world has ever seen and, when our own king dies, Princess Elizabeth will be our queen and I'm sure she will be a very good one.'

Stephen frowned, 'Yes but I meant in modern times.'

'Well, I just mentioned Princess Elizabeth, but what about Agatha Christie, she's the world's best and most famous author, and what about Amy Johnson, she flew solo all the way to Australia.'

'I wondered who she was,' Harriet said quietly. 'Our teacher has a picture of her on her desk at school.'

'Listen to your Aunty Alice,' Amy interceded. 'The world is changing, not before time either. Women are proving they can do all the jobs that men used to do, now they're away with the army.' She patted Stephen on the arm. 'When this is all over, it's going to be a very different country, so you, take heed, mister. It won't just be a man's world any longer.'

'I did say she could be a doctor in my hospital,' Stephen looked aggrieved.

Amy gave him a big smile and ruffled his hair. 'So you did,' she said.

We were quiet for a while as we all thought about the discussion we'd just had. Then, suddenly, Miriam placed her knitting in her lap and looked across at Amy.

'Ooh, I knew there was something I meant to ask you.'

Amy held her mug between both hands and lifted her head.

'It's like this, I bumped into Freda Palmer today, you know who I mean? You were at school with her daughter, Vera... anyway, Vera's got a young man who's just been called up and they want to get married before he's sent abroad.'

'Poor Vera,' Amy replied, 'imagine having to say goodbye straight after your wedding day.'

'I know, but she's determined to do it. She's set the date for the end of January; he goes in the first week in Feb.'

Amy pulled a sad face.

'She, erm... Freda, this is... was wondering if you would knock up a wedding dress for her out of some of the silk panels you have?'

Amy's jaw dropped. 'Miriam!'

'She said it needn't be anything fancy, just a plain white dress... made of silk... whatever you can manage...'

'Does every woman in the town know I've got a few lengths of silk?'

Miriam shook her head.

'I don't think so, lovely, but Joanne Sharp was standing with us when we were talking outside the wool shop, and she asked if you'd consider making a Christening dress for her little Pauline, she's just coming up to six months and she'd like to get her done soon.'

Amy was speechless. I bit my cheek in an attempt to stop laughter bursting out of me.

'I think you're going to need more silk. You'd better have a word with that Jimmy the rope man.' I turned away and looked out of the window, shaking with silent laughter.

Amy got to her feet, dragged on her coat and opened the back door.

'I'm going home now,' she said.

Chapter 13

Alice
Saturday 21st December

On Saturday, the kids accompanied me into town again to buy a few last-minute bits and bobs and to pick up the portraits. We stopped at the photographer's first. Mr Jenkinson was in negotiations with a rather loud, very posh sounding lady wearing a fur stole.

It was Harriet who saw my picture on the feature wall first.

'Aunty Alice,' she cried excitedly, 'you're all lit up.'

Stephen looked up at what was, I had to admit, a very clever piece of photography. I really did look like I had come straight out of the pages of a Hollywood magazine.

'Why aren't you wearing any clothes, Aunty?' he asked a little too loudly.

The posh woman turned around before I could answer. Her mouth dropped open as her eyes followed mine up to the feature wall.

'So, that's the sort of thing you do here?' She glared at me and turned back to Mr Jenkinson. 'You can forget the idea of my daughter's portrait,' she stormed.

Mr Jenkinson looked puzzled as the woman stormed past us leaving the glass door swinging in her wake.

'I was wearing a dress, Stephen. You remember the one you saw me in on Sunday? It just looks like I'm not wearing anything because all you can see is my head and shoulders.'

'And your thingies,' he added, nodding towards my breasts.

I half smiled and walked to the back of the shop where Mr Jenkinson was waiting for us.

'I'm sorry about that, I hope it didn't cost you a customer.'

'It's all right. She'll be back. There's no one else she can go to unless she takes a drive down to Gillingham.'

'That's all right then. I was beginning to feel guilty.'

The photographer stepped across to a rack of shelves next to his cash register and picked up two brown paper bags with the picture of a camera printed on them above the words 'Jenkinson's Portraits'. Placing one of the bags on the table at the side of the till, he slid out a twelve by eight frame and held it in front of him so that we could see.

'Wow!' Stephen exclaimed. 'That's so good, we look like we're really on the pirate ship.'

'The parrot came out particularly well, I feel,' said Mr Jenkinson as he slipped the photograph back into the bag. He tapped it as he handed it to Harriet. 'There's a smaller six by four print in there too as a bonus, but it will need a frame.'

'That's very kind of Mr Jenkinson isn't it, children?'

The kids nodded in unison.

'This bag has your own portrait, plus a six by four version, and also a six by four of Amy's study. I hope she likes the way it came out; I certainly do.'

I paid the photographer, slipped the pictures into my bag and waving, we left the shop and returned to the High Street where we made our way to the café. Mrs Timothy, the owner, gave us a bit of a look as we entered, but said nothing. I gave her a big smile as I ordered tea and 'three slices of your wonderful sponge cake.'

From the café we made our way along the bustling pavement to Woolworths, where Harriet, as she had promised, bought Stephen a penny bag of chews before spending the remaining five pence of her pocket money.

The weather had begun to turn as we left the famous red fronted shop and we hurried to the bus stop on Middle Street as the freezing rain began to fall.

'Wrap up well tonight,' I said to Amy as I handed the photograph to her in the hallway of Honeysuckle Cottage. The rain dripped from my hair onto the hall carpet as she held it out at arm's length.

'What do you think, Alice? Is it really good enough for a national competition?'

'I think you're a shoo in,' I replied. 'It's a beautiful picture, Amy. I haven't seen the large version but it must be stunning if the little one is anything to go by. You look so natural, so... so, beautiful, he got the lighting just perfect.'

'It is good, isn't it,' she said happily. 'I just don't think I'm model material, that's all.'

I pulled out my own picture and showed it to her.

'OH MY GOD... I mean goodness,' Amy shrieked. 'Mum, Mum, look at this.' Amy threw the living room door open and rushed inside to show her mother my photograph.

'Oh, Alice, you look just like the actresses in Amy's magazine.'

I grinned. 'I am rather pleased with it.'

'It's very glamourous, Alice,' said Mr Rowlings, taking the picture from his wife. He took off his reading glasses and squinted at the picture.

Amy picked up the latest edition of her Photoshoot magazine and flicked through the pages until she came to a black and white study of Katherine Hepburn, pictured in an almost identical pose to mine.

'You see? Hollywood awaits you, my darling. All you need is the boat fare.'

'Ha!' I scoffed. 'Stephen asked me why I didn't wear any clothes for the picture while we were in the shop. I could have died.'

Amy snorted, then burst into laughter. Mr Rowlings handed back the photograph and nodded to the boy.

'I can see why he thought that. You must have been freezing, Alice.'

'I was wearing...'

'Am I coming to you or are you coming to me this evening?' Amy cut in.

'It's up to you, love,' I replied sliding the photograph into my bag. 'I think I'll just tape the ends up and give it to him in the brown bag rather than wrap it up in newspaper,' I said, absent-mindedly.

'Who's he? Do you have a new boyfriend, Alice? Amy didn't say anything?' Mrs Rowling's eyes lit up as she looked at me.

'No, no, nothing like that,' I said turning for the door. 'It's for...' I mumbled something incoherent and pulled the door open. 'Come to mine,' I said hurriedly, not wanting to face the prospect of a grilling about my love life from Amy's parents.

Amy winked at me as she saw us off.

'Good idea,' she said.

We arrived at the cinema in good time to see Henry Fonda playing the beleaguered Tom Joad in the story about America's great depression, The Grapes of Wrath, but we never did get to find out whether he and his family would manage to overcome the horrendous circumstances they found themselves in, as the projector broke down about fifteen minutes into the film.

The proprietor announced that he would issue us all with a ticket for a free showing on the following Saturday, by which time he hoped to have the projector fixed. Those who preferred it could queue for a refund.

Amy and I took our tickets from the usherette as we walked through the big main doors of the theatre and out onto what was by now, a very icy street.

We slipped and slid our way along the pavement and got to the stop just as the bus pulled up. As it was still only eight o'clock, we decided to skip the Old Bull and go straight home because we would almost certainly have too much to drink after arriving at the pub at such an early hour, and the half mile of sheet ice that now made-up Long Lane wasn't something we would feel safe traversing after a long session in the snug.

We got the first real snow of the winter overnight. I woke up to find the farm covered in a white blanket. Shivering at the mere sight of it, I pulled on a set of my father's old long john's and an extra jumper before slipping into my work overalls.

The pigs took much longer to sort out than usual and despite the extra layers, I was shivering like I'd developed a dose of flu by the time I made my way back to the luxuriant warmth of the kitchen.

I sent the lads home after milking and feeding the cows. Barney and George took a sled load of silage and hay down to the bottom pasture where our sheep were almost invisible against the backdrop of snow.

Bray and Bessie were confined to the stables for the morning. In the afternoon I covered their backs with blankets and let them out for an hour to feed on the hay that Barney had strewn around earlier that morning. I broke the ice on the water trough for the second time that day so they could drink their fill. After their hour's exercise I took them back to the stable and fed them an oats and corn mix before shutting them in for the night.

On Monday morning I was called into the house by Miriam who stood on the top step making phone call movements with her hand against her ear.

'It's Godfrey,' she shouted. 'He says it's important.'

I hurried into the kitchen, kicked off my wellies and in my thick black socks, half ran, half skidded my way across to the front room.

'Godfrey, how lovely to hear your voice. What's the weather like in London? We're snowed in up here.'

'We've had a bit of the white stuff, Alice, but it's not the weather I'm calling about. I er, I have some rather bad news I'm afraid.'

'Oh, Godfrey, don't say you're not coming home after all.'

'No, I'm still coming, Alice, but I think I'll be coming on my own. I doubt Rose will be joining me for the trip.'

'Why, what's happened?' I put my hand on my brow, dreading the next few moments.

'I had an hour to spare between meetings this morning, so I thought I'd make a dummy run to Rose's house so that I'd know exactly where to go tomorrow afternoon.'

He was silent for a few moments.

'Godfrey?' My voice was shaking.

'There was... look, there's no easy way of saying this, Alice... There was no house, merely a pile of rubble. The street was bombed in the night. There's nothing left standing.'

Chapter 14

'Oh my goodness, poor Rose.' My voice broke. 'What am I going to tell the children?'

'I'm so sorry, Alice.'

'Are you sure she was in there? I mean, she could have been in a shelter.'

'She wasn't, Alice. I spoke to a neighbour. The sirens hadn't gone off. The bombers were over another part of the city all night, then in the early hours, all hell broke loose. The word is, it was a lone bomber, dumping its load before flying home. It wasn't picked up. Amazingly the houses on the other side of the street came through it pretty much unscathed. She told me that the ARP and firefighters worked through the night to get the survivors out. Only a dozen people survived from the twenty houses that have been destroyed. There is a chance she was one of the lucky dozen, I suppose, but I wouldn't get your hopes up, Alice.'

'Oh, Godfrey, could you do a bit of digging? Ask around. Someone must know if they got her out.'

'I'm sorry, Alice, I'm back in the office now. I've got a big meeting with Herbert Morrison and his civil servants later this morning, then we're meeting with Winston soon afterwards. I can't get out of meetings with members of the government, much as I'd like to help.'

'I'm sorry, Godfrey, I understand. You've got the welfare of the entire country to think about. I thought you might still be in the area.'

'I would have phoned from Lambeth if I could have found a working phone box, Alice, but the exchange has been hit. None of the public call boxes are working, the one at the end of her street was damaged beyond repair in the air raid. Government departments, hospitals and the like are still working as we were all moved to the new switching system earlier in the year. It hasn't reached all parts yet. A lot of London still relies on the old exchange operators to connect calls.'

'So, there is a chance she got out alive? We can't be one hundred percent sure?'

'No, as I said, she may have been one of the lucky dozen. All the neighbour knew, was that she was in the house when the bombs began to fall.'

I made a quick decision.

'Right, I'd better let you get to your meeting, Godfrey. Thanks for calling. I'll get a few things packed.'

'Why? Alice, you can't come down here, the raids are worse now, especially over the East End and around the Thames.'

'I have to do something, Godfrey, I can't just tell the kids their mother is dead, when she might not be.'

'No, I understand that.'

'I'll ring you when I get to London. I might need to bunk up with you overnight.'

'All right, Alice. I'll tell my secretary to expect a call from you. I'd better go now, I'm so sorry to be the bearer of such bad news.'

I walked into the kitchen still in a state of shock. Luckily, Stephen and Harriet were out in the yard feeding breakfast scraps to the chickens. Miriam took one look at my face and knew there was something wrong.

'It's Rose. Her house has been bombed, Godfrey doesn't know if she got out alive or not.'

'Oh, no, those poor children, as if they haven't had enough to put up with.' She paused as she took in the devastating news. 'What about their dad?'

'I've no idea, he wouldn't have been with her, they separated earlier in the year.'

'Is there a hospital or some other service we could ring? Someone must know if she got out or not.'

I was about to tell her that I intended going down to London myself to investigate, when the back door opened and Amy breezed in.

'Morning all, I've just...' Her voice tailed off as she saw the look on our faces.

'What's wrong? Come on, out with it.'

'It's Rose,' I said, wiping at my leaky eyes with the back of my hand. 'She's missing in the bombing. Her house was flattened. Godfrey just rang.'

Amy was the voice of logic as usual.

'It doesn't mean she died in the rubble though, does it? She could have made it to a shelter. Was there an Anderson in her garden? Did a neighbour have one? She might have been sheltering under the stairs like you had to when you were caught in a raid, Alice. Missing doesn't mean dead. Think positive.'

I hugged her. 'Oh, Amy, I've been trying to do that since I got the news but...'

'Right. Amy clapped her hands. This calls for some serious thinking. Put the kettle on. Brains always work better on a cup of tea.'

'If you're going to be discussing it in here, I'd better get the kids out of the way. We don't want them to walk in while we're talking about what might, or might not have happened.' Miriam grabbed her coat and opened the back door. 'We'll go for a walk up the lane.'

My hands were still shaking as I poured tea into two big stripey mugs. Amy added milk to them both and we sat down next to each other, holding hands.

'I mean it, Alice,' Amy said when I had given her the full details of the phone conversation. 'We only have the word of one neighbour and the thing we can realistically rely on about her testimony is that she was in the house when the bombs started falling. A dozen people were rescued on the street overnight. There would have been a big search team and a lot of confusion. Who's to say she didn't just walk out of the house after or during the raid?'

'You're right of course,' I replied. 'That's why I'm going down to London. I have to know one way or another before I tell the children. I can't let them think there's a chance she might be alive if there isn't. We have to know for sure.'

'Absolutely right. They can't be told anything until we know for certain. Which is why you can't go to London.'

'I have to, Amy, I have to find out what happened.'

'You can't go,' Amy repeated. 'Look, Alice, if you go rushing off to London the kids are going to be suspicious. They'll know something's going on, they're bright little things.'

'I know, Amy, but...'

'No buts, you can't go. What if something were to happen to you while you were there? What if you were caught in a raid too? The kids would not only have lost their real mother, but their stand in mother, too. You can't risk that. It really isn't fair on them.'

I hadn't even considered that eventuality. My heart sank. 'But we have to do something, Amy.'

'You don't have to do anything. Keep calm and carry on, as the posters say. Just try to keep everything as normal as possible here. I'll go to London. The kids won't see anything wrong in that. You can tell them I'm visiting my aunt.'

'But you don't know anything about London, Amy,' I protested.

Amy patted my hand. 'I know more about London than you think. I've been there before, remember?'

'That was a school trip to the British Museum,' I replied.

'It's still London,' she retorted. 'I kept my eyes open on the bus.'

I shook my head. 'Amy, a lot has changed since nineteen thirty-two. I was there in September. You can't get around a lot of it, some of the bus services have been cancelled, many of the railway lines have been damaged. Parts of the city are in ruins. You don't get to see the reality on the newsreels.'

Amy shrugged. 'I'll be fine. Anyway, this case will require brains to crack it and my extraordinary sleuthing powers will be needed. Come on, you know I can spot a clue in a barrel of red herrings.'

'I don't want you to put yourself in danger either, Amy. I really don't think I'd ever get over it if I lost you.' I pulled her to me and hugged her close, my tears dripping onto her shoulder.

Amy put her arm around me and we rocked together for a few moments.

'I'll be back in time for Christmas,' she said. 'Don't worry about me, you know I'm the luckiest person alive and this situation needs all the luck we can throw at it.'

We were quiet for a while, each lost in our own thoughts, the silence highlighted by ticking of the big clock on the wall.

'You know this is the only viable solution,' she said eventually, patting my hand again.

I nodded. It did seem to be the only card we had to play.

'When will you go?' I said quietly.

'I'll get the noon train from town. I only have to change once at Gillingham then straight on to Victoria in London.'

'Have you got a street map?' I asked.

'Yes, Dad's got one. He spent a lot of time in London in the thirties.'

'You'll need a torch too; it's pitch black at night and you don't know your way around. You have to cover your torch with—'

'Tissue paper to dampen the beam down. Yes, I know that, Alice, we have to do it up here too, remember?'

I laughed nervously. 'Of course you do.' I got to my feet and walked through to the front room where I opened the safe and took out my petty cash tin. Fishing out three, one-pound notes and four, ten-shilling notes, I pressed them into her hand.

'Five pounds! I can't take your money, Alice and that's far too much. I'm coming back tomorrow, whatever I find out, so I won't need anything like that amount. I've got savings, I can—'

'Take it,' I demanded, giving her a stern look. 'If you're taking my place then you're taking my money too. You never know what you might need when you get there.'

Amy knew I'd never let her get out of the house without my money in her pocket, so she gave in with dignity, smiled at me, then gave me a hug.

'I'll need her address,' she said.

Chapter 15

Amy
Monday 23rd December

After leaving the farm, Amy hurried along Long Lane, slipping, skidding and sliding on the ice that seemed reluctant to thaw despite the presence of the pale winter sun. After a couple of hundred yards, she found Miriam and the children who were on their way back to the farm.

'Hello, and goodbye,' Amy said, her breath hanging in the cold air. 'I'm off to London to see my old aunt for a couple of days.'

'They're bombing it you know?' Stephen said, seriously.

'I know, but they aren't bombing the part I'm going to, it's right on the outskirts, don't worry.'

'When will you be back? Santa won't know where to leave your presents,' said Harriet.

'Oh, I'll be back before Santa comes. I'm only staying overnight.'

'Will we see you on Christmas Day?'

'I wouldn't miss it for the world, darling.' Amy kissed Harriet on the forehead and bent over to kiss Stephen, who flinched and stepped backwards, holding out his hand as he moved.

Amy smiled and shook it. 'I'll be back soon. Have a lovely Christmas Eve. Make sure you're asleep for Santa.'

At home, Amy gave a quick explanation to her mother, then, almost running upstairs, she packed an overnight case, threw in a lipstick and foundation pack before taking a last look around the bedroom to see if she had forgotten anything.

Back downstairs, Amy tested her torch, then taped new strips of tissue over the end before tossing it into her case.

'Do you know where Dad's London Street map is, Mum?'

'It's in the bottom drawer in the kitchen. Oh, I don't think this is a good idea, Amy. Why don't you wait until your dad gets home, see what he thinks?'

'There's no time for that, Mum. The kids have to know the truth about what happened to Rose. If I can find her, it will put their minds at rest. The one good thing about all this is that they didn't know she was supposed to be coming home tomorrow. It was going to be a surprise.'

'Well, at least take a flask and some sandwiches.'

'I haven't got time to wait, Mum. The train goes at twelve. If I miss that one it will be dark by the time I get there and I'd like to do a bit of digging this afternoon, if possible.'

Amy left the house carrying her small brown suitcase leaving her mother in tears on the doorstep.

'Please take care, Amy and get to a shelter before dark. Don't take any chances, please don't take any chances.'

The main road at the top of the lane was pretty much free of ice and Amy stood, stamping her feet impatiently at the bus stop as she tried to build some sort of plan in her mind. Thankfully, the bus was slightly early and Amy arrived at Spinton station in good time for the London train.

There was a small queue at the ticket office and Amy nodded to a few acquaintances as she shuffled forward towards the ticket master's window.

'Single to London, please,' she said, pushing a ten-shilling note through the gap.

'Are you staying there for Christmas? You must be barmy,' the ticket master replied. He pointed to a large poster at the back of the office that read; *Is Your Journey Really Necessary?*

'I wouldn't be going if it wasn't,' Amy muttered under her breath, then smiling at him, she replied. 'I'm only there overnight. I'll be coming back tomorrow. I have urgent business to attend to.'

He handed her a green ticket with her change. 'Don't miss the last train back. Five forty-five from Victoria. There's nothing after that as it's Christmas Eve and the authorities want to get some repairs done to the line during the break. Change for Spinton at Gillingham.'

Amy smiled again, then stepped away and walked through to the platform, presenting her ticket to the guard as she passed through the double doors. The train was already on the platform, steam hissing from the sides of the engine, smoke puffing from the chimney.

She climbed into the third-class carriage wondering why she had never seen a second-class carriage on the train network. There was only ever, first and third.

The compartment wasn't too busy and after stuffing her little case onto the overhead rack, she sat in a seat by the window and looked out over the almost empty platforms.

The train made good time and they were only a few minutes late when they reached the bomb-damaged Gillingham station. Amy followed the detour signs and had to take the over-line bridge to reach her platform. She stared straight ahead as she took the stairs, not wanting to look at the gaps between the steps as she climbed.

The train was packed, men in business suits sat alongside soldiers and navy personnel. Feeling claustrophobic in the narrow aisle and after having her bottom felt twice, Amy decided to sit on her case in the clear space just outside the toilet.

After twenty minutes, the guard came past.

'Tickets, please,' he called as though he were shouting to a carriage load of people.

Amy produced her ticket, then went to sit down again. The guard looked at her pityingly. 'A bit rough in there is it?' He nodded towards the carriage.

'People can't keep their hands to themselves,' Amy replied, bitterly.

'I did wonder why you were sitting out here,' he said with a frown. 'Then again, I don't suppose some of those lads will ever get the chance to be near a pretty girl again... not that I'm excusing their behaviour.'

He thought for a few moments then came to a decision. 'Come with me, Miss,' he said with a wink.

Amy picked up her suitcase and followed the guard as he led her through the next packed carriage and out the other side. In front of them was a door marked 'First Class'. He ushered her in and held out his hand towards a table of empty seats.

'This is very kind of you,' Amy said, 'but what if I'm asked for my ticket?'

'I've already seen it,' the guard replied. 'I won't say anything if you don't.' He smiled, touched the peak of his cap, then left the carriage.

Victoria station was its usual bustling self. Porters pushing trolleys loaded with cases, hurried up and down the platforms as passengers both civilian and military, stood around in small groups or sat on benches reading newspapers as they awaited their connections.

After showing her ticket at the gate, Amy stepped out from beneath the big station clock and looked along the long line of buses that stretched out in front of her. Unsure of which one she needed, she approached a man wearing a fawn gaberdine mac and a black trilby.

'Sorry, love, I'm not from these parts,' he said with a tip of his hat. 'Try asking one of the conductors.'

Amy strolled along the line of red double decker buses until she found a conductor standing with his driver as they smoked and chatted.

'Which bus will take me to Lambeth, please?' Amy asked.

The conductor placed his hand on his ticket machine, lifted his cap and smoothed back his dark hair.

'I wish my bus was going that way, can I persuade you to go to Paddington instead?'

Amy smiled sweetly and put her case down. 'Sadly, not today, I'm in a hurry. Maybe another time.'

The conductor put his cap back on and pointed towards the front of the line of buses. 'Any bus that goes over Westminster Bridge will suit, Miss, so jump on any one of the first three.'

Amy smiled again, picked up her case and strolled to the front of the line. The big red bus sported a poster that ran the full length of the vehicle beneath the upstairs windows advising her that *Loose Lips Sink Ships*.

Grabbing hold of the steel pole, she stepped onto the open platform, took a seat on the lower deck and waited for the conductor to finish handing out tickets to the people at the front. He was a scrawny, untidy looking man in his fifties wearing an ill-fitting jacket and crumpled trousers. He touched the peak of his cap as he came back down the aisle.

'Where to, Miss?'

'Um, well, I'd like to get to Drews Avenue, I believe it's just off the Lambeth Road.'

'You're in luck, then,' said the conductor, cheerily. 'I'll give you a shout when we're close by. Drews is just off Lambeth Walk if I remember rightly. We don't go down there but we do go past it.'

Amy passed him a shilling and the conductor set his machine and wound out a threepenny ticket. He handed her the change before walking up the stairs whistling the tune to the famous Lambeth Walk song from the film, Me and My Girl.

Amy Looked out of the window as the bus trundled along Victoria Street, passing Westminster Abbey, Big Ben and the Houses of Parliament before crossing Westminster Bridge and the recently bombed St Thomas' Hospital. As the bus drove slowly past Westminster, Amy crossed her fingers and sent up a silent prayer, asking God to look kindly on Mr Churchill and his ministers as they plotted the defeat of the Nazis from the meeting rooms of parliament.

'Next stop for Lambeth Walk, then Kennington Road.'

Amy got up from her seat, picked up her case and stood on the open platform as the bus came to an easy halt. Thanking the conductor, she stepped onto the pavement and waited until it had pulled away before spotting a gap in the traffic and crossing the road.

Like the conductor, Amy found herself whistling Lambeth Walk as she strolled along the street. There was quite a bit of bomb damage with huge open craters and empty spaces where working people's houses once stood.

As she walked, a sharp wind blew plaster dust from the piles of broken bricks into her face. Amy coughed and dug into her pocket for a handkerchief. Holding it front of her mouth, she walked on, past the side roads she had memorised from her father's street map. When she reached Drews Avenue she stopped and held her breath as she surveyed the damage that the bomber had cause.

The entire left-hand side of the avenue was nothing more than a couple of dozen piles of bricks and broken timbers, but, apart from a few blown-out windows, the right-hand side was remarkably untouched.

Amy walked along the rubble strewn street, trying to work out where number 37 might have been. A telephone kiosk, its windows in shards, lay on its side in the middle of the pavement. The plinth of what was once a post box sat cracked and broken on the bend of the avenue. She checked the door numbers of the houses on the right and stopped when she got to number 36. Standing on the dusty pavement she looked across to the twelve-foot pile of bricks and beams that had once been someone's home. Amy sniffed and was sure she could smell gas in the air. She was just about to pull her gas mask out of the cardboard box that hung over her shoulder when she heard a voice behind her.

'Are you looking for someone, love?'

Amy turned to find herself facing an elderly woman wearing a flowered pinny and a headscarf made into a turban.

'I'm trying to find out what happened to someone who lived over there.' She pointed vaguely at the piles of bricks that lined the road. 'A Mrs Wakelin?'

'Ah, Rose. Poor Rose. She was so excited about going up to see her kids. They were evacuated you know.'

'I do,' said Amy. 'That's the reason I'm here. We got a message this morning saying that her house had been bombed but we don't know what happened to her. Whether she made it to a shelter or not.'

'She didn't,' said the old woman, folding her arms beneath her ample bosom. 'As I told the posh gentleman this morning. She was inside when the bombs rained down.'

Amy sighed deeply. 'The posh gentleman was the person that gave us the message about the bombing. He said that a dozen people were dug out alive?'

'I don't know how many got out, love. The ARP moved us all out while they shut the gas supply off. We were only allowed back at ten this morning. We stood in the freezing cold on Lambeth Walk for over four hours.'

'I'm sorry to hear that,' Amy replied. 'It can't be very nice for you, living through this night after night.'

The woman sniffed. 'We're Londoners, what else would we do? We can't let that Hitler think he's got us beat, can we?'

Amy felt a lump rise in her throat. Her part of the world had been spared the Blitz, she found herself feeling immensely proud of the old woman and the thousands like her who flatly refused to let the enemy make them cower. She reached out and touched the old lady on the arm. 'Bless you,' she said, quietly.

'I'll tell you where you might find out who got out and who didn't,' the old girl said. She pointed beyond the row of broken houses. 'There's a shop on Fuller Street. The lady who owns it looks after the ARP, makes them sandwiches, cups of tea, that sort of thing. She's a good woman. We all shop there so she'll know Rose. She might have some idea what happened to her.'

'Thank you,' Amy said, quickly. 'I'll go there now.'

'Tell her Gladys Partridge, sent you,' the old woman shouted as Amy crossed the street. 'She doesn't take kindly to strangers.'

Chapter 16

Alice
Monday December 23rd

Miriam and the children arrived back soon after Amy had left. I had just about enough time to compose myself as I heard them coming through the gate at the back.

'Aunty Alice. Amy is going to London,' Harriet burst into the kitchen with the news.

'I know, she just told me,' I said.

'It's a bit sudden, isn't it?' said Stephen who always liked a full explanation for everything.

'Amy hasn't seen her aunt for a long time,' I said, hating myself for lying.

'She should just write her a letter,' said Stephen practically. 'It doesn't matter if a letter gets blown up.'

'Amy isn't going to get blown up,' I replied, crossing my fingers and sending up a quick prayer for her. 'She'll be back before we know it.'

'I wish I could go with her,' he said quietly. 'I'd love to see Mum for Christmas.'

Harriet nodded in agreement. 'It's not fair. I hate this war.'

I crouched down in front of her. 'We all hate it, sweetheart and we're all praying for it to end as soon as possible.'

'It can't end until Mr Hitler has gone,' Stephen said. He was an avid listener to the news bulletins and pored over the newspapers whenever he could get hold of one. 'We're going to need the Americans, but they don't want to come.'

'They might, one day,' I replied, putting my hand on his shoulder. 'They were late coming in last time but when they did, they made all the difference.'

Stephen pulled out a chair and sat at the table, swinging his feet.

'I'm not going to get my hopes up.' He looked across to Miriam who was standing by the sink studying him carefully. 'What's for lunch?' he asked.

Because the kids had broken up from school for the holidays, Miriam and I hatched a few plans to keep them occupied and to keep their Christmas excitement under some sort of control. Stephen could become hyperactive if left to his own devices. Harriet was much calmer but even she was beginning to let the Christmas spirit get the better of her.

We set them a series of tasks, devised to keep them occupied for the afternoon. Firstly, they were to accompany me on a tour of the yard, barn, cattle shed and stables. After feeding apples to Bessie and Bray, we strolled down through the still frost laden grass to the bottom acre to check on the sheep. From there we walked up the hill to the top field where we found Barney, George Foulkes and John Postlethwaite repairing a gap that had somehow appeared in the hedge that separated the farm from Long Lane.

'We've shored it up short term, Missis,' my foreman said as we approached, 'but we could do with planting some hawthorn in the gaps come spring if we want to move the sheep up here.'

I nodded. 'Stick some Blackthorn in there too, Barney. I'm thinking of having a go at making our own gin this year.' I looked at Stephen with a smile on my face. 'Stephen knows all about Blackthorn, don't you?'

Stephen nodded and held up his thumb to show the evidence of his recent encounter but the scratch had long healed.

'My missis will be pleased when she hears that news. She loves a drop of gin does Myrtle. She's so looking forward to the party tomorrow night. She's talked of nothing else for days.'

'We're looking forward to it too, aren't we kids?'

Harriet and Stephen nodded in unison. 'Can we have some gin too?' she asked.

'A sip, possibly. You're not old enough to have alcohol.'

'How do you make gin from thorns?' Stephen wanted to know.

I laughed. 'You'll see, you can help me make it.'

'I bet it tastes a bit sharp,' he replied seriously, making us all laugh with his unintended joke.

At three-fifteen, I went into the front room and called Godfrey's office. To my surprise, the secretary put him straight on the line.

'Hello, Alice. Have you arrived?'

'No, I'm still at home, Godfrey, Amy's coming instead.'

'I can't say I'm too disappointed by that news, Alice. It would have been lovely to spend a little time with you, but I'd much rather wait until Friday and know that you're not in danger.'

'Amy talked me into letting her come instead. She was right, too. I wasn't thinking clearly. We can't risk the kids losing their guardian as well as their mother.'

'She's a clever girl is Amy,' Godfrey replied. 'Where is she going to stay? It wouldn't really be seemly to invite her to stay with me.'

'She's going to try to find a little B and B if there's anyone with a room free.'

'She'll struggle. All the cheap hotels and bed and breakfast establishments are full of people who have lost their homes in the bombing. The councils can't cope with the demand.'

'Poor Amy, I don't think she's fully realised what she's letting herself in for,' I replied.

'She can always come to mine if she's stuck, Alice. I'll have a word with my landlord. He'll let me kip on the sofa in the front room, I'm sure of it. Besides, with the way it's been recently, it might be another night in the shelter anyway.'

'How did the meeting with Winston go? I'd be so star struck I wouldn't be able to get a word out.'

'He's not the easiest man to get along with,' Godfrey replied. 'He thinks he knows best, whatever the topic of conversation. As far as the war is concerned, he is generally found to be right, but we were talking about new civilian regulations that might need to be brought in. He got bored pretty quickly and just told us to get on with it.'

'So, can you tell me what restrictions we're going to be facing now or is it all top secret?'

'I'd love to fill you in on the minutiae of civilian travel restrictions but I'm afraid they might lock me up if I do. They don't want to annoy the general population until we absolutely have to. The details would probably bore you to death anyway.'

'All right, you convinced me,' I said with a laugh.

Godfrey laughed along, then suddenly became serious.

'You'll let me know if you hear anything about Rose, or if Amy requires a bed?'

'I will, Godfrey. Thank you.'

'I'm in the office until late tonight. Herbert Morrison wants to come back to go over things in depth. I can't see me getting away before eleven, though if the planes come early as they have been doing recently, our meeting might have to be held in the underground station instead. The government have had some offices built into a few of the non-public areas.'

'All right, Godfrey. Take care, please. This business has really made me think about how precious life is.'

'Goodbye, Alice. Try not to worry too much about Amy. As I said, she's a very resourceful young lady. She'll be just fine.'

I crossed my fingers as I put the handset back on the cradle, and looked up at the clock. *Three-thirty. Amy must be there by now.* I glanced up heavenward. *I hope she can find a phone that works.*

Chapter 17

Amy
Monday 23rd December

Amy walked carefully through the ruins, hardly daring to look down in case she saw something she'd rather not see. As she stepped across a flattened length of fencing, she found herself in the alleyway that led to Fuller Street. She turned at the corner and looked along the street for signs of a shop, only to find that she was standing right outside of it.

Mrs Pettigrew's corner shop was a red brick house that had had two of its downstairs rooms knocked into one. The two sash windows on the lower floor had been boarded up, presumably to prevent having to replace shattered panes. As Amy pushed the wooden panelled door open, she heard the tinkle of a bell. Inside, the walls were full of shelves holding everything from cigarettes and tins of baked beans to cans of Brasso metal polish and carbolic soap.

Mrs Pettigrew was standing behind the long, glass counter as she entered. On her right was a large white weighing scale. She lifted two slices of ham from it and laid them out on a piece of greaseproof paper before folding it carefully and laying the flat package on one of the glass shelves beneath the counter. On the wall behind her was a hand written sheet that listed all of the items and amounts that could only be purchased with ration books.

'What can I get you, dear?' she asked, looking up.

The shopkeeper was a small framed woman of about thirty-five years of age with patches of hair going prematurely white. Her almond shaped eyes and high cheekbones hinted at an Asian influence in her pedigree. She rested her slender fingers on the counter and smiled a genuine smile as Amy approached.

'I'm not looking to buy anything, for the moment at least. I was sent here by Mrs Partridge... Gladys.'

'Oh yes?'

Amy took a deep breath. 'It's quite a complicated story, I'm afraid. My name is Amy Rowlings and I live in Spinton in North Kent.'

'Spinton?'

'It's a small industrial town near the estuary, just outside Gillingham.'

'You're a long way from home, Amy. What brings you here?'

'I've come to find Rose Wakelin. Her children were evacuated to my friend's farm and she was going to come up for Christmas, but we heard the news yesterday that her house had been bombed flat and we don't know what happened to her, so I've some to find out.'

'Roger!' the shopkeeper shouted.

A brown-haired lad of about Stephen's age, wearing a hand knitted jumper, stuck his head through the open door behind her.

'Watch the shop, son.' She smiled at Amy. 'You'd better come through, dear. I'll put the kettle on.'

Mrs Pettigrew's kitchen was small, but warm and welcoming. She took Amy's coat and hung it on a peg on the back of the door, then put two carefully measured spoons of tea into a brown pot before taking the already steaming kettle from the Aga range and splashing the hot liquid over the tea leaves.

'Hope you don't like it strong. We don't do strong these days,' she said with a sorrowful look on her face.

'So, tell me, how did you find out about Rose?' she asked when she had poured the tea.

'Alice... she's Harriet and Stephen's guardian, got a phone call from Godfrey Wilson... he's a lawyer working at the War Office. He was going to give Rose a lift to Spinton tomorrow afternoon as he was heading home for Christmas. Anyway, he took a drive out this morning so he would know where to pick her up and just found a pile of bricks instead of a house. We were all flabbergasted by the news and we had to find out what has happened to her for her children's sake. They don't know anything about it yet.'

'They'd be devasted,' the shopkeeper replied. 'They've been caught in the bombing themselves. They know how serious it can be.'

Amy nodded. 'They didn't know she was coming up. It was going to be a surprise.' Her eyes filmed over. 'The poor things...'

Mrs Pettigrew reached across the table and took Amy's hand.

'So that was the posh man that Gladys saw. I was wondering who he was. She said he had government written all over him. I was beginning to wonder what our Rose had been up to, getting involved with the high ups.'

'Mrs Pettigrew, I was—'

The shopkeeper patted Amy's hand then withdrew her own. 'Call me Lois,' she said.

'Lois, I was wondering if you'd heard anything about the aftermath. Gladys seemed to hint that you might.'

'Not much happens around here without me getting to hear about it,' Lois said with a short smile. 'As it happens, I can tell you that Rose survived the raid. She was the last person pulled out from the rubble at six o'clock this morning. I can't say how bad her injuries are, but she was conscious when they pulled her out.'

Amy leapt to her feet. 'That's wonderful news!'

Lois motioned her to sit. 'As I said, I only know she was conscious when they pulled her out. Kevin told me that she was rambling.'

'Kevin?'

'Oh, Kevin is the head of the local ARP team. In case you didn't know, ARP stands for Air Raid Precautions. His main job is patrolling the streets checking on the blackout etc, but he's also involved with the rescue teams and the firefighters. He uses my phone to report in sometimes if the street phone is down.'

'Does Terry Wakelin work with him a lot? He's a firefighter I believe.'

'Don't talk to me about that low-life scum,' Lois spat. 'He's led poor Rose a merry dance over this past twelve months. I doubt the man has ever seen a fire, he's more concerned with taking advantage of any shell-shocked women he can find after an air raid.'

She curled up her lip and continued. 'Kevin got him the job, he's only doing it because it keeps him out of the army, the cowardly so and so. I don't know why Kevin is so protective of him, but he won't hear a word against Terry. Kev's is a local councillor; he owns a small milk processing plant. A few of the fire crew work for him. I honestly don't know why they let Terry do as he pleases. It's like he's got a hold over them all.'

'I had heard that Rose had chucked him out,' Amy said.

'Best thing she ever did too. He comes in here most nights for his cigarettes. I only serve him because Kev asked me to go easy on him.'

'Do you think I could get to meet Kevin? I'd like to know what happened exactly, and where they took her after they pulled her out.'

'If you hang around for a couple of hours, you'll get to meet him. He always pops in before his night shift, but, as it happens, I can tell you where they would have taken her. The nearest hospital is St Thomas'. It was bombed back in September, the nurses' quarters were flattened, but it's still functioning to a degree. All the injured from around here are taken there. Mind you, I don't think they keep most of them. They're sent across London to bigger, fully functioning hospitals after being assessed.'

Amy looked up at the wall clock. It was already three-thirty.

'St Thomas'? I think we drove past that on the bus, it isn't far away, I could get there before dark.'

'It's only a shortish walk,' Lois said.

Amy sighed. 'The thing is, I still have to find somewhere to stay for tonight.'

'I can sort that out for you if you like,' said Lois brightly. 'My sister only lives a couple of streets away. She's been taking in some homeless people for the past year. It helps boost her income now she's got the new baby and her Peter has gone to war. I know for a fact that she has an attic room free, she'll only charge you four bob and you'll get breakfast thrown in for that. An evening meal too if you're lucky. Oh, she's got an Anderson shelter by the way, so you'll have somewhere to go if the sirens go off.'

'That sounds fabulous. I'll go straight after I've been to the hospital; I hope she hasn't let it by then.'

Lois tutted. 'Never mind that, dear, I'll send my Roger over.' She turned her head towards the shop and shouted.

'Roger!'

'Yes, Mum?'

'Get yourself over to our Emily's, will you? Tell her I've got someone for the attic room tonight. Tell her she'll need something to eat if she's got enough spare.'

'Okay, Mum.'

'Roger, while you're there, ask her if she's all right for soap powder. Tell her I've got some Oxydol for the nappy bucket coming in tomorrow. Oh, and tell her I've got a few bars of Lifebuoy soap if she's short.'

When Roger had gone, Amy got to her feet. 'Thank you so much for your kindness, Lois. Do you think I could leave my case here until I get back from the hospital? Save me carting it about.'

Lois smiled, picked up Amy's little case and placed it behind the door. 'It'll be safe enough there, don't worry.'

'I wasn't about to,' said Amy, smiling again. 'Right, I'd better get off if I'm going to get back before the blackout.'

When Amy set off, she was feeling much better about things. The news that Rose had at least been conscious when they lifted her from the rubble surely meant that she had a fighting chance of pulling through. As she walked along Lambeth Road, she began to feel much more positive. She crossed her fingers and hoped to get more good news from the staff of St Thomas' hospital.

On the approach, she passed a line of street sellers, all shouting out their offers. Amy passed a makeshift stall containing pairs of wool socks, on another plank table, a man was selling packs of American cigarettes. On the other side of the street a young boy stood lookout watching for the police.

'Here you go, darlin, just what you need for those lovely long legs of yours.'

A man with a dark stubble-covered chin, beamed at her from under his grey trilby. He looked right and left, before pulling out a brightly coloured, cardboard-backed packet with a cellophane window from beneath his overcoat.

'Nylons!' he proclaimed. 'All the way from the USA. Come on, love, ten bob a pack.' He stepped back and looked Amy up and down. 'Medium size, just the ticket.'

'Ten bob! That's a day's wages for me,' Amy replied. 'I can't afford ten bob.'

'All right, because you have the face of an angel and because I'm about to knock off for the day, you can have them for seven and six, how about that?'

Amy thought about it, she was severely tempted. Working class girls from Kent couldn't even dream of getting their hands on nylon stockings.

'I'm sorry,' she said eventually. 'I'm very tempted but it's still too much. I honestly can't justify spending that amount on a pair of stockings.'

She smiled at him and turned away, only to feel his hand on her arm.

'Look, love, I've only got four pairs left. I want to get rid of them ASAP and I don't fancy trawling the pubs looking for custom tonight.'

'Where do you get them?' Amy asked. 'We don't even make them in this country, do we?'

'We don't and that's why they are such a bargain.' The man looked right and left again conspiratorially, then tapped the side of his nose. 'I know this bloke you see? He works as a driver at the American embassy. He knows a man who imports American goods that are delivered on the Lease Lend ships. You know, the ones that run the gauntlet of the German U-boats to get essential supplies into the country?'

Amy nodded. 'I get it, so they're not stolen then?'

The man feigned shock.

'Look, love, I'm an honest man, trying to make an honest living before the blooming army come and press gang me into service. These are all I've got left until the New Year. Come on, darlin, do me a favour. I've got to buy Christmas presents for the wife and kids.'

Amy sucked air through her teeth.

'I'm sorry, but I can't afford it.'

'I'll tell you what, love. Take the lot, all four pairs for a quid, how's that? I'm robbing myself but at least I'll be able to buy little Johnny the toy truck he's set his heart on.'

Amy thought hard. She had more than enough money in her purse, but it was Alice's money. *I could always pay her back from my post office account.* Turning away from the spiv, she pulled her purse out of her pocket and slid out a pound note.

'Four pairs? I want to look at them before I hand this over.'

The man beamed. 'There you are, love.' He pulled the four separate packets from his inside pocket and handed them to her.

Amy examined the packets carefully, looking through the cellophane at the flesh-coloured stockings, checking for any visible snags or pulls. Finally satisfied she held the packs to her chest with one hand and passed over the banknote with the other.

'Nicely done, darlin, I'm sure your fellah will appreciate them. Come back again after Christmas if you want any more.'

Amy stuffed the precious packs inside her coat and with a huge smile on her face, she turned towards the bombed-out entrance of St Thomas' hospital.

Chapter 18

St Thomas' hospital had been hit by bombs six times during September and October. The first wiping out the nurses' quarters and the third, the main corridor of the hospital which also destroyed the out-patients department.

Amy walked along a path that had been cleared through the devastation, looking right and left at piles of twisted metal, bricks, roof timbers and slate. Although the raids had been reported in the newsreels at her local cinema, nothing could have prepared her for the amount of damage that had been inflicted on the Victorian hospital. How it was still functioning at all was something of a miracle.

At what used to be the main entrance, she followed an arrowed sign around the side of a mound of rubble and found herself on a dirty, paved path that led to a set of double doors at the side of which was a hand written sign: 'Do you worst, Adolph. We are still here.'

Amy stepped inside and made her way to a desk on the left-hand side of a long, wide, cream painted corridor. There was a small queue in front of her so she stood patiently for fifteen minutes as a receptionist worked her way through the requests.

'How may I help?' she asked as Amy stepped forward. 'You don't look injured, are you just visiting?'

'Actually, I'm after a bit of information about a patient,' Amy said, truthfully.

'Are you a relative of the patient?'

'I'll be honest. No, I'm not, but I do have a very good reason for asking about her.'

The receptionist pulled a face. 'We don't hand out patient information willy-nilly.'

'I wouldn't ask if I wasn't desperate for news of her,' Amy replied. 'Please help, her children will be distraught. They were evacuated to Kent you see; she was supposed to be coming over for Christmas.'

The receptionist looked at Amy sympathetically. 'Who is this lady? When was she admitted?'

'It was sometime this morning,' Amy replied. 'She was pulled out of a bombed house in Drews Avenue, it's only just down the road, I've just come from there.'

'I know Drews,' the woman said. She looked through a sheaf of papers until she found the list she wanted.

'What's her name?'

'Wakelin.'

'I don't have a Wakelin listed. Are you sure she was brought here?'

'I was told this would be the place she would be brought. There were twelve injured people altogether. It would have been early this morning when they came in.'

'Ah, I wasn't here until nine. Wait a moment.'

The receptionist got up from her desk and walked along the corridor for twenty yards or so until she came to a side office. After a couple of minutes, she returned with a nurse in tow.

'This is Nurse Banks,' she said nodding towards the uniformed woman. 'She may be able to help you.'

The nurse led Amy back to the green painted office and sat down behind a desk covered in tan coloured files as Amy went through her story again.

'The lady's name please?'

'Wakelin.'

The nurse frowned. 'I can't remember a Wakelin but that doesn't mean she wasn't here.'

'Her first name was Rose, if that helps?'

'Ah, Rose, I've got her. A pretty lady, about thirty, dark hair. She was very confused, asking us to let her go, but she was in no condition to be released.' She pulled a list of names from a small pile on her desk. 'Here she is, Rose, no surname, just a question mark.'

'Thank goodness,' Amy breathed a sigh of relief. 'How was she? Was she badly injured?'

'She got off remarkably lightly, I'd say,' replied the nurse. 'She had a broken leg and a damaged knee, but apart from a few cuts and bruises and her confused state of mind, she was all right. She was under a table in the kitchen apparently. Good old English oak, eh?'

'Do you think it would be possible for me to see her?' Amy asked.

'I doubt it, she's not here anymore. We couldn't deal with the number of patients coming in and we just don't have the beds for most of them, so we sent her over to Guy's in an ambulance. They've got the facilities and the beds over there.'

Amy checked the clock on the wall.

'Do you think I'd make it before the blackout?'

'I wouldn't rush, dear,' the nurse said with a smile. 'She won't be going anywhere tonight. They'll keep her in for certain. You'd be better off paying them a visit in the morning. The same staff that admitted her will more than likely be on duty then too.'

Amy let out a huge sigh of relief. 'Thank you, I honestly can't tell you how relieved I am to hear this.' She looked down at the phone. 'Is that working?' she asked.

'It usually is, we aren't routed through the local exchange. We're switched to a government run one.'

'Do you think I could make a quick call. I just want to put her family's mind at rest.'

The nurse pursed her lips.

'Be quick then, but, if you're caught. I don't know anything about it.' She got out of her seat and headed for the door. 'I'll be five minutes. I need to use the ladies.'

'Mollison Farm, Alice speaking.'

'Hello, Alice speaking, this is Amy speaking.'

'AMY! What's the news? Please tell me you have some good news.'

'And how are you in that strange town, Amy?' Amy said, trying to stifle a giggle.

'I was going to ask,' Alice replied. 'But...'

'I understand, dear heart... and... the news... is ... GOOD! In fact, it's better than good, it's GREAT!'

'You found her? Oh, Amy you clever girl.'

'Erm, not exactly. I know where she is, but I haven't seen her yet. I'm calling from St Thomas' Hospital. She was brought here after she was rescued but she's been sent over to Guy's now.'

'How is she? Not badly hurt, I hope?'

'She got off lightly, Alice. A broken leg, cuts and bruises. She's a bit confused, obviously, but apart from that she's fine. The nurse said she's going to make a full recovery.'

'Oh, Amy.' Alice began to sob into the phone.

Amy had to clear her own throat before she could reply.

'So, I'm heading over to Guy's in the morning. I've got digs set up for tonight. With a bit of luck, I'll be on the train home by mid-afternoon. I'm not sure yet whether Rose will be with me. It depends if the hospital discharges her.'

'Fingers crossed they do,' said Alice. 'They must need the beds for the more seriously injured. There will be more being admitted every day because of the bombs.'

'That reminds me, I'd better get back to Mrs Pettigrew's shop before the blackout.' I'll ring you again tomorrow when I know more. But for now... well, it's better news than we could ever have hoped for.'

'Goodbye, Amy, take care, my darling. I'll see you on Christmas Eve.'

Amy put the phone back on the cradle and opened the office door as the nurse was returning.

'Thanks so much for your help,' she said. 'I honestly can't tell you what it means to us.'

The capital was bathed in twilight and the impromptu market traders had disappeared leaving their make-do plank and beer-crate benches behind them as Amy stepped out of the ruined gates of the hospital and turned right heading towards Lambeth Road. On the streets, blackout curtains were being drawn in readiness for another night of enemy attacks. Householders stood on their front steps calling in their cats, Amy suddenly realised she hadn't seen a single dog since she'd arrived in London. Maybe people couldn't afford to keep them anymore because of the meat ration, maybe cats didn't need as much food, or maybe they supplemented their diets with one of the many rats that scurried about in the ruins. She hastily switched her train of thought away from the dogs, not wanting to think about what sort of cruel end the poor creatures had met.

Mrs Pettigrew's shop boasted a double blackout curtain on the door. The first was fixed across the doorframe itself meaning that customers had to find one of its edges and pull it to the side to allow themselves to enter. Inside, a second curtain had been set up across the open entrance to the shop, a system that stopped any light at all escaping from the interior of the building.

Amy dragged aside the thick second curtain and blinked in the sudden light, provided by a single, clear glass, one-hundred-watt bulb.

'Mum, that lady is back,' Roger called over his shoulder.

Suddenly, Mrs Pettigrew's head appeared through a dingy-looking curtain that separated the shop from the kitchen.

'Come on in, love? Did you find her?'

Amy stepped behind the counter and Mrs Pettigrew held the curtain aside to allow her to enter the kitchen.

'Cup of tea, Amy?'

'If it's no trouble,' Amy replied, pulling off her coat and retrieving the four packs of stockings from inside her cardigan.

The shopkeeper took Amy's coat, hung it on the back of the door and grinned as she nodded at the stockings. 'Someone's been shopping on the black market,' she said.

Amy's face coloured. 'Have I bought contraband? I sort of knew the man was a bit dodgy but I didn't know that the stockings are illegal.'

'No, they're not illegal, they're not really black-market goods like some of the other stuff that Clarence Dobson sells. They are virtually impossible to get hold of though. I've been tempted myself but I refuse to pay ten bob a pair.'

Amy handed a pair to the shopkeeper.

'For being so kind to me,' she said.

Lois shook her head. 'I couldn't take them off you, Amy. It's very kind of you, but ten shillings...'

'I only paid half that. He wanted to get rid of the last few pairs before the blackout.' She waved the pack in front of the shopkeeper. 'Please, take them. I really am grateful for sorting me out with digs and pointing me in the right direction to find Rose.'

Lois hesitated, then took the stockings from Amy's outstretched hand. 'There really was no need, but I'm not going to look a gift horse in the mouth. I'll put them in my knickers draw until my Sam comes back from sea.' She winked. 'All my silk ones have been darned to within an inch of their lives.' She pursed her lips and thought for a moment. 'Do you know, I get offered all sorts of black-market stuff, being a shop owner and all, and I will admit, just between the two of us, that I do take the odd pack of ciggies or a few bars of soap, but no one ever offers me stockings.' She placed the pack on the table and stroked it. 'I'll feel like Greer Garson when I wear these.'

Amy opened her case and slipped the remaining three pairs inside. 'My best friend is a dead ringer for Rita Hayworth. If you put them side by side, you'd be hard pressed to tell them apart, and she is going to be over the moon when I hand her a pair of these. She's got legs to die for.'

'Roger!'

'Yes, Mum?'

'Bring in that bit of ham I put under the counter earlier on will you. I think we'll have an early tea.'

For the next hour, Amy listened with amusement to the shopkeeper as they sipped at a seemingly endless supply of tea and bit into thick-cut bread covered with a finely spread layer of margarine and wafer-thin strips of ham.

At six, the bell tinkled and a man's voice called out.

'Lois, it's Kevin.'

'Come on through, we're in the back.'

A few seconds later, the curtain was drawn and a man in his fifties stepped through into the kitchen. He was a thin-faced man with bristling eyebrows and dyed black hair. He wore a blue, serge uniform and carried a steel helmet under an arm which sported an armband that read, ARP.

'Hello, Lois, hi, Roger...' the man's voice tailed off when he saw Amy sitting at the thick, plank table.

'This is Amy. She's been waiting for you. She's come all the way from Kent.'

Kevin sat down uninvited and Lois placed a green tea cup in front of him. 'Help yourself, it's a fresh pot,' she said.

Kevin poured tea and added a dash of milk. 'How can I be of service, young lady?'

'It's not so important now as I've found out what I needed to know, but I was looking for information on the whereabouts of Rose Wakelin.'

'Ah, I see. Did you find her at St Thomas'?'

'No, they moved her over to Guy's. They couldn't cope with the demand up the road there.'

'How is she? Her leg was a bit of a mess and she was a bit confused when we pulled her out. We only knew she was there because old Gladys Partridge insisted that she'd been inside when the bombs started to fall.'

He sipped his tea and looked absent-mindedly at the ceiling as the lights flickered and dimmed before returning to full brightness. 'She kept saying, 'where are my kids?' over and over. We couldn't find any kids. Didn't they get evacuated?'

'They did, they're safe and sound in Kent,' Amy replied. 'Poor Rose.'

'Poor Rose, indeed. She'll have lost everything; she wasn't even wearing a coat and we couldn't see one in the rubble. This is the second time she's been bombed out, isn't it?'

Amy nodded. 'Last time the bomb hit a gas main and it took half the street out. She was living in the East End with the kids and Terry, then.'

'Ah, Terry. I was very disappointed in him. I told him about Rose when we had the debrief with the fire service and the rescue teams this morning. He didn't seem the slightest bit bothered.'

Lois scowled. 'That doesn't surprise me. He only ever thinks of himself.'

'He'll be in for his pack of ciggies soon, I suppose,' Kevin said. 'He's not all bad, Lois.'

'He's scum, I've wiped better things off my shoe,' Lois spat.

Kevin finished his tea and got to his feet. Picking his helmet up from the table, he stuck it under his arm. 'Right. I'd better go and make sure no one's inadvertently signalling to the enemy. If that Evans woman hasn't shut the blackout curtains properly tonight, I'm going to issue her with a summons. I've let her off twice in the last couple of weeks. You can see her attic light from the bottom of the street.'

When Kevin had gone, Amy stretched and smiled across the table at Lois. 'Thanks so much for the lovely tea and the gossip. I came to London not knowing anyone and now I feel like I've made a very good friend.'

Lois reached across and took her hand. 'You're more than welcome, love. Our Emily lives at number two, Tavistock Gardens, it's a posh name for what it really is,' she laughed, then nudged her son. 'Get your coat on, Roger, you can show Amy where she lives.'

'It's quite all right, I'll find my way if it's close by. I don't like to think about him all alone in the dark.'

'Oh, he's been out and about many a time, don't worry about him.'

'No, honestly, I'd only feel guilty about it.' Amy picked up her case and placed it on the table. 'I've got my torch in here, just give me directions.'

Lois frowned. 'If you're sure? All right. Turn left outside the shop door. Walk to the end of the road, it's only about a hundred yards. Turn right at the bombed-out ruin on the corner and go straight across Shaw Street. Tavistock Gardens is directly opposite. You honestly can't miss it; Emily's is the first house on the right-hand side.'

Amy nodded as she pulled on her coat and slipped the torch into one of the big side pockets.

As she was fastening her coat, the shop bell tinkled.

'Lois?'

The shopkeeper snarled. 'Here he is now, the louse.'

Amy picked up her little case and followed Lois through the curtain into the shop.

Without bothering to greet him, the shopkeeper turned to the left, picked up a ten pack of Players Navy Cut and tossed them onto the counter.

'Sixpence,' she demanded, holding out her hand.

Terry suddenly lost interest in the cigarettes. His eyes were fixed on Amy.

'Well, well, what have we here? Good evening, pretty lady, what brings you to these parts?'

Amy opened her mouth to speak but was cut off by Lois.

'Never you bloody mind what she's doing here. Take your fags and get out.'

'Now, now, don't be like that, Lois,' Terry said evenly, never taking his eyes from Amy.

Amy stared back at him as he winked at her. He was a tall man, around six foot in height. His chestnut hair was slicked back with Brilliantine or Brylcreem. He had a handsome, oval face with piercing blue eyes, a straight nose and a wide smile that showed off a good set of teeth. He wore a blue boiler suit with a buff-coloured belt but no helmet. His right arm sported a band that informed residents that he was a member of the Auxiliary Fire Service, or AFS. Amy could see why women would be attracted to him.

'Hadn't you better get off and find a fire to fight?' Lois said with a look of distaste on her face.

'You're a sour old cow.' Terry replied as he picked up his cigarettes. He dropped a sixpenny piece onto the counter and watched it roll across the surface before looking back towards Amy. 'Nice meeting you, love. Perhaps we'll bump into each other another time.'

He turned and left the shop, waving his hand in the air.

'Does he actually fight fires?' Amy asked. 'His uniform looks brand new.'

'It would, my dear. He never gets his hands dirty let alone his uniform. He'll be spending the night in the Underground or some unfortunate bugger's Anderson shelter. I really don't know how he manages to get away with it. They actually pay him you know?'

Amy shook her head and walked from around the counter. At the curtain she looked back and smiled at Lois and her son. 'I hope we'll meet again one day. Please let's keep in touch.'

Lois jotted something down on a scrap of paper and handed it to Amy.

'That's my address and phone number, much good that is at the moment, but hey, we live in hope that the service will be restored one day.'

Amy tucked the paper into her pocket.

'I'll write as soon as I get back, to let you know how everything worked out. My friend Alice has a telephone. I've been trying to persuade my dad to get one for ages but he won't. I can always call you from Alice's though.'

Lois gave Amy a hug and held the blackout curtain aside until she had stepped though. 'You take care out there in the dark,' she said.

Despite living on a country lane that had no streetlights, Amy had never seen dark quite like it. At home, there was usually the odd twinkle of a light inching through the corner of someone's window, but here the streets were pitch black. It was a moonless night with thick, heavy cloud that blanked out the merest hint of starlight. Amy pulled her torch out of her pocket and switched it on, making sure it was pointing down at her feet, then, feeling the hairs on the back of her neck stand up, she pointed the torch beam three feet ahead and began to walk along the cobbled street.

Amy could hear the click of her own heels as they echoed around the empty streets. The night was cold but the cloud cover meant there would be no frost. She took a deep breath as she counted her steps, trying to work out how far she had come. Catching her foot on a raised cobble, she lurched forwards but managed to steady herself before she fell. Standing still for a moment she shone the torch a little further ahead to try to spot any other raised obstacles that might be in her path.

Then she heard the noise, a scraping sound from behind.

'Come on, Amy, it was probably just a rat or something,' she whispered to herself and not really wanting to know what was behind her. She lengthened her stride and began to half walk, half run along the blacked-out street, shining her torch right and left as she went, not really caring anymore about the regulations. She had just reached the bombed-out building on the corner of the road when she felt a hand on her arm.

Chapter 19

Amy screamed.

'Steady, steady,' said a man's voice. 'There's no need to scream, I'm not going to hurt you.'

The pressure on Amy's arm increased as he turned her around to face him.

'You shouldn't creep up on people like that,' she said, her nerves still in shreds.

Terry Wakelin lifted a leg and stuck out his foot. 'I'm wearing rubber boots, love. It's not my fault they don't make a noise.'

Amy shook off his hand and took a step back.

'Okay, well, I'll be on my way now then.'

Terry grabbed at her arm again. 'Don't rush off, darlin, we didn't get a chance to talk back there because of that miserable old sow. Let's have a bit of chat, eh?'

'Sorry, Terry, I've got to get to Emily's before—'

'Ah, you're staying with her are you. That's good, she keeps a nice clean house. I used to knock around with her old man before he volunteered for the army, the daft sod. I've been meaning to drop in to see how she is. I haven't seen her since she had the baby.'

'I think he's a brave man if he's volunteered to fight,' Amy replied.

'Not when you've got a brand-new nipper. It's stupid. He should be at home looking after them.'

Amy tried to step back again but Terry held onto her arm.

'Look, Terry, I'm not going to argue the point. I just want to get to my bed. I'm shattered, it's been a long day.'

'I'd like to see you to your bed,' Terry leered, leaning in so close that Amy could smell stale beer and cigarettes on his breath. She lifted her case to try to push it between them.

'Get off me!'

Terry ignored her plea. 'Come on, darlin, let's have a bit of a cuddle. I know a nice quiet little corner.'

Amy swung her case up at his groin, the metal corner catching him on his upper thigh.

'That wasn't very nice, was it?' His grip on her arm tightened as he tried to pull her towards the ruined house.

'Stop it. Leave me alone,' Amy dropped her case and swung her fist towards his face, the blow catching him on his shoulder.

Terry laughed as he turned sideways on to face her. Pursing his lips, he put his hand around the back of her neck and pulled her face towards him.

'Terry Wakelin, leave that poor girl alone.'

Terry pulled away swearing as he turned.

'Oh, bugger off, Lois. We were only having a bit of fun, weren't we?' He looked back to Amy for confirmation.

'I know your idea of a bit of fun, Terry, now piss off and leave her alone. She doesn't want anything to do with a louse like you.'

Terry took a step towards her but Rose lifted a heavy looking steel torch.

'Try it,' she said. 'Just try it.'

Terry backed away towards the bomb site.

'Look, Lois. I didn't mean her any harm. I only followed her to make sure she got to your Emily's in one piece.'

'Well, that's a coincidence, Terry, because that's exactly the same reason I followed her.'

Terry grunted. 'Right, I'd better be off, somewhere, there's fire that needs fighting.'

'Ha!' replied Lois, scornfully. 'If there is, you won't get within a mile of it.'

She took Amy's arm and led her down the street, past the ruined house and across the road at the next junction. When they reached number two Tavistock Gardens, she rapped on the door and waited until her sister answered it.

'This is the lady Roger was telling you about, Sis. Look after her, will you? I've just had to rescue her from that scumbag, Terry Wakelin.'

Emily nodded and stepped away from the door, her arm pointing into the dark interior of the house.

'Come on in, sweetheart. You must be ready for a cuppa.'

'Thanks for rescuing me, Lois,' Amy said. 'I don't think he'd have done anything nasty but it was kind of you to come after me.'

Lois nodded. 'He's just a bully. If you stand up to a bully, they tend to back down.'

'Will you be all right going home on your own?' Amy asked.

'He won't come near me, love. Half the policemen in the area drop into my shop to say hello when they're out on the beat. He wouldn't dare risk me reporting him for harassment.'

Amy waved goodnight, then stepped inside the house allowing Emily to draw the blackout curtain across the door before switching on the light.

'Come through,' Emily said, leading the way around a table that had a wooden beer crate perched on top with half a dozen pint bottles inside.

'It's Dad's birthday tomorrow, he's coming round for tea. Lois got the beer for him; he loves his Nut Brown does Dad.'

She pulled open a door in the far corner of the room and stood aside so that Amy could go through first. 'Watch out for the nappy bucket as you step into the kitchen. You wouldn't want to spill that lot over your feet.'

The kitchen was small and lit by a single bulb hanging from an uncovered light fitting. Three cupboards lined one wall, one of which was missing a door. On the opposite side was a white Belfast sink and an ancient electric cooker with a burnt enamel hob.

Emily stopped at the side of a three-foot-long, Formica topped table and motioned Amy to sit. She pointed to a wicker basket that sat on the draining board next to the sink.

'Only just got her off, she's not having a good day.'

The young mum plugged in a battered electric kettle with a dangerously worn cable. Picking up a red patterned tea caddy, she scooped two spoons of tea into a brown and white striped tea pot, before turning her face towards Amy.

'Did Lois tell you it's four bob for the room?'

'She did, yes.' Amy pulled her purse from her coat pocket and counted out four one shilling pieces. Emily scooped them up and slipped them into the pocket of her faded dressing gown.

'That'll buy the little one's milk tomorrow,' she said. 'I'll be able to go back to work in a few months and earn a bit so things won't be so tight then.'

'You're doing the B and B thing to keep you going then?'

Emily nodded. 'I've got a whole family in one room upstairs. A woman and three kids, bless them. I can't charge them a lot because they've got bugger all either. When Kitty is a bit older, the mother says she'll look after her for me while I go back to the factory.'

'I work in a factory,' said Amy, brightly. 'I'm a sewing machinist.'

'That's what I do too. Or did until Kitty came along. It's been a bit of a struggle since then. Pete had a good job at the docks, but of course, he's away fighting now and a soldier's pay isn't as good as a crane driver's.'

The two women chatted about their work as they sipped their tea. At eight, Amy's eyes began to close and her head fell forward as she listened to Emily talking about Lois and the shop.

'I'm so sorry,' she said as her head jerked back up.

Emily laughed. 'Please, don't apologise. I was beginning to wonder if I'd bored you to sleep though.'

'No, no, not at all, it's just been a long day,' said Amy.

Emily led her up two flights of stairs to a small attic room containing only a single wardrobe and a metal framed bed covered by a thick, flower-patterned eiderdown.

'It's not much, I know, but it's clean. There are no bed bugs and the mattress is comfortable enough.'

'It's just perfect,' said Amy as she dropped her case on the floor and laid her coat across the bottom end of the bed.

'The lavvie's outside I'm afraid, and you'll have to wash in the sink downstairs in the morning. We don't have a bath.' Emily opened the wardrobe door and produced a large ceramic chamber pot. 'For emergencies,' she said.

Emily left the room, closing the door behind her and Amy stripped to her underwear, unpacked her nightie and after pulling it over her head, she climbed into the bed. Within a couple of minutes, she was fast asleep.

Amy woke at ten with the air raid siren howling only slightly louder than Emily's baby, Kitty. She dragged herself out of bed as Emily hammered on the door. 'AIR RAID!' she shouted.

She found her shoes and picked up her skirt, but deciding there wasn't time to get properly dressed, she dropped it again and grabbed her coat as Emily's hammering became more urgent. Pulling her coat over her shoulders, she yanked open the door and hared down the stairs, catching up with the lodger family at the back door. Overhead, the arc lights lit up the sky and the sound of explosions filled the night.

Emily appeared carrying Kitty in her wicker basket. She nudged Amy as she came down the steps leaving the door open behind her.

'Come on, quickly now,' she called over her shoulder.

Amy pulled her torch out of her pocket and aimed it just in front of Emily who almost tripped over a small pile of bricks as she hurried down the garden. At the bottom, in front of the outside toilet, was a corrugated iron structure, with an open gap at the end. Emily stepped down into the dugout and took a seat on a short wooden bench which was covered by a pile of folded blankets. Placing the basket on her knees, she shuffled along as Amy stepped into the pit and slumped down next to her. The mum and her three children sat on the bench opposite, looking remarkably calm. When Amy was settled, the woman leaned to the side and pulled a thick, blanket over the entrance.

'I'm Noreen,' she said through the darkness.

Amy introduced herself as she wriggled her backside to try to get comfortable. A few seconds later a match was struck and the short stub of a candle was lit and placed in a saucer on the floor between the two benches.

'That's better.' There should be a box of candles under your seat, dear.' Noreen pointed to Amy's knees. Amy bent down and fished around under the bench until she found a battered metal biscuit tin. Passing it over to Noreen, she leaned back against the rough planks that held up the earth wall and blew out her cheeks.

'I've never been in an Anderson before. We don't really have any need for them where I'm from.'

'Lucky bugger,' said Noreen. 'I wish I'd never seen one, we seem to spend half our lives in here.' She rattled the open tin. Spare candles, matches, a screwdriver, a tube of Germolene and a tin of ant powder.' She placed the tin on the seat next to her. 'So, what brings you from the safety of your home to this living hell?'

Before Amy could answer, the blanket was pulled back and a man, carrying a crate of beer, stepped down into the shelter.

'Hutch up,' he ordered, as he dumped the rattling crate onto the dirty, plank floor.

Amy twisted her head to the side to find Terry leering at her. He leaned forward, lifted a bottle of brown ale from the crate, then using the tin opener blade from the Swiss army knife in his pocket, he eased the cap from the beer. Taking a deep slug, he turned back to Amy and grinned.

'Do you come here often?' he slurred.

Chapter 20

Alice
Monday 23rd December

In the evening, Harriet and Stephen disappeared upstairs for twenty minutes. When they came back down, they were each carrying a small flat package that had been carefully wrapped in newspaper.

They waved them under my face, grinning, then did the same to Miriam.

'No touching or feeling until Christmas morning,' said Stephen. 'These have got to go to Santa.'

I nodded seriously. 'I won't touch them. I promise.' Miriam nodded her agreement.

'We made them at school,' said Harriet.

'Shhh,' Stephen put his finger to his lips. 'No clues, walls have ears and all that.'

'But this isn't anything to do with the war, it's Aunty Alice's Christmas present.'

Stephen put his finger to his lips again. 'Shh.'

The children carried their parcels carefully to the Christmas tree and slid them underneath.

'When do you think Santa will pick them up?' Harriet asked.

'In the night, I would think,' I replied. 'He won't come while we're here.'

'But how will he get in, there's a fire in the grate.'

'Santa Magic,' I said with a wink. 'He can get in and out of any room. Fires are no obstacle to Santa.'

Stephen pushed his parcel a little further under the lower branches. 'No touching,' he said again.

'Have you written your letter to Santa yet?' Miriam asked as she emptied the tea pot into the sink, and swilled it out with hot water from the Ascot.

Stephen shook his head. 'Not yet, we were wondering where to put them. At home we used to stick them up the chimney but we didn't have a fire there, we had an electric heater.'

'You can leave them on the mantlepiece,' Miriam suggested.

Harriet nodded her head eagerly. 'Can we have some paper, Aunty Alice?'

I walked through to the front room and pulled two cream envelopes and two sheets of my precious stock of notepaper from my desk drawer and took them back to the kitchen.

'Wow, proper writing paper,' said Harriet, running her fingers over the silky, lined sheet.

'Only the best for Santa,' I replied.

Stephen sucked on the end of his pencil. 'What shall I ask for?' he mused.

'Don't expect Santa to bring you everything you write down,' Miriam warned. 'He can only fit so much in his sack despite his magic, and there is a war on, remember. Some toys are hard to get hold of.'

'I hope he manages to dodge the planes when he's flying about on his sleigh tomorrow night,' Harriet said with a look of concern on her face.

'They won't even see him,' I reassured her. 'Santa Magic. He'll fly right over the top of them and they won't even know he's there.'

Harriet smiled at me. 'Santa Magic,' she said, and sticking her tongue out of the side of her mouth as she always did when she was concentrating, she began to make her list.

When the long lists were complete, the children folded their sheets of paper, slid them into the envelopes, then licked the gum on the triangle folds and stuck them down, checking to make sure the glue had taken hold.

I took the proffered letters and placed them carefully on the mantlepiece, leaning against the wall of the fireplace.

'He'll find them there easily enough,' I said. 'Now, who's for a milky mug of Ovaltine?'

After the hot drinks, Miriam led the children into the bathroom to wash and clean their teeth before bed and I tiptoed across to the Christmas tree and slid the kid's presents out from underneath. Carrying them carefully across to the fireplace, I picked up both letters and held them on top of the parcels. Taking a quick look into the parlour to make sure they were still safely inside the bathroom, I turned around and unlocked the cupboard under the stairs where I had secreted the rest of their presents, and placed their gifts and cards onto a low shelf, then, backing out with a satisfied smirk. I locked the door again, and plucking a little bell decoration from the Christmas tree, I walked quickly into the parlour and stopped just outside the bathroom door. Opening the door an inch, I waited until the kids had finished brushing their teeth, then tinkled the bell three times before slipping it into my pocket.

I turned away and made out I was searching for something in the parlour as the bathroom door flew open and two puzzled faces looked out.

'What was that tinkling noise, Aunty Alice?'

It was my turn to look puzzled. 'I didn't hear a tinkling,' I said.

'It was a bell, a little pixie bell, thingy.'

I looked at Miriam and shrugged. Miriam shook her head. 'I didn't hear a thing.'

Stephen hurried past me and rushed into the kitchen.

'They've gone!' he shouted. 'Santa's letters have gone.'

Harriet ran in after him, her mouth agape.

'So have the presents! Look, Stephen.'

Stephen lay on his stomach and searched under the tree. 'They've gone. Santa must have been to collect them.'

'But how? ... SANTA MAGIC!' the children shouted together.

'Well, I never,' I said holding my hands to my face. 'It must have been Santa, I've only been in the parlour for a few moments, he must have slipped in when I wasn't looking.'

'That's what the tinkling noise was,' said Harriet. 'I don't think grownups can hear it.'

'That must be the answer,' I said, thoughtfully. 'Come on now, if you've finished in the bathroom, it's time for bed.'

When the excited kids had been tucked into bed, Miriam picked up her knitting and I picked up my Agatha novel and read a few more chapters, still unable to fathom who had killed Simeon Lee. After an hour, I put the book down and walked over to the back door. Opening it an inch or two, I looked outside at the snow-covered yard before turning my eyes skywards.

'Blimey, it's been coming down tonight,' I said. 'It's a white out.'

'Lovely, just what I like at Christmas,' Miriam replied. 'I hope it's still around for the party tomorrow. I always love standing in the yard singing carols by lantern light.'

I shivered as I thought about another freezing cold morning in the pigsties, then put the thought aside as quickly as it had entered my head. I lived on a farm where we took the rough with the smooth. Martha would have piglets in the playpen again in the morning. I smiled at the prospect. I loved to hear her squeals when I carried the animals into the kitchen. Martha was over two now and was beginning to understand a little bit about the concept of Santa Claus. I had bought her a wooden dog on a rope that she could pull along behind her for Christmas, but, because the animal had fold over ears, in a moment of creative brilliance, I had painted it pink. An adult might see it as a pink dog, but I was hoping a toddler might accept it for what it was meant to represent.

I closed the door, shutting out the bitter cold of the night and began to think about Amy, hoping fervently that the diggings she had found enabled her to get a good night's sleep. Then I thought about my own experiences in London a few weeks before and offered up a prayer, beseeching any deity who happened to be listening, to keep her safe until morning.

I slept fitfully that night, waking in a cold sweat around two o'clock, my dream still in my mind. I switched on the bedside lamp and shook my head to clear it. After taking a deep sip of water from the glass next to the lamp. I lay on my back and stared up at the ceiling as I tried to make sense of the jumble of thoughts that ran though my head. My dream had been full of bright lights and the sound of explosions. Standing in a bomb crater, smiling and waving towards me was Amy. She was shouting something I couldn't quite make out, then a bright searchlight lit up the sky above the rooftops behind her and line of brilliant white tracer bullets began to pierce the night sky like arrow shaped fireflies.

I switched off the light and tried to put the dream into the background of my thoughts, but as I was drifting off, Amy's words finally made their way through the tangled web of dreamland and into my head.

'I'm all right, Alice, dear heart. Don't fret.'

Chapter 21

Amy
Tuesday 24th December

Amy found herself beginning to feel a little anxious in the claustrophobic atmosphere of the Anderson shelter. Her anxiety was replaced by a flash of anger as Terry pulled a cigarette from his pocket and lit it with a brass Ronson lighter.

'Can't you go outside and smoke that horrible, thing,' Amy spluttered as he turned towards her and exhaled a thick cloud of smoke.

'I'm not going out there with a fag on,' Terry replied, taking a swig from his brown ale bottle. 'I'd be like a target. They'd home straight in on it. They're bloody good those German pilots.'

The air in the shelter was soon full of the acrid smoke. Noreen did her best to waft away the worst of it from her children's faces but they soon began to cough and splutter. Terry, unfazed, took another deep draw and blew the smoke across the shelter towards them.

Noreen snapped, leaning forwards she snatched the half-smoked cigarette from Terry's mouth, dropped it on the floor and stamped it out under her shoe.

'Oi!' It was Terry's turn to be angry. 'I'll only light another one.'

'And the same thing will happen to it,' Noreen snarled at him. 'Look, Mister, whatever your name is, I'm a smoker too, but I wouldn't expect other people to smoke the same cigarette as me. It's just selfish.'

Terry gave her the finger, but his cigarettes stayed in his pocket. Draining the first bottle of beer, he dropped it with a clink into the crate before pulling out and opening another one. He took a long gulp, then offered the bottle to Amy.

'Here you go, love. Have a swig. It'll put hairs on your chest.'

'I don't really want hairs on my chest thanks,' Amy replied with a frown.

'No, I bet you don't.' Terry looked down at Amy's bosom with a leer. 'Forget I said that.' Taking another slug, he put his hand on her thigh, leaned back against the timber wall and closed his eyes.

Amy pushed his hand away angrily, but a few moments later, he put it back.

Noreen pulled a disgusted face and reaching into the biscuit tin, pulled out the six-inch-long screwdriver, nodding down at Terry's hand as she passed it to Amy.

Amy pushed the hand away again. 'Do that again and you'll wish you hadn't.'

Terry snorted and wrapped his palm around her thigh, this time a little higher up.

Amy brought screwdriver down with more force than she intended. Terry shrieked and pulled his hand away, holding it up to his mouth before lifting it in front of his eyes to inspect the damage.

'I did warn you,' Amy said, sternly.

'I might need bloody stitches in that,' Terry complained. 'I could have you up for this, it's assault.'

'And what do you call what you were doing to her?' Noreen spat.

'I was just being friendly,' Terry said in a whiny voice. 'There was no need for that response.'

Amy slipped the sharp screwdriver into her pocket and pulled her coat over her naked knees as Terry sucked at his injured hand again.

'You might have given me Tetanus,' he moaned.

'I'm sure the beer will take the pain away.' Amy almost had to shout as the sounds of the exploding bombs got closer.

The children seemed unfazed by the noise as they lay across the bench, leaning against each other.

Emily had been dozing, she woke with a start as the deep WHUMP of a bomb hit something nearby.

Terry showed her his injured hand before draining the contents of his latest bottle and dropping it into the empty side of the crate.

'Well, this is nice and cosy,' he slurred, as he opened up a third bottle. He leaned forwards and tried to focus as he looked past Amy to Emily. 'That's ten pints tonight, not bad for a weekday.'

When no one seemed eager to congratulate him on his feat, he grinned to himself then continued to talk to Emily.

'Have you 'eard from Pete? Bet it's a bit warmer where he is than it is here.'

'I got a letter a couple of weeks ago. How do you know he's out in the desert?'

Terry tried to tap the side of his nose, but missed and hit his cheek instead.

'I have my ways, my sources,' he said drunkenly. 'I get to know a lot of stuff.' He waved his hand in the air nonchalantly.

'You ought to be out there fighting yourself, you coward,' Emily hissed as another loud whistling was followed by a huge explosion.

'I've got important work here,' Terry replied. 'Mr Churchill can't spare me.' He began to snigger, then laugh.

'Lois often wonders how you manage to get away with skiving on the backs of real firemen.' Emily had to shout to make herself heard about the noise of the air raid.

'I have friends in high places,' Terry boasted.

'Kevin the ARP man? He's hardly highly placed.'

Amy looked up as the sound of planes hummed overhead.

'It's not Kevin I'm talking about.' Terry lifted his arm and the beer spilled onto his chest. 'Bugger.' He pulled the material towards his mouth and sucked on it. 'Waste not want not,' he muttered to himself.

They sat in silence for a while listening to the sound of heavy bombing in the distance.

'Some poor sods are getting it bad tonight,' Noreen said, sadly.

'Sooner them than us,' Terry replied, taking another long slug from the bottle.

'Come on then, Terry, out with it, who's this highly placed official keeping you in the manner to which you have become accustomed?'

Terry smirked, lifted the bottle to check how much remained, then looked past Amy to Emily.

'Larry Groves,' he said, smugly.

'Larry Groves? Who the hell is Larry Groves when he's at home?'

'That's the point,' Terry sniggered. 'He isn't often at home, not with his poor, neglected wife anyway.'

'What are you blathering on about?' Emily frowned as she leaned forwards to look past Amy.

'Larry Groves is the head of the Civil Defence Committee for Westminster and Lambeth. What he says, goes, he has a lot of afflu... influence.'

'And just how did he get to know about your value to the war effort?'

'I told him, myself,' Terry boasted. 'Right after I caught him canoodling with Kevin the ARP man.' He suddenly burst into laughter which ended up in a coughing fit.

'Kevin? Isn't he married?'

'Nope,' Terry took another sip of beer then waved the bottle in the air. 'At least he's honest about it, unlike that Larry Groves.'

'So, you blackmailed them? Terry you're even more disgusting than I thought you were.'

Terry shrugged, then squinted at the bottle.

'You've got to look after number one,' he replied.

'Maybe you should try looking after your wife and kids instead,' Amy said quietly, through a lull in the air raid.

'What do you know about it?' Terry glared at Amy.

'I happen to know your children, and I'm very fond of them,' Amy replied. 'Harriet is a very clever little girl and Stephen would be a credit to any half-decent father.'

'I miss my kids,' Terry sniffled and wiped his eyes on the back of his sleeve. 'It's her I can't abide.'

'Her! I assume you mean, Rose, your wife? The wife who almost died in last night's air raid.'

Terry shrugged again. 'Look, I wouldn't wish that on her, but then I wouldn't wish it on anyone. Not even that queer, Larry Groves and Kevin.'

'You make me sick,' Emily shouted as the air raid picked up again.

'Why would you stick up for a Nancy boy like that? You reckon I'm disgusting but what about them? You can't get any more disgusting than that, sticking their—'

'Shut it, there are children here remember?' Noreen stared hard at Terry.

'You're right, kids shouldn't have to know about filth like that.' He tried to take another drink but the bottle slipped from his hands and hit the crate with a clunk.

'How do you know my kids?' he asked Amy after a long silence.

'They were evacuated to my friend's farm,' Amy replied. 'They're being well looked after; they're living with people who care about them.'

'I care about them,' Terry wagged a finger at Amy. 'Don't you go saying I don't.'

'All right, I believe you, but a letter or two wouldn't go amiss.'

'I've been busy,' Terry said, defensively. 'I will write though. Tell them I love them and I'll write soon.'

'I'll tell them not to hold their breath,' Amy muttered to herself. The next thing she knew, Terry's head had slumped onto her shoulder and the gentle sound of his snoring was in her ear.

The all clear sounded at six o'clock and Amy eased herself away from the still sleeping Terry and followed Emily, as she carried her baby in a basket, out of the shelter. Amy flashed her torch to light up the path as she held open the blanket door for Noreen and her half-awake children.

Back in the house, Emily laid the wicker basket down on the Formica table and stretched.

'Well, we survived another one,' she said. 'I'll nip out in an hour or so to get Kitty's milk. Anything I can get for you, Noreen?'

'I need to check what I've got on the coupons, love. My ration book is on the table in the front room with yours.'

Emily opened the kitchen door and walked through to the living room. A few seconds later Amy heard an angry shout.

'Someone's taken the ration books. They were here last night.'

Amy and Noreen rushed in to the front room as Emily held her hands to her face. 'What the hell am I going to do? Kitty needs her formula.'

'Are you sure you didn't take them into the kitchen or upstairs?' Amy asked, looking around.

'I'm positive, they were on the table next to Dad's beer... Oh, shit. It's him, isn't it? That beer he was drinking last night, it was Dad's.' She stormed back into the kitchen. 'I'll swing for the bastard.'

'Don't confront him, Emily,' Amy said in a calming voice. 'Let him sleep on, get the police in. Catch him in the act. If we go storming in, he'll just deny it and get rid of the evidence.'

'Good thinking,' Emily replied, nodding at Amy. 'I can't risk a busted nose anyway.'

She turned back into the front room, pulled away the thick blackout curtain and opened the front door. She looked right and left along the street, then down at her watch.

'Rodney Berry is usually patrolling about now. Noreen, can you keep your eye on Kitty while I try to find him?'

'I'll come too,' Amy volunteered.

'No, honestly, Amy, I know the streets around here, you stay with Noreen in case our drunken hero wakes up in a bad temper.'

Emily slipped out of the door and pulled it shut behind her.

Noreen ushered her sleepy children upstairs, then returned as Amy was plugging in the kettle.

'This thing is lethal,' she said, trying to avoid the bare copper wire that protruded from the flex.

'Needs must,' Noreen replied. 'She can't afford a new one, or even a second hand one until she gets back to work.'

Emily was only gone for fifteen minutes, she returned via the back door with a tall, broad police constable in tow.

'Is he still in the shelter?' she asked quietly.

'He is. We've been keeping an eye out,' Amy replied.

PC Berry turned away and marched down the garden towards the Anderson. 'Come on, Sleeping Beauty, let's be 'avin you,' he called as he pulled the blanket aside and aimed the beam of his torch into the shelter.

Terry came out, squinting at the light from the policeman's torch.

'What? I 'aven't done anything wrong.'

'I'll be the judge of that,' the policeman replied. 'Now, empty your pockets.'

'I've got nothing in my pockets, just my fags and lighter.'

'He has, he's got my Kitty's milk ration,' Emily yelled.

'What!' Terry looked up the garden towards the entry between Emily's house and the one next door. 'How would I get hold of your ration book?'

'I know it was you,' Emily snarled. 'You went in my house before you came to the shelter. You stole Dad's beer too. Some of it is still in the crate.'

PC Berry shone his torch into the shelter. The half crate of beer lit up in the beam.

'Well?' The policeman shone the torch into Terry's face again. 'Pockets,' he commanded.

Terry's right hand dipped into the side pocket of his boiler suit pulling out his cigarettes and lighter.

'Other side,' Berry ordered.

Terry gripped the packet of Players and his lighter in his right hand and lifted the flap on the wide, side pocket with his left. Before anyone could react, he pulled out a wad of ration books, hurled them into the policeman's face and took off up the yard.

Startled, the policeman was frozen to the spot for a second, but then he turned and ran after Terry, shouting, 'Stop,' as he hurried up the yard. By the time he came out of the alley onto Tavistock Gardens, Terry had crossed Shaw Street and was rounding the corner onto Fuller Street.

PC Berry, lifted his whistle to his lips and blew on it three times before hurrying after the miscreant, but by the time he reached the destroyed house on the corner of Fuller Street there was no sign of Terry.

'Did he have your ration books?' Berry asked when he returned to Emily's kitchen.

Emily waved them at him. 'He did, and he had Noreen's too, and there are a few more here. I reckon he's been nipping into people's empty houses while they've been sheltering from the raids.'

The policeman checked the books. 'I'll see these get returned to their rightful owners,' he said.

'Can I keep my coupons? You don't need them for evidence?'

Berry shook his head and waved the other books at her. 'I've got these, it will be all right. You will have to make a statement at the station later on today though.'

'Thank God,' Emily blew out her cheeks. 'I was getting worried for a moment.'

'You'll need to drop in at the police station too, Miss.' Berry turned his attention to Amy.

'I can't, I mean, I'd like to, but I have to get over to Guy's hospital this morning.'

'I'm sorry, Miss, but you will have to make a statement. I'll expect you all at one o'clock.'

The policeman touched the brim of his helmet and left the kitchen.

'You've got plenty of time to get to Guy's and back before one,' Noreen said, handing Amy a cup of tea.

'I suppose so,' Amy replied with a yawn. 'I need to get an hour's sleep first though. I didn't get a wink last night with that drunken so and so breathing his disgusting fumes into my face.'

She took a couple of sips of tea, then walked to the stairs.

'Can you give me a shout about nine-thirty? I really do need to get my head down.'

'Nine-thirty it is,' Emily said with a nod. 'Now, Noreen, I'm off to the shop, Lois will be opening soon. What can I get you?'

Amy climbed the stairs wearily. When she got into the attic, she took off her coat and threw it over the bottom of the bed, then kicking off her shoes, she pulled back the eiderdown and slipped between the sheets. She was asleep within minutes.

At twelve-forty, she was dragged out of her slumbers by Emily, who tugged urgently at her shoulder.

'Amy, get up. I'm so, so sorry.'

Amy opened one eye, then blinked and risked the other one. 'What's wrong?' she asked, sleepily.

'I nodded off in the chair after I fed, Kitty,' Emily explained. 'I'm so sorry, Amy.'

Amy sat up and stretched. 'Not to worry. What time is it?'

'It's twenty to one, we've got to be at the police station in twenty minutes.'

Chapter 22

The police station was only a short walk along the Lambeth Road and Amy arrived with Emily, Noreen and Kitty almost bang on time.

A desk sergeant checked their names and addresses against a list on the counter and asked them to wait while he alerted the investigating officer to their presence.

Emily and Noreen were interviewed first and Amy was left sitting in the cold police station reception, studying black and white, wall mounted, photographs of previous generations of police officers to pass the time. At one-thirty, PC Berry stuck his head around a door on her right, and called her name.

'Miss Rowlings? This way please.'

Amy followed him along a short corridor to a wood panelled office where a uniformed sergeant was reading Berry's report from earlier in the day. He placed it on the desk in front of him as she approached.

'Good afternoon, Miss Rowlings, thank you for attending this interview. It shouldn't take long to sort this out. I've already spoken to your friends and I have a good idea of how the events of last night panned out. I'd just like to have your take on things, seeing as you were the only one who wasn't affected by the alleged theft.'

Amy smiled nervously and sat down on the opposite side of the desk to the sergeant.

'If you wouldn't mind explaining what you saw last night. Take your time.'

Amy took the sergeant through the sequence of events from when she first bumped into Terry at Lois's shop to when Emily had brought PC Berry to the house earlier that morning.

'So, you didn't see Mr Wakelin take any of the ration books that were found in his possession?'

'No, I wasn't aware he had them until he pulled them out of his pocket and threw them at the constable.'

'Thank you. Now, you said that Mr Wakelin was in a drunken state when he arrived at the shelter.'

'He was drunk before then. I could smell beer on him when he stopped me on my way round to Emily's house.'

'I see.'

'Have you arrested him already then?'

The sergeant nodded slowly. 'He wasn't hard to find, Miss Rowlings. We sent an officer round to his flat and waited for him to come home. He was arrested at eight o'clock this morning.'

Amy sighed with relief. She really didn't want to bump into Terry again if she could help it.

'We found another twenty stolen ration books at his residence. To be honest we were expecting to find a lot of black-market stuff as well, you know, cigarettes, etc, but there was none of that. We did recover some jewellery, bottles of scent, that sort of thing. It appears he's been nipping into people's houses while the residents were in the shelters.'

As he mentioned the black market, Amy was relieved that she had left her case with the packs of stockings in Emily's bedroom. She wouldn't have liked to explain how she got hold of them to the policeman.

'Isn't that looting? Can't he be hanged for that?' Despite Amy's dislike of Terry, she couldn't bear the thought of his children discovering that their father had been executed.

'No, it won't happen. He'll be charged with burglary and he'll get a big fine and a few months in prison, maybe six if the magistrate is in a bad mood. We can but hope.'

Amy breathed another sigh of relief.

'The best thing to come out of all this is, he won't be able to dodge the military any longer. He'll be called up the minute he gets out of prison.' The policeman flashed a quick smile.

'Good, it's what he deserves,' said Amy, sternly.

'Now, Miss Rowlings. The thing is... Mr Wakelin has made a serious allegation against you.'

'Against me?' Amy's mouth gaped.

'He claims you assaulted him while you were all in the Anderson shelter. He has a wound on his hand which he claims was inflicted by you.'

Amy stared wide eyed at the sergeant. 'But... Yes, but he kept putting his hand on my leg, higher and higher up, I told him to stop a couple of times but he wouldn't. There was a screwdriver in the shelter, so in the end I stuck him with it. I didn't use that much force; it can't have been much more than a scratch.'

'Nevertheless, you admit the assault?'

'I... it wasn't an assault; it was done in self-defence.'

'I'm not sure the courts would see it that way, Miss Rowlings.'

'Are you really saying that a woman can't defend herself against the unwanted attentions of a man?'

'I'm not saying that at all, what I'm saying is, it's going to be difficult to prove. He was drunk and he claims he put his hand on your leg to steady himself.'

'Three times in the space of a minute?'

The sergeant held up both hands. 'I understand, Miss Rowlings, but he does have a wound and that might prove difficult for you if the case was ever to go to court.'

'This is so unfair.' Amy felt tears well in her eyes.

'Now, now, don't cry. I'm sure this can be sorted out to everyone's satisfaction.'

He got to his feet and called for PC Berry.

'Constable, would you pay a visit to Mr Wakelin in the interview room opposite please. Just ask him once again, whether he intends to continue with his allegations against Miss Rowlings.'

When Berry had left the room, the sergeant asked Amy why she had come to the area during such a dangerous time. Amy explained about Rose and how she still, as yet, hadn't found her.

'I was supposed to be at Guy's Hospital this morning, but because of the air raid, I slept in. I'm going round there as soon as I leave here.'

'I hope she makes a speedy recovery from her injuries. A few nights away from the Blitz will do her the world of good, I'm sure. Now...'

The sergeant was interrupted when PC Berry came back into the room, rubbing the knuckles of his right hand as he entered.

'Mr Wakelin has decided to withdraw the allegations against Miss Rowlings, Sergeant.'

'Excellent, well done, Berry.' He got to his feet and held out his hand to Amy. 'Good day, Miss Rowlings, I hope your search is successful. Show the lady out, please.'

When Amy stepped out of the police station, she found Noreen and Emily waiting for her.

'That took a while,' Emily said, as she gently rocked her wicker basket.

'It was something and nothing,' Amy replied. She looked up at the clock on the wall of the Baptist Church opposite. 'Oh, my goodness, it's gone two, I really must get on.'

'You'll get a bus just over the road,' Noreen said. 'I had to take our Jimmy to Guy's a couple of weeks ago when he ripped his knee open playing on a bomb site. The buses run every few minutes.'

'What about your suitcase?' Emily asked.

'Oh, I don't have time to come back for it, can I pick it up later?'

'I'll be out all afternoon,' Emily replied. 'I've got to go to Dad's to pick him up for his birthday. I've decided to take him round to Lois's now. She always keeps a bit of beer in the back. I can take your case with me and you can pick it up from there if you like?'

Amy reached out and gave her a hug. 'Thanks so much for taking me in at such short notice.' She turned to Noreen and hugged her. 'It's been lovely to meet you and the kids, stay safe, won't you?'

'We'll do our best,' Noreen said as she returned the hug. 'Now, you'd better run, there's a bus coming.'

It was two twenty-five when Amy stepped off the bus outside Guy's hospital. She walked through the imposing pillars at what was the main gates until the Ironwork had been recycled for the war effort, and walked across the main quadrangle, past the statue of Thomas Guy, the founder, and headed for the main entrance.

Inside she followed a sign for reception and found herself at the end of a long queue of people.

Fortunately, the desk was well manned and twenty minutes later, Amy was facing a stern looking woman wearing horn-rimmed spectacles. Her dull, grey hair was swept back into a severe bun.

'Yes?'

'I'm enquiring as to the health of Rose Wakelin; she was brought here from St Thomas' yesterday. She suffered a broken leg and other injuries after being caught in an air raid.'

The woman stared at Amy for a few moments, before shuffling through a pile of papers. Without looking back to Amy, she raised her arm and pointed along the corridor.

'Straight to the bottom, turn left, then straight on, first right. That's where you'll find anyone who's come in over the last twenty-four hours. They're treated and assessed before being found a bed on a ward if they need one.'

Amy thanked her and hurried along the corridor, relieved that her search was finally over.

After following the receptionist's directions, Amy found herself in what was little more than a wider extension of the corridor. People with arms in slings, or thick bandages around their heads, sat on a series of benches, while those in a slightly worse condition were laid out on mattresses on the floor. Amy walked along the lines, looking for the face she had memorised from the photograph on Alice's mantlepiece, she had even rehearsed her greeting in her mind. *'Rose Wakelin, I presume.'*

Finding no one who resembled Rose, Amy did another tour of the area, looking a little more closely at the faces of the injured. When she was convinced that Rose wasn't among them, she walked back to the main corridor and searched for a nurse, finding one in a little office just a few yards away.

Amy knocked on the open door and waited until the staff nurse looked up. She was a pretty woman in her early thirties wearing her nurses' cap and a white, ward dress.

'How may I help?'

Amy told her story once again as the nurse listened attentively. When she had finished speaking, the woman picked up a thick file and thumbed through the pages.

'Ah, Rose Wakelin, formally of 37 Drews Avenue... Next of kin, Mrs Felicity Hargreaves.... blah blah blah... Ah, here we are... treated for a tibia shaft fracture and knee ligament damage. Right leg set in plaster of Paris from knee to ankle. Treated for minor cuts and bruising to the face and arms. Confused when admitted, blah blah blah... Yes, we admitted the lady you're looking for.'

'Phew,' Amy replied.

'We did try to get in touch with a relative but it proved impossible. Her mother isn't on the telephone network. According to the added note here, we tried to ring a number of people in the Gillingham area, called Morrison. She kept rambling on about a Stephen and Harriet, so we assumed they were related to her in some way. We scoured the Kent directory but the three Stephen Morrisons we contacted had never heard of her.'

'The name was actually Mollison, not Morrison,' Amy replied, 'and Harriet and Stephen are her children. They're the evacuated kids I mentioned a few moments ago.'

'Ah, that explains why no one we rang knew her then.' The nurse made a few extra notes on the file and crossed out two lines of information. 'Right,' she said, eventually, picking up the sheet with Rose's details on and getting to her feet. 'Let's go and find her, shall we? She's in temporary ward three by the looks of it.'

An increasingly excited Amy followed the nurse out of the office and back the way she had come along the main corridor. About thirty yards on, she turned right and pushed open a set of double doors. A nurse looked up from her desk as she entered.

'Mrs Wakelin. She was brought here after treatment, I believe?'

'She was, Staff... but she's not here now.'

'Why on earth not? Has she been admitted to a ward? I didn't think her injuries were that serious.'

'She discharged herself, Staff. About...' she looked down at the register on the desk...'just over an hour ago.'

Chapter 23

Alice
Tuesday 24th December

'It's Christmas, Aunty Alice!' Harriet came rushing down the back steps with Stephen close behind.

I shut the gate of the whelping pen with my heel and tried to stabilise the two squirming piglets I held under my arms.

'Technically, it's Christmas tomorrow, it's only Christmas Eve today,' I corrected her.

'Yes, but Santa comes TONIGHT!' she screamed.

Stephen ran around in the snow with an imaginary rifle, shooting the enemy wherever he found them.

'Come on,' I said. 'Let's get breakfast and drop these two in with Martha.'

'Santa's ears must be burning,' I said after listening to Harriet and Stephen wax lyrical about the person of the moment. 'You've spoken about nothing else since you got out of bed.'

'It's exciting, that's why,' Stephen explained.

'I understand that,' I replied, patiently. 'But I think we're going around in circles now. We've already discussed the route he might take and what he might have in his sack, three times.'

'What shall we talk about then?' Stephen asked.

I sighed. 'I don't know, what about your mum and dad, you should be thinking about them today, having to work while you're running around shooting Germans.'

'We're always thinking about Mum and Dad,' Harriet said, seriously. 'We never stop thinking about them.' A sad look came over her face and I instantly wished I hadn't mentioned them.

'Dad will have to work tonight if the bombers come,' Stephen said. 'He's a very brave man, fighting fires when the bombs are falling.'

'He is,' I agreed. 'He's a very brave man.'

'Mum's brave too,' Harrier blurted. 'She makes bullets and bombs. You have to be brave to do that.'

'Indeed you do,' I said, nodding my head. 'I don't think I'm brave enough to do either of those jobs.'

'I'm glad you don't, or we wouldn't see you for Christmas either,' Stephen said.

I smiled. 'Who's up for a walk? Let's leave Miriam to get on with her baking.'

Miriam waved a flour covered hand towards us. 'Homemade sausage rolls. Be back in an hour and you can have a warm one.'

'What time does the party start?' Harriet asked as we trudged our way along the edge of the middle field. Stephen marched in front, taking the odd handful of snow from where it had drifted in the hedgerow and throwing it like a hand grenade at his invisible enemies.

'They'll all be here for about five-thirty,' I replied. 'But the ladies all bring a little bit of something for the party and they'll spread it all out on the big table before we start officially.'

'BANG!' shouted Stephen as his latest projectile exploded against a gate post.

We came out of Middle Field about half way along Long Lane. 'Where to now,' I said, looking right and left.

'Can we have a bottle of pop at the Old Bull?' Harriet asked.

I nodded. Stan would let the kids stand in the foyer to drink their fizzy pop. They hadn't been in there since the summer.

'Bring them into the snug, there's no one in there yet,' Stan said as I stuck my head around the door.

I ushered them into the lounge bar where a merry fire was already blazing in the grate.

The children had never been in the snug before and rushed across to two seats on either side of the fire that had been made out of old leather saddles.

'Giddyup!' Stephen shouted as he leapt onto his imaginary horse.

'Shhh,' I hissed. 'You'll be thrown out if you make too much noise.'

Stephen pointed his gun at the picture of a farmhand standing next to a cart full of hay and let loose a volley of bullets.

'Oi! Keep that racket down,' a deep voice called from the bar side of the pub.

'Oh, shut up, Ken,' Stan said as he pulled the tops off two bottles of lemon crush and pushed in a couple of straws. 'You were young once.'

'I can't remember ever being young,' Ken replied and went back to studying the race cards in his folded newspaper.

'Sorry, Stan, but I've left my purse at home. I thought I'd got a few coppers in my pocket.'

'That's all right,' Stan replied. 'I'll add the pop onto your party drinks bill. I'll hand it to Barney when he comes up to collect it all.'

We left the pub at twelve and headed back up the snowy lane to the farm, Stephen kicking up snow at Harriet, who got her own back by throwing a superbly aimed snowball at the back of his head.

The kitchen was warm and inviting and smelled of cooked pastry.

Miriam, as promised, pulled out a plate from the top oven and placed it on the table. 'Only one each. You don't want to lose your appetite for the party food tonight.'

The sausage rolls went down in no time and I licked the tips of my fingers as I swallowed the last mouthful.

As I got to my feet, Miriam nudged past me and placed a silver cake stand in the centre of the table, then turned and went into the larder, returning a few moments later with a large, gorgeous smelling, fruit cake.

'No icing this year, sadly, but I'm sure it will be well received. What's left of it, that is.'

She stared at me through narrowed eyes. The children looked at the picked at edges of the cake, then their eyes followed Miriam's accusing finger as she pointed it at me.

'Have you been piggling at the cake, Aunty Alice?' Harriet looked aghast.

'Not exactly piggling,' I replied, averting my eyes from Miriam's glare.

'She does it every year,' Miriam complained. 'She just has to piggle at it. She can't help herself.'

'I only had a bit... a few crumbs,' I responded, trying not to look at the kids.

'I'm putting it in the safe next year,' Miriam said turning away towards the sink.

'Aunty Alice has the key for the safe,' Stephen said.

'Then I'll... Well, I don't know what I'll do, maybe I'll hide a mouse trap under the muslin cover.'

Stephen and Harriet laughed at the prospect of me having my fingers caught in a mouse trap and I tried to change the subject. I didn't succeed.

'No more piggling.' Miriam slapped at my hand. 'There'll be nothing left for the families if you keep at it like that.'

I held both hands in the air. 'No more piggling,' I promised.

Finally free of accusatory stares, I clapped my hands and told the kids to go upstairs for an hour's nap. 'You're going to be up a bit later tonight and I don't want you getting all grumpy on us.'

'Aw, Aunty Alice,' Stephen didn't like the idea at all.

'Up!' I commanded, pointing towards the stairs.

'Don't let us oversleep, Aunty Alice,' Harriet said as she walked obediently across the kitchen. 'We don't want to miss the party.'

'I'll give you a shout in an hour, don't worry.' I looked at the big clock on the wall. 'Go on, I'll call you down at three.'

When the kids had gone upstairs, I stood beneath the garlands in the middle of the kitchen floor and collected my thoughts.

'Right, I'd better get the lads wage packets made up. We had a decent year what with the government taking control of prices. They'll be pleased with their Christmas bonus this year. I'll be in the front room if I'm needed.'

'I'll bring you a cup of tea in a bit later,' Miriam replied, wiping her hands on her pinny.

An hour later, I had just sealed the last brown wage packet and laid in onto the silver tea tray I always used to carry the lads' earnings into the kitchen at the start of the party, when the phone rang.

'Mollison farm, Alice speaking.'

'Alice, it's Amy, I'm at Guy's hospital but—'

'Hello, Amy, have you found her? How is she? Will she be able to withstand the journey home?'

'She's not here, Alice. She discharged herself about an hour ago.'

'Disch... What do you mean? Where would she go? She can't walk, can she?'

'She can... sort of. She's got broken tibia so she's in plaster from the knee down on her right leg, but she's got a pair of crutches, so she'll be able to get about... ish.'

'In the snow?'

'It's not snowing down here, it's very chilly though, which is why I'm a bit worried, Rose doesn't have a coat on.'

'Where would she have gone, Amy?'

'I do have some idea; I managed to get hold of her mother's address. She lives relatively close by. I'm going down there as soon as I hang up.'

'Oh, dear, I'm sorry you're getting all this bother, Amy.'

'It's no trouble, dear heart, I've met some lovely people on my travels, I've survived a letch and my first bombing raid and I was nearly arrested for assault, so it's been an interesting time.'

'Assault... what...'

'I'll fill you in when I get back, Alice. I'm running out of time, it's a quarter past three already, and the last train back is at five forty-five. I have to find her well before then or it's all been a complete waste of time.'

After Amy had put the phone down, I walked into the kitchen and gave Miriam the news. When I had finished my report, Miriam's usually calm face took on a look of horror. I turned around quickly to see Stephen standing on the bottom step of the stairs.

'Why didn't you tell us about Mum?' he asked, looking at us sternly.

'We didn't want to make you worry, Stephen,' I replied. 'We didn't know the full extent of what had happened, that's why Amy went to London to find out.'

'You should have told us. She's our mum.'

'Stephen, you'd have been worried sick about her. We do have better news, don't we? We know that she's all right, that she survived the bomb. That's good, isn't it?'

'But she has a broken leg and she's left hospital. Where has she gone?'

I walked across the room and put my arm around his shoulders.

'We think she's gone to your gran's house, love. Amy's going there now. She'll find her and make sure she's all right. Don't worry.'

Stephen shook his head, 'She won't go to gran's, they don't get on any more.' He looked me straight in the eyes and bit his lip. 'I want to help,' he said.

'You can help best by explaining the situation to your sister. Don't go worrying her now. She can come and talk to me if she needs to ask anything. I'll be in the front room working on the accounts. Now, don't fret, Amy will call us as soon as she learns anything.'

Stephen turned back towards the stairs but stopped on the second step. 'I mean properly help,' he said.

Chapter 24

Amy
Tuesday 24th December

Amy hurried out of the hospital and turned onto Newcomen Street studying the hastily drawn map, the staff nurse had given her. When she reached the Borough High Street she turned left and began to scan the streets as the passed them. Finally spotting Marsden Terrace, she waited for a gap in the traffic before crossing to the other side.

Marsden Terrace was a row of Victorian red brick houses half of which had been destroyed by the bombing. Amy hurried along the rubble strewn street until she came to the very last house on the right-hand side. Pausing to get her breath back, she walked through a gap between two four-foot-high brick pillars, and climbed the three stone steps that led to the front door. Smoothing down her coat, and pushing her hair away from her face, she lifted the iron door knocker and rattled it, twice.

Felicity Hargreaves was a trim woman with peroxide hair rolled up in curler clips, partly covered by a faded green headscarf. Amy put her at about fifty years of age. Her face brightened when she saw her on the step.

'Hello, love, what can I do for you?'

Amy smiled, 'Are you Mrs Hargreaves?'

'I am indeed.' The smile dropped from her face and she looked at Amy anxiously.

'If it's about breaking the blackout, it only happened once and I fixed the curtains as soon as the ARP had gone.'

'No, it's not about the blackout curtains, Mrs Hargreaves. I'm Amy Rowlings and I'm looking for your daughter, Rose. I was told she might have come here.'

'Oh, sorry, love, I thought you were from the council.' Felicity frowned suddenly. 'What do you want with Rose?'

'Stephen and Harriet... your grandchildren, have been evacuated to my best friend, Alice Mollison's farm over in Kent. Rose was due to pay them a visit for Christmas... but... I'm sorry you must know that already.'

Felicity sniffed. 'No, I didn't know, as it happens.'

'Oh, I thought Rose might have...'

'I haven't seen Rose for eighteen months.' Mrs Hargreaves stuck her head out of the door space and looked up the road before stepping back inside. 'Come on in, love. I don't want to wash my dirty laundry in public.'

Amy stepped into a neat front room with a square of carpet in the centre on which sat an oval, mahogany table which was partly covered by a folded tablecloth. Against the back wall was a well-worn sofa. Perched on the arm rest, was the biggest, blackest, cat Amy had ever seen.

'That's Rameses,' said Felicity, affectionately. 'He's a big bugger, isn't he?'

'He certainly takes up a lot of room,' Amy replied.

'He's a champion ratter, he easily earns his keep,' Mrs Hargreaves said. 'My Harry is a fishmonger, so he brings home all the scraps from the shop. We don't have to give him anything bought with ration coupons.'

Amy thought about crossing the room to stroke the cat but decided against it when the animal pulled back it's ears and hissed.

'Can I get you a cup of tea?' Felicity asked.

Amy looked across to the brass carriage clock that sat on the mantlepiece.

'No, thanks so much for offering but I'm running really short of time now. It's ten to four. I've got to be back at Victoria by a quarter to six. That's the last train back you see. I was hoping to find Rose here.'

'She and my Harry don't get on, Miss Rowlings. There was a misunderstanding.' Felicity tugged at her headscarf to pull it a bit further towards her brow. 'I lost my husband, Rose's dad, back in 'thirty-one. It was such a struggle bringing up two kids on my own, what with the Great Depression and everything. Anyway, I met Harry when I nipped in to his shop to buy a bit of fish for my tea a couple of years ago. We hit it off straight away, but Rose never liked him... she even accu... well, never mind, let's just say, she was wrong, it was a total misunderstanding.'

'I see, well...'

'He was drunk, we'd just got home from a wedding, Harry was just full of the joys of spring after seeing his younger sister married. He went to give Rose a hug, but she moved as he came towards her and he ended up grabbing her... Well... he apologised straight away. Rose had had a few herself and was angry with that louse of a husband of hers for flirting with every woman in sight at the wedding.'

'Oh dear, that's such a shame. Have you tried to talk to her since?'

'I sent letter after letter, begging her to drop in and clear the air. I missed her. I still do,' she said, wiping her eyes.

'I'll tell her if I find her. Life's too short for a misunderstanding to split up a family.'

'That blooming Terry made it worse. He called Harry an old letch and swore to Rose that Harry had deliberately grabbed her where he did. Then I heard from Janice that he's been filling her head with lies about things I'm supposed to have said about her... I wouldn't... couldn't say such things.'

'Well, I doubt she'd believe him now, they've split up.'

'Have they? That's the best news I've had in years. Is he still dodging the army?'

'He won't be after he gets out of jail. He's been arrested for stealing ration books during the air raids.'

'Now, why doesn't that surprise me.'

Amy checked the clock again. 'Look, Mrs Hargreaves. The thing is, Rose was injured in the bombing yesterday. She's not too badly hurt, in fact she's just discharged herself from hospital. She's got a broken leg... she was lucky.'

'Oh my goodness. That's the second time she's been bombed out. Poor Rose.'

'I'm desperate to find her. I tracked her all the way to Guy's, but I haven't got a clue where to look now. You were my last hope. She gave your address as her next of kin.'

'Did she? Oh, that's wonderful. She hasn't totally forgotten me then?'

'I doubt she'd ever do that, Felicity,' Amy said, softly. 'Do you have any idea at all where she might have gone? She wasn't wearing a coat and she has no money at all.'

'She'll be at Janice's,' said Felicity.

'Janice's?'

'She's her best friend from school. She married a really nice man... he's away in the navy now. She lives at Parkside Court, it's only a fifteen-minute walk away.'

Amy checked the clock again. 'It's after four now, I'd better get the bus.'

'By the time you get back up to the High Street and queue for a bus, you could have walked it.'

'Okay, if you can give me directions that would be great.'

Felicity opened the front door and led Amy out onto the top step. Pointing across the road to the gap between two, partly destroyed houses, she gave Amy detailed instructions.

'Through the gap onto Harris Street. Turn right, then, about twenty yards on, look over the road. You'll see an alley, opposite. Go to the end, turn right again, follow the bend around and you'll come back out onto the Borough High Street. Straight across you'll find Parkside Court. She's got a ground floor flat. Number three. Rose will be there if she's anywhere.'

'Thanks so much,' Amy went over the directions again, then stepped back down to the street.

'Please... tell her I love her. I miss her so much.'

Amy smiled, sadly. 'I'll tell her, don't worry.' She crossed the road to the bomb-damaged houses, then turned back and waved. 'I'll tell her,' she repeated.

Parkside Court was a block of nineteen-twenties style flats that had a loose, art deco feel about it. Amy entered through a pair of double doors and found flat three on the right-hand side. After knocking on the door, she took a step back and waited.

Janice was a good-looking woman with dark hair hanging in curls around her shoulders. She arrived at the door wearing a knee-length pinafore and holding a toddler in her arms.

'Yes?'

'Hello, I'm sorry to disturb you, I'm Amy Rowlings and I'm looking for Rose Wakelin.'

The woman looked at her suspiciously. 'What do you want with Rose?'

'It's all right, I'm not with the council or anything.' Amy gave a short laugh. 'Rose's mum thought I was.'

'You've seen Felicity?'

'Yes, I've just come from there. She told me where you lived. I was hoping to find Rose here.' She looked over Janice's shoulder as she saw a movement in the shadows behind her.

'What do you want her for? that's the question.'

Amy went over the story again, leaving out the part about Terry and the police.

'Bless you for trying to find her,' Janice said, when Amy had finished her story. She reached out and touched her arm. 'Bless you.'

'So, is she here?'

'No, love, you've missed her again, I'm sorry to say. She left about half an hour ago. I gave her my spare coat and lent her five bob to get a cab. The poor woman was out on her feet when she arrived here.'

'So, she left in a taxi? Do you know where she was heading?'

'Oh yes, she said she was going home.'

'Home? You mean to her mum's or to Drews Avenue?'

'Drews, love. She said she had to meet a lawyer who was giving her a lift to see the kids.'

'Godfrey!' Amy exclaimed. She glanced down at her watch. 'This was what time, exactly?'

'It was a quarter to four. I know that because I heard the church clock chime as I waved her off.'

'She was supposed to meet him at three-thirty, so she would have been late,' Amy said, more to herself than to Janice.

'Yes, that's right, she was worried about being late, but she said she had a backup plan. I have no idea what that was.'

Amy stepped away from the door and flashed a smile. 'Thank you, Janice. I'll see if she's still there. Do the buses to Lambeth run past here?'

'On the High Street. Turn left at the junction there, the bus stop is about thirty yards down. Any bus will do, they all go along Lambeth Road. You'll have to get off at Lambeth Walk though.'

Amy waved, hurried out of the entrance and ran to the junction with Borough High Street. As she turned the corner, she flashed a look to the right to see a big, red double decker bus with Westminster in the destination window trundling down the street. Sticking out her arm to alert the driver that she wanted to get onboard, she rushed towards the stop, arriving just as the bus pulled up.

Chapter 25

Godfrey
Tuesday 24th December

Godfrey Wilson started up the engine of the government-owned, black Humber Super Snipe and pulled away from the kerb outside his Westminster lodgings. On the back seat was his case and a spare suit that he had folded neatly and wrapped in cellophane film. Checking his watch, he drove along Victoria Street and turned to drive across Westminster bridge. His meeting with the War Ministry official had gone on much longer than he had expected but he had still managed to get away for three-fifteen which was a bonus.

'There's a chance she might still turn up,' he muttered to himself as he turned right onto Lambeth Palace Road. Humming along to a tune on the car radio that the mechanics had installed that week, he turned left onto Lambeth Road, then right, onto Lambeth Walk. When he arrived at Drews Avenue, he slowed to allow a small truck carrying a fire crew to pull out, before turning into the bomb-damaged street. Godfrey drove to the end of the road and performed a three-point turn manoeuvre before parking up outside the ruins of number 37, facing the way he had come.

'Three-thirty, on the dot,' he said, checking his watch as he looked up the street past the flattened houses. 'I'll give her another twenty minutes.'

He reached over to the passenger seat, picked up his briefcase and pulled out the minutes of a meeting between War Office officials and his office junior,

Michael Pembroke. He had just finished reading the third page when he heard someone tap on the window. He looked up to see the figure of Gladys Partridge hugging a shawl around her shoulders as she bent down to look into the car. Godfrey wound down the window and nodded to her.

'Hello, Mrs...'

'Partridge. I saw you here yesterday morning.'

'Ah, yes, I was looking to see where Rose Wakelin lived. I am supposed to be giving her a lift to Kent.'

'Does she know you're coming?' Gladys asked.

'She knows all the arrangements, but I am aware of what happened to her, so I only came on the off chance that she'd turn up.' He looked at his watch. 'It's almost ten to four now. I don't think she's going to make it.'

'Not with a broken leg she won't. She'll be in hospital for Christmas, that's for sure.'

Godfrey smiled, grimly.

'Thank you for the update, Mrs Partridge. I'll be on my way then. Merry Christmas to you.'

Godfrey started the engine and after winding up the window, he pulled slowly away from the kerb. At the junction with Lambeth Road, he turned right, and headed towards the Old Kent Road, thinking about Alice. If the roads were clear enough, he might be able to find time to drop in at the farm on his way home. He patted his pocket, feeling the long, black jewellery box he has slipped into it before setting off, and smiled to himself.

'I hope you like your present, Alice,' he said aloud.

As Godfrey slipped the car into third gear, he checked his rear-view mirror and turned up the radio as, on the opposite side of the road, a black taxi slowed to turn into Drews Avenue.

Chapter 26

Stephen
Tuesday 24th December

Stephen turned out of the farm yard and, clutching his small, brown case in his hand, he took a quick look over his shoulder to see if he had been spotted before hurrying along the icy path towards the bus stop at the Old Bull. The sun never really got to that side of the lane until too late in the day to aid a thaw, and Stephen found himself slipping and sliding along sections of the rough path between the hedgerow and the road. When he reached the bus stop at the junction of Long Lane and the Gillingham Road, he put his case down and fished around in the pocket of his coat for the penny and ha'penny he would need for his half price bus fare.

He winced as a sudden bitter gust of wind whipped up the powdered snow from the hedgerow and sent it swirling around the bus shelter, stinging his eyes. Rubbing his sleeve across his face, he stepped forward and stuck out his arm as he saw the green single decker bus approach.

'Penny ha'penny to the station please,' he said with more confidence than he was actually feeling.

The bus driver wound his machine and handed Stephen a ticket. He nodded towards Stephen's case. 'Are you running away from home?' he asked.

Stephen forced a smile.

'No,' he said, bluntly.

'Where are you off to then?' the driver asked.

'London,' Stephen replied, honestly.

'London? On your own?'

'Not on my own.' Stephen thought frantically. 'I'm erm, meeting my aunt at the station.'

'London,' the driver mused. 'Well, son, rather you than me, I have to say.'

Stephen took a seat at the front of the bus and put his case on his knee as he fixed his gaze out of the side window so he wouldn't have to look at the driver. He hoped that Harriet had held on long enough to give him time to get to the train. He knew that she'd buckle under pressure eventually and tell Aunty Alice about his plans, but he also knew that she'd do her best to keep his secret as long as she could. Mum needed help and they had come to the conclusion that Stephen was the only one that could provide it.

At the station, he got off the bus and stood for a few moments in front of the imposing stone façade, then summoning up every ounce of courage he possessed, he walked through the wide entrance and approached the ticket office.

'How much is a ticket to London?' he asked the bespectacled man on the counter.

The ticket master looked past Stephen into the foyer.

'Are you with your mum or dad... an aunt... uncle, grandmother?'

'No, it's just me. My mum is meeting me at the other end.'

'Really? Well then, she'll have given you a letter, explaining why you're travelling alone.' The man held out his hand towards the glass screen.

'No... I mean, she did, but I've lost it.'

The man looked suspicious. 'That's a shame, son, but I can't let you on the train without it. We've got rules you see. No one under fourteen can travel alone on the network unless they have written permission.'

Stephen considered buying some stationary from the little shop in the foyer and writing his own note but decided against it. He didn't want to bring more suspicion on himself. He stood back as a man wearing a thick winter overcoat and a felt hat walked towards the counter.

'London, third class please.'

The ticket master produced a green ticket and put the man's money into his cash drawer.

'Change at Gillingham,' he said.

Gillingham? Stephen thought. *I can get a bus to there, they'll let me on the bus, surely? I've just been on one.*

Under the intense scrutiny of the ticket seller, Stephen backed away from the counter and made his way out onto Middle Street, where he turned right and walked up the hill, past the cinema towards the High Street.

The bus station was busy and Stephen had to queue to get to the ticket counter. He had already scoured the empty bays looking for a board that had London written on it and was disappointed to find that he couldn't get a bus that would take him directly to the capital.

'How do I get to London, please?' he asked nervously when it was his turn to be served.

'You can't get a direct ticket. You have to travel to Gillingham and buy another one there. It's a different bus company,' the clerk explained.

'Oh, right. Well can I have a ticket to Gillingham then please?'

The man studied him carefully.

'Hang on a minute, son. I'll just get the inspector. I don't think I can sell you a ticket unless you're fourteen.'

Stephen panicked. The last thing he wanted was an inspector prying into his business. Turning away from the counter he ran out of the bus station and hurtled along the main street, past the bustling market place and the café where he had tea and cake with Alice on Saturday mornings. Unsure where to go next, he looked over his shoulder to make sure he wasn't being followed, then spotting a policeman on the opposite side of the road, he slowed to a walk and tried to make himself look as though he knew where he was going. Thankfully, the policeman had other things on his mind and Stephen was able to make it around the bend without being spotted.

Leaning against the wall of the photographer's shop, Stephen took stock. Gillingham was out, it seemed. He was sure he'd only have the same problems if he tried to buy a ticket there. He wondered how far London actually was. *Ten miles at least. Can I manage to walk that far in the snow in one day?*

Weighing things up in his head, Stephen decided that the Gillingham Road might be too obvious. He was sure that Harriet would have given up the secret by now and Aunty Alice, Miriam, or even Barney and some of the farm lads might be out looking for him in the old truck.

But if not the Gillingham Road, which one would be best to take? Stephen had only lived in the area for about a year and only came into town with Alice and Harriet on Saturday mornings so he had no idea where many of the lanes and narrow country roads led. Then he had a moment of inspiration. In the back of his mind, he remembered coming out of the photographer's shop and having to wait for a bus to pass before they could cross the road. When the vehicle had passed, he had noticed a narrow road, little more than a wide path that only one car at a time would be able to drive along unless there were passing places at points along its length. Suddenly a light went on in his head and he knew he had found the route he must take.

Stephen crossed the street and bent low to read the worn lettering on the battered, weather-beaten stone road sign.

Old London Road.

Taking one look back towards the High Street, Stephen turned his attention to the ancient, snow-covered roadway. There being no sign of a pavement and not wanting to risk spraining an ankle by falling into a ditch, he stepped smartly onto the centre of the medieval cart track, and steeling himself against the long journey he knew lay ahead of him and with the snow coming half way up his wellington boots, he took a deep breath and began to walk.

Chapter 27

Alice
Tuesday 24th December

At a quarter past four, I flipped the cover of my account book closed and stretched to ease my aching shoulders before entering the kitchen.

'Oops, I said I'd shout the kids at four. Harriet will be annoyed with me. I wonder how she took the news.'

'Oh they're not asleep, Alice, at least Stephen isn't. He came down just after you went through to do the accounts.'

'Where is he then? Has he gone back up?'

'No, he's gone to play with young Timothy Denton... you know, his friend from school, he lives just above Amy on Long Lane.'

'Good, that might help him take his mind off things,' I replied, moving my shoulders in a circular motion. 'Right, I'll nip up and make sure Harriet's awake before our guests start to arrive.'

Upstairs, in the kid's bedroom, I found Harriet sitting on her bed cuddling Miss Moffit, her doll. I had bought it for her last birthday and she always turned to her in times of crisis.

'Are you coming down? Miriam thought you might like to help lay the table.'

Harriet shook her head. 'I'm not bothered about the party.'

I walked slowly across the room and sat on Stephen's bed to face her.

'Harriet, darling, I know it's going to be difficult, but please don't worry about your mum. She's fine... all right, she's hurt her leg, but she's going to be all right, I promise you.'

'But she's all alone in London with a broken leg. Where will she go? She hasn't got a house anymore.'

'Amy will find her, darling. Don't worry too much.'

'But what if she doesn't?'

I thought for a moment, I hated the thought of lying to her, but I had to set her mind at rest.

'She will find her. Amy is a very clever young woman. She helped solve a murder mystery a few months ago, remember? And finding someone has to be easier than that, doesn't it?'

Harriet nodded once. 'I suppose so.'

'It has to be easier. Amy is the cleverest person I know. You've been her partner when we listen to the detective mysteries on the radio. She can spot a clue when no one else can. If there's a clue in London, no matter how small, Amy will spot it.'

Harriet slid off her bed, put down her doll and reached out towards me. I pulled her into my arms and hugged her for a full minute before she spoke again.

'She might get some help soon anyway, then it will be easier.'

I smiled as I pulled away. 'There you go, positive thinking, that's what I like to see.' I patted her on the back. 'Come on now, we've got a party to organise.'

At five o'clock, the first of the guests arrived and after greeting us heartily, began to unpack their little baskets and place the few items they could afford to bring, onto the table. I was beginning to get more than a little concerned about Stephen.

'He does know what time the guests are coming doesn't he?' I asked Miriam.

'He does, lovely. He promised to be home for a quarter to five but with the weather being what it is, it might take him a bit longer.'

'Agnes Denton is on the telephone network, isn't she? I'll give her a quick call.' Turning on my heel, I hurried into the front room and picked up the phone.

'Hello, Mrs Denton, it's Alice from the farm. Is Stephen still there?'

'Stephen?'

My heart sank, but I had to ask the question anyway.

'He came to play with Timothy a couple of hours ago, didn't he?'

'No, love, Stephen hasn't been here. Tim's been in all day because of the weather. We've been playing games in front of the fire.'

'All right, Agnes, thank you.'

I hurried back to the kitchen, grabbed the truck keys from the shelf and dragging my coat from the pegs I hurriedly pulled it on.

'He's not there, Miriam, he never went to the Denton's.'

Miriam stared at me with a horrified look on her face. 'But...'

'Did you actually see him leave?'

'No, he told me he was going as I was heading for the bathroom; I was burst... I didn't actually see him go out of the door.'

My gaze turned to Harriet who was standing looking at her feet. I hurried across the kitchen and crouched down in front of her.

'Harriet, this is really important. You have to tell me if you know anything about this.'

Harriet shook her head, avoiding my eyes.

'Harriet. I mean it. It's freezing out there, it only stopped snowing this morning and there's more forecast for tonight. You have to tell me what you know.'

'I promised I wouldn't,' Harriet said with tears welling up in her eyes.

'You have to tell me,' I said, doing my best not to snap at her. 'Please, Harriet, we have to find him. He's in danger out there.'

'He's going to London to find Mum,' she said, quietly. 'He packed his case with some clean clothes, and he said he was going to take some sandwiches from the table if he could get them without Miriam seeing.'

'How is he planning to get there, love?'

'He took all the money from his piggy bank. He's going to get the train.'

'They won't let him on the train on his own, will they?' Miriam asked.

'I don't think so. I'll drive up now. They'll have seen him for sure, if he tried.'

After telling Harriet she had done the right thing, I hurried out of the back door, threw open the big barred gate and crossing the snowy yard to the barn, I leapt up into the cab of my old truck and slipped the key into the ignition. It took four attempts to start it but finally the engine roared into life and I drove carefully through the gate and out onto the lane. Half a dozen party goers waved to me as I drove slowly past them. Lifting one hand in greeting, I concentrated on the road, and driving as quickly as I dared in the conditions, I made my way along the icy lane towards the Old Bull.

Chapter 28

Amy
Tuesday 24th December

Amy jumped down from the bus platform near the junction of Lambeth Walk and walked quickly to the Drews Avenue turn. Hurrying past the bombed-out buildings, she eventually slowed her pace as she approached the remains of number 37. There was no sign of Rose.

She sighed deeply.

'Now what?' she said aloud.

Deciding that the best course of action would be to check in with Lois Pettigrew, Amy turned away from the brick-littered street and walked towards the gap between the two ruined houses that led to Fuller Street.

'Coo-eee! Ooh Ooh!'

Amy turned to see Gladys Partridge waving to her from her gate across the street.

'You missed her.'

'I can see that,' Amy muttered to herself as she crossed the road towards the waiting woman.

'It's been like Piccadilly Circus around here today,' Glady said as Amy reached the gate.

'Really?'

'Oh yes, first we had the fire crew, damping down a fire that started up again in one of the bombed-out houses, then that posh man turned up again. He was looking for Rose, he hung on a while but then decided she wasn't coming, and took off.'

'What time was that?' Amy asked.

'It was about ten to four when he left, the silly man. If he'd hung on another few minutes, he'd have found her.'

'You saw her?' Amy asked, excitedly. 'Did you speak to her; did she say where she was going?'

'I didn't get the chance to be honest, dear. By the time I noticed her in the back of the taxi, it was already pulling away. I came out to the gate, waving, but she didn't see me, or if she did, she didn't ask the driver to stop.'

Amy sighed.

'I always seem to be half an hour behind,' she said.

'Sorry, love, but I have no idea where she's gone.'

Amy thanked Gladys and after pulling out her torch, walked slowly back over the road and made her way to the little shop on Fuller Street. The night was already drawing in and the first snowflakes of winter had begun to fall. Despondent, Amy pushed open the door of the shop and stepped inside.

Roger looked up from his place at the counter as the little bell tinkled.

'Mum, that lady is back again.'

A few seconds later, Lois's head appeared through the curtain. 'Hello, Amy. Did you have any luck?'

'I've been about half an hour behind her all day,' Amy replied as she walked behind the counter, invited by Lois's beckoning finger.

In the kitchen, Lois pointed to a chair by the table and picked up the tea pot. 'I bet you're ready for one of these then? You just missed Dad and Emily.'

Amy looked at the clock. 'I've nothing better to do now. My train goes in an hour and I've totally failed in my mission.'

'When was the last news of her?'

'Gladys spotted her waiting in a taxi on Drews, but it pulled away as she came out of her gate. Rose missed the man she was looking for by five minutes... Poor Rose.'

Lois added a dash of milk to Amy's tea and offered her the cup. 'Where do you think she'll have gone?'

Amy shrugged.

'Do you think she'll have gone to the station?'

Amy shook her head. 'She only had enough money for the taxi she was in. She won't have anything left over for a train ticket.'

'Maybe she got the taxi driver to follow the lawyer's car... like in the films, you know... Follow that cab... only it was her in the cab...' Lois tailed off.

'She'd missed him, she wouldn't have anything to follow,' Amy replied, taking a big sip of tea. 'Ooh, I was ready for that.'

Lois sipped at her own tea. 'Emily dropped your case off, it's behind the door there.' She sipped her tea again. 'You had an interesting time of it round there, it seems?'

Amy shook her head. 'I couldn't believe that Terry actually tried to get me charged with assault when he had his hands all over me in the shelter.'

'He'll get what's coming now, and not before time too,' Lois said with a grim smile.

'I don't suppose the telephones are back up yet, are they? I'd like to get in touch with Alice to let her know the bad news.'

'Sorry, love, it'll be days yet.'

'Ah well, I thought I'd ask.' Amy finished her tea, then checked her watch before standing up.

'Five o'clock. I'd better make my way to the station.' She slammed her hand down hard on the table in frustration. 'I hate being beaten. I came so close to finding her.'

'Well, at least you know she's all right,' Lois replied.

'Could you do me a favour if she turns up here again in the future?' Amy asked.

'Of course, you only have to ask.'

'Tell her that her mum loves her, misses her and feels so bad about the way they parted. Please ask her to get in touch with Felicity. It would mean so much to her.'

Lois patted Amy's hand. 'I'll tell her, don't you worry. I bet she's missing her too. We all need our mums when we're in trouble.'

Amy picked up her case and turned to Lois, wrapping her free arm around her shoulders.

'Thank you so much for the help and the friendship. I'll be in touch as soon as I can. Maybe you could spend some time with us in Kent, have a bit of a holiday.'

'Oh, I'm a London girl, through and through, I belong in the crowded streets and the smoke,' Lois replied. 'Our Roger might like to try a bit of country air at some point though. He was due to be evacuated last year but when the bombs never came, we thought we wouldn't need to send him away... it's too late now of course.'

'He'd be welcome any time, as would you if you do change your mind.'

Lois nodded and gave Amy a peck on the cheek. 'How are you going to get to Victoria?'

'I've just about got time to get a bus,' Amy replied, checking the clock again.

'Hang on a minute, I've got an idea,' Lois said pulling back the curtain.

'Roger. Nip around to Gary's, he'll be up and about by now. Ask him to bring his van around, will you?'

'Yes, Mum,' Roger said as he hurried out of the shop.

'I don't want to be any bother,' said Amy. 'I'm sure Gary has better things to do.'

'He's on nights, which is why he'll have been sleeping today, but, as it's Christmas Eve he won't have to go in tonight.' She led Amy into the shop. 'Gary's my brother, he only lives a hundred yards away.'

Five minutes later, Roger arrived back at the shop with a tall, greying man wearing a hand knitted jumper and a pair of black trousers that had a patch on both knees.

'Gary, do me a favour, love. Give Amy here a lift up to Victoria, will you? She's in danger of missing her train.'

'Righto, Sis.' Gary smiled broadly at Amy. 'Oh, can I have my dinner with you tonight? Pam's going over to her mother's.'

Outside, Gary opened the passenger door of his bottle green van which had the words Post Office Telephones, stencilled on the door.

Amy climbed in and sat her case on her knee. 'This really is very kind of you.'

'It's not a problem, Amy,' Gary replied with a smile.

'Do you work for the Post Office then?' she asked as they drove along Fuller Street.

'No, I got the van from them though. It's a nineteen-thirty model, they upgraded their fleet about two years ago and I bought it off them. I can't afford to get the lettering sprayed out. Anyway, it comes in handy when I drive around. The police tend to let the service vans into places they wouldn't let an ordinary car go through.'

The pair chatted until they arrived at Westminster Bridge where they joined a long queue of traffic. As she saw the Houses of Parliament coming up, Amy suddenly had a brainwave.

'Gary, do you know where the War Office is?'

'Yes, it's in Whitehall.'

'Can we get near it?'

'We could go down Horseguards Avenue, but I doubt they'll let us park up right outside the War Office, it's pretty heavily guarded.'

'Can you get me as close as you can... please? I've just had an idea.'

They were stopped at a sentry post half way along the wide avenue that was lined with government buildings. A grim-faced soldier demanded Gary's identification, then looked into the cab to ask Amy for the same.

'Can we park up anywhere?' Amy asked, producing her brown covered document. The soldier checked it and handed it back, then, spotting the Post Office logo on the door of the van he pointed to the verge on the other side of the road.

'Park up there, but I'll need to see your paperwork before you go inside any of the buildings.'

Gary opened his mouth to begin an explanation but closed it again after being dug in the ribs by Amy. She flicked her head to the left. 'Park up, I want to have a quick look around,' she hissed.

Gary nodded his thanks to the soldier and pulled up on the opposite side of the road.

'I won't be long,' Amy said as she pulled the lever to open the door.

Outside, it was dark and Amy had to pull the torch from her pocket to see much of the area. The snow, which had been sporadic when she had entered the shop was coming down a lot heavier now and Amy pulled the lapels of her coat together and held them at her chin as she walked back along the road they had driven in on. Some fifty yards along, she risked raising her torch beam from the floor and aimed it across the street to the square where the War Office was situated. Spotting a long row of benches, Amy crossed the road and began to walk along their length but found them all to be empty. She was just about to return to the van when she heard the choking sob of a woman.

Lifting her torch again, Amy walked back the way she had come and found the prone figure of a woman, stretched out on one of the solid backed benches. Her body was wracked with sobs. On the floor, in front of the bench were two wooden crutches.

'Are you all right?' Amy asked softly as she shone her torch onto the back of the woman's snow-covered head.

'He's gone. I missed him.' The distraught women began to weep again.

Amy walked around the bench and crouched down next to the distressed woman.

'I missed him; I won't see my children now. Oh dear... oh dear...'

Amy laid a comforting hand on the woman's right shoulder, then began to stroke her hair.

'Rose?'

The woman's head turned and she looked at Amy through red, tear-soaked eyes.

Amy smiled and pushed the wet, matted hair away from the woman's face.

'Rose, I'm Amy Rowlings. Alice sent me to find you.'

Chapter 29

Godfrey
Tuesday 24th December

Godfrey drove carefully along the newly improved A2 highway, his slatted, blackout headlights angling the beam down to the road in front, his wipers only partially clearing the heavy snow that landed on his windscreen.

It had taken him an hour and a half to lose some of the traffic and to finally see the town of Rochester appear on the infrequent road signs. Rubbing his tired eyes, Godfrey turned off the car heater and wound down his window an inch to let some of the cold air into the cab.

After ten minutes, feeling a little more awake, he turned on the radio again to listen to the evening news bulletin.

The traffic picked up again as he approached Gillingham and came to an abrupt halt when he was still five miles away from the town. Realising he was going nowhere any time soon, Godfrey turned off his engine and listened to the bulletin, turning his wipers on now and again to clear the windscreen.

After fifteen minutes, he looked to the side to see a man dressed in a military uniform walking past the line of cars. Winding down his window, Godfrey shouted across the road to him.

'Any idea what the holdup is all about?'

The army officer stopped and crossed to Godfrey's Humber.

'It's a mess up there. Two lorries and an empty bus are blocking the road. It will take a couple of hours at least to open it up again.' He sighed. 'Christmas Eve, too.'

Godfrey thanked him for the information, then reached forwards and pulled a map out of the glove box. Spreading it out over the steering wheel he plotted his course from London to Gillingham, then worked his way back to see if there were any detours he could take that would enable him to find a way around the road block. Spotting a thin, wavy squiggle on the map and at first thinking it was a stream, Godfrey followed the wriggly line until, with a shout of 'Eureka' he noticed that the track led to Spinton High Street.

'Well, well, lady luck isn't against me after all,' he said as he folded the map and stuffed it back into the glove box. Starting the engine, he wound down his window, stuck out his head to see what clearance he had behind, then, after reversing three feet, he swung the car to the right and pulled out onto the opposite side of the road.

Five minutes later, he slowed to a crawl and looked through the line of traffic until he spotted the narrow, tree lined opening. Waiting patiently for the car blocking the road to ease back, Godfrey held up a hand in thanks and pulled onto what seemed to be nothing more than a farm track. As he straightened up, his headlights flashed across a snow-topped stone marker. Godfrey slipped the car into second gear and drove slowly and deliberately along the snowy track, trying to keep a steady line between the two lines of trees.

Chapter 30

Alice
Tuesday 24th December

I found my heart in my mouth a few times as I sped along Long Lane, the tyres of the truck unable to cope with the amount of snow that stuck to the treads. It was easier going on the Gillingham Road and I made good time in what little traffic there was.

Parking up right outside the station, I left the engine running and hurried across the pavement, slipping and landing on my backside with a thud before picking myself up and walking gingerly into the entrance hall.

The ticket office was empty and I had to wait a frustrating five minutes before a peak-capped man arrived at the counter.

'Sorry about the wait, my dear. Call of nature.'

'Have you seen a small boy, about ten years old. He would have been wearing a dark grey overcoat and carrying a small brown suitcase?'

'No, love, sorry, I haven't seen him. Hang on though, I'll ask Joe, he took over for a couple of hours this afternoon.'

The man walked slowly through the office door at the back of the room, and when he reappeared, he had Joe with him.

'Yes, I saw him. Little lad, reckoned he was trying to get to London.'

'That's him!' I cried. 'Did you sell him a ticket?'

Joe shook his head and pulled on the peak of his cap. 'No, love. We can't sell tickets to minors without seeing a letter from an adult giving them permission to travel alone. It's against the—'

'Where did he go? Did you see?'

'He shot off up Middle Street. I came out after him but he was up past the cinema by the time I got onto the pavement. I reckon he was heading for the bus station.'

'Thank you,' I called over my shoulder as I hurried out of the station. Picking my way carefully towards the truck.

The bus station was almost deserted with only one bus waiting in the bay to depart as I rushed towards the ticket counter, arriving as the man was just about to close for the Christmas break.

'Sorry, love, unless you want that bus to Rochester, we're done for the evening.'

'No, I don't want to buy a ticket. I just wanted to know if you've seen a small boy carrying a suitcase this afternoon. He would have been trying to get to London.'

'Yes, he was here. He ran off when I said I'd get the inspector. He looked a bit jumpy. What's he done... run away from home?'

'Something like that,' I replied. 'Do you know which way he went?'

'Sorry, Miss, I don't. But he was trying to buy a ticket to Gillingham. You can't buy one from here all the way to London. So, I suppose he's either gone to try his luck at the train station or headed off down the Gillingham Road. He seemed quite a strong-willed young lad.'

'He is,' I replied as I turned and ran back to the truck. I had received one bit of good news at least. The Gillingham Road ran straight between Spinton and its bigger cousin. If he was on it, and providing he hadn't hitched a lift, which I doubted he'd try as he wasn't that confident around strangers, I had a pretty good chance of catching him long before he got anywhere near his destination.

So, with more hope than I'd had since I left home, I jumped back into the truck, turned right out of the bus station and made my way back down the Middle Street hill towards the Gillingham Road.

I drove deliberately slowly, my eyes darting left and right, hoping against hope to spot his small, wiry frame against the backdrop of the snow. My heart sank as the first flakes of new snow hit my windscreen and ten minutes and a mile further on, it almost seemed like I was driving through a blizzard.

I gave up and turned back when I was two miles outside Gillingham. There was no way that a small boy could have walked so far in those conditions, so I drove back, with the wind behind me, scouring the sides of the road for any sign of him.

Arriving back in Spinton with my heart in my boots, I pulled up outside the police station and climbed slowly down from the truck. The snow had eased off again and was now nothing more than a light flurry. I brushed the wet flakes from my hair as I stood at the counter and pressed the bell.

'Yes? Oh, it's Alice, isn't it? Merry Christmas.'

I had met the constable twice before, he was a friend of PC Ferris, who occasionally used to accompany Amy and me to the cinema.

'I want to report a missing child.'

'Missing... in this lot? Blimey, that's not good.'

'No,' I said measuredly. 'It isn't.'

I spent the next ten minutes giving the policeman a detailed account of what had happened that afternoon. When he had finished writing out his notes, he turned away and hurried into the bowels of the station, reappearing with a sergeant at his back. After reading the report, the sergeant called for yet another officer and ordered him to put out an urgent missing person's bulletin.

'Ring Gillingham first. Get them to check out the railway and bus stations. If he got that far, they'll know.'

I spent the next twenty minutes tapping my fingers on the counter as I waited for Gillingham to report back.

'He didn't go through Gillingham, Miss. I'm confident of that. We've heard back from them. No one matching... erm... Stephen, is it? No one matching Stephen's description has attempted to buy a ticket at either station.'

'Then where is he?' I wailed. 'He's out in the snow somewhere, the poor little thing. He'll be terrified by now. Anything could happen to him out on the dark roads.'

'Now, now, don't go thinking gloomy thoughts. We're sending out patrol cars to check every road out of Spinton. I know you've already done the Gillingham Road but we'll check it again in case he took shelter while the storm was raging. Now it's stopped, he may well be on the road again.'

I put my hand on his arm. 'Thank you so much.'

The sergeant smiled softly.

'You go home, Miss. We've got your telephone number. We'll give you a call when we find him... And, we will find him.'

I drove home unable to stop those gloomy thoughts, imagining all sorts of terrible outcomes.

As I walked into the crowded kitchen, the murmur of conversation stopped and all eyes turned to me.

'Any news?' asked Miriam in a shaky voce.

I shook my head and looked at Harriet's horrified face.

'It's my fault, isn't it? I should have said something.'

Her eyes flooded with tears as I rushed across the kitchen towards her.

Chapter 31

Amy
Tuesday 24th December

'Alice? Alice, from the farm?' Rose's face lit up in hope.

Amy nodded eagerly. 'We were all so worried about you when Godfrey told us your house had been bombed. Alice asked me to see if I could find out what had happened to you. I've been chasing your shadow since yesterday.'

Rose struggled into a sitting position and placed her head onto Amy's shoulder. 'I thought... I thought I'd missed my chance of seeing the kids... Oh, thank you, thank you.'

'I was lucky to find you if I'm honest,' Amy said. 'I've been half an hour behind you all day. I've been to two hospitals, your mum's house, Janice's, Mrs Pettigrew's shop...'

'Mum's? Is she all right?'

'She's fine, she just misses you so much. She asked me to give you her love when I found you.'

Rose began to cry again. 'Poor, Mum, I've been so horrible to her.'

'Never mind that now,' Amy said softly. She took her arms from around Rose's shoulders and looked into her scratched, tear-soaked face. 'Listen, Rose, we have to go. We'll miss the last train.'

'I don't have any money for a ticket,' Rose replied, lifting her hands with the palms facing up. 'I've lost everything, my money, the kid's presents, my clothes... everything.'

'You don't need money, Rose. Alice is paying for your ticket.' Amy stooped and picked up Rose's crutches. 'As for the rest of it, I'm sure we can do something about that.'

Amy helped Rose to her feet and passed her the wooden supports. Rose put one under each arm, and turning, put the rubber feet of both crutches a couple of feet in front of her, then pushing off with her good foot, she swung herself forwards. Amy walked slowly alongside, shining her torch in front of Rose in case she came across any obstacles.

Back at the van they found Gary suffering an interrogation by the same soldier he had already spoken to.

Amy walked along the passenger side of the van and pulled open the door to allow Rose to get in, but soon realised there wasn't going to be enough room in the cab for her protruding, plaster covered leg.

'Here they are,' she heard Gary say. 'We'll be away in a minute.'

'Make sure you are,' the soldier replied grumpily before returning to his guard post.

Noticing Rose's problem, Gary jumped out of the van and hurried around to the passenger side. Pulling open the side door, he took off his big coat, folded it up and formed a make-do seat. Easing her into the van, he waited until she had got herself comfortable before grabbing hold of the door handle.

'I'll drive as carefully as I can, Rose, but the roads aren't as good as they used to be. You might get tossed about a bit, back there.'

'It will be fine, Gary,' Rose said with a smile. She placed her hand gently on his arm. 'Thank you so much for this.'

Gary slammed the van door shut and hurried around to the driver's side as Amy clambered onto the passenger seat. Waving to the soldier, Gary turned the van around and drove along the embankment before skirting around Parliament Square and onto Victoria Street where he found a queue of traffic being supervised by a lone police officer. Tapping the steering wheel in frustration, he checked his watch and blew out his cheeks.

'It's going to be a tight run thing, Amy.'

After what seemed an interminable amount of time, but was, in reality, only a few minutes, the policeman waved Gary forwards and he put his foot to the floor and sped past the angry PC.

They pulled up under the big clock at Victoria at five thirty-five. Amy opened the door as the van was still moving, and dragging open the passenger door, she helped Rose out onto the road.

'I hope it wasn't too bad a journey, Rose,' Gary said as he walked around the back of the van. 'I had to pull away a bit sharpish back there.' He looked up the road, half expecting to see the policeman giving chase. 'I think I'll take the long way back.'

Amy gave Gary a hug and a peck on the cheek as he picked her little case up from the floor well of the cab and passed it to her.

'You're an angel, Gary. You'll get your reward in heaven.'

Gary blushed. 'Go on. You'll miss it if you don't hurry.'

With Rose shuffling along behind on her sticks, Amy ran for the ticket office and breathed a sigh of relief to find there was only one person in front of her in the queue. She looked back over her shoulder and pointed, guiding Rose to the platform entrance where a guard stood, checking tickets as people headed for their trains.

'Two single tickets for Spinton, please,' she said as the woman in front stepped away from the window.

'You're cutting it fine, love,' the ticket master said, checking the price on a chart before winding on the ticket machine.

Amy pushed a pound note over the counter and waited impatiently as the man meticulously counted out a handful of coins.

'Change at Gillingham for Spinton. You'll have a half hour wait between trains if this one is on time.'

He looked into Amy's eyes as he handed over the coins and two, green tickets.

'Not that it's ever on time these days, there's damage on the line so it might be a bit tight.'

Amy thanked him for his advice and hurried across the open foyer to the gate where Rose was waiting, chatting to the guard.

'You'll have to run, love,' he said as he tore off pieces of the tickets and handed the stubs back.

Amy stepped through the gate and looked across forlornly towards platform six where a five-carriage train was puffing smoke and hissing out steam. *Run... how on earth are we going to do that?*

With Rose swinging herself along on her sticks as best she could, Amy began to run for the platform. When she was still thirty yards away from the back of the locomotive, she spotted the train guard standing with a red flag raised in his right hand. A station guard walked along the length of the train slamming doors shut.

'STOP! Please, STOP!' Amy screamed at the top of her voice. She looked around for Rose who was still some distance behind.

It was instantly obvious that the guard hadn't heard her plaintive cries.

'Run, Amy, run,' Rose yelled as she wobbled on her sticks and almost fell.

Amy looked to the guard, then back at Rose. *It's no good, we'll never make it.*

Then, help came from an unexpected source. A porter, seeing their distress, pushed an empty baggage trolley alongside Rose.

'Hop on, love,' he said with a big grin. 'You're not done yet.'

Rose clambered onto the trolley and the porter grinned again. 'Hold on tight,' he shouted.

Rose stuck both crutches under one arm and grabbed the rail of the trolley with her free hand as the porter began to push. Amy whooped as the trolley hurtled past her at speed. Picking up her case she gave chase, shouting along with the porter as she ran.

'Stop, Stop!'

The train guard, who by now had lowered the red flag and lifted the green one, put his whistle to his lips, then, hearing the commotion from the platform, turned his head to the right.

'Please wait,' Amy screamed from fifteen yards away.

The guard lowered the green flag and raised the red one again. Taking his whistle from his lips he smiled in recognition.

'You again,' he called as Amy puffed to a stop. 'We'll have to stop meeting like this.'

Amy suddenly realised that it was the same guard who had sneaked her into the first-class carriage the day before.

'Hello again,' she panted. 'Sorry, we're in a bit of a flap.'

As the porter helped Rose down from the trolley and steadied her on her crutches, the train guard made a hand signal towards the front of the train, then led Amy and Rose to the last carriage.

'You'll be lucky to get a seat this evening, ladies. The train is packed.' He looked at Amy and winked. 'No first class this time I'm afraid, it's full of Military brass.'

'We're just happy to be on the train, thank you so much for waiting.' She pulled her purse out of her pocket and offered a shilling to the porter who shook his head and looked towards Rose.

'Just doing my job, Miss. Merry Christmas to you.' He touched the peak of his cap, turned the trolley around and whistling a jolly tune, headed off up the platform.

The guard opened the door of the last carriage to find standing passengers almost filling the space inside.

'There isn't enough room to swing a cat in there,' he said, closing the door again.

Amy's mouth gaped. 'Oh no, not after all she's been through.' She looked towards Rose whose eyes were brimmed with tears.

'Fear not,' said the guard with another wink. 'Follow me.' He led them to the very end of the train and pulled open the door to the guard's van. 'This is my little haven. I sit in here after I've checked all the tickets.'

He helped Amy up the steps. She put her case on the floor and reached out to grab hold of Rose, who was being manhandled up the step by the guard. 'You'll find a pile of mail sacks in there,' he called up. 'They'll be a more comfortable than a seat, most likely.'

The guard slammed the door shut and stepped back. After checking that the line of carriage doors was closed, he raised his green flag and blew his whistle. Then, as the train began to inch forwards, he pulled open the last carriage door and stepped inside.

In the guard's van, Amy stacked up a couple of mail bags and eased Rose onto them before doing the same thing for herself. 'He was right,' she said with a little laugh. 'These sacks are really comfy.' She looked towards the door of the carriage and frowned. 'I just hope neither of us needs to use the lavvy.'

Chapter 32

Stephen
Tuesday 24th December

Stephen stepped out from the shelter of a huge, old oak tree and resumed his journey through the tree lines feeling less and less sure of himself. The snow storm that had thankfully just blown over, had begun to make him think he had made the wrong decision, taking the route he had. He had seen no sign of life since he stepped off the High Street and he had no idea how far he had travelled. It could be five miles, or only a single mile. While sheltering under the tree, he had eaten two of the small triangle sandwiches he had taken from the table in the kitchen and he was now concerned as to how long the remaining two would last him. He was already hungry, and thirsty.

Pulling off a woollen glove, he scooped up a handful of fresh snow and stuffed it into his mouth. *I won't go thirsty at least*, he thought as he trudged along. Dying of thirst was the thing that terrified him most. He'd had nightmares about it since reading a book about a small band of French Foreign Legion troops who got lost in the desert.

He squinted and brushed snow from his face as a sharp wind picked up and whistled through the trees from the left. Ahead, the lane meandered between the snow laden trees, looking much like it had for the last, however long it was. Stephen patted his pocket to make sure his torch was still there, he hadn't needed it since the storm ended, as a full moon had poked out from between the broken clouds, shining an eerie light through the canopy of branches, reflecting on the brilliant white of the snow.

He had been lucky to remember seeing the marker at the end of the lane. Despite his misgivings about the path he had chosen, he was pretty sure that this road, although much more difficult to traverse than the main road, would lead him all the way to his destination. *Why call it Old London Road if it didn't lead all the way to London?* He wondered which part he would arrive at. The East End would be good, he knew his way around there.

Ten minutes further on, the snow became deeper as the tree line receded. Stephen's legs ached like they never had before, even more than that time Mum had run out of money and they'd had to walk all the way to Southwark to visit Gran to see if she could lend her some.

Spotting a fallen trunk at the edge of the tree line, Stephen decided to rest his legs for five minutes. Brushing a pile of snow from the frozen bark, he sat down, rested his elbows on his knees and put his head in his hands. Looking up the lane, he fancied he had seen a flash of light, but he dismissed the thought quickly. *It's probably a mirage, like the Foreign Legion troops see in the desert.*

Closing his eyes, Stephen willed himself to carry on. Then, in the distance, he heard the roaring of a car engine.

Chapter 33

Amy
Tuesday 24th December

The train was only ten minutes late pulling into Gillingham station and Amy had to wake Rose to tell her that they had arrived. As she sat up, rubbing at her eyes, the carriage door opened and the train guard stuck his head into the compartment.

'Wakey Wakey,' he called. 'All change for Spinton.'

Amy helped Rose to her feet and after passing down the crutches, she steadied her as she stepped backwards out of the carriage and onto the step.

On the platform, Amy put down her little case and held out her arms to the guard. 'We really can't thank you enough for your kindness... I don't even know your name.'

'It's Briggs,' he replied, 'and you are very, very welcome. I wish all my passengers were as friendly as you.'

'I can't call you Briggs,' Amy said with a frown.

'All right, it's Luther, but please don't tell anyone. You can't be known by a German name these days, can you?'

'Well, Mr Briggs,' Amy replied with a courtesy, 'Rose and I thank you from the bottom of our hearts. We wouldn't be here without you. Could I give you something for your trouble?' She reached for her purse but Luther put his hand on her arm.

'I don't do good deeds for financial gain,' he said, giving her a stern look.

'I'm sorry, I didn't mean to offend you,' Amy slipped the purse back into her pocket, then stood on her tiptoes and planted a kiss on the guard's cheek.

'Now, that's better than any financial reward,' he said. 'I won't wash my face for a week.'

He looked across the rail lines to the adjacent platform.

'It's not in yet, but that's where you'll get your next train.'

Amy pulled a face.

'So it is. I suppose I'm going to have to face that scary, open step bridge again.'

'Don't you like it?'

'It makes me feel as though it's about to open up and drop me into the depths,' Amy said with a shudder.

'You'll be fine,' said Luther. 'Just close your eyes as you climb the steps.'

He moved aside as a huge man jumped down from the train and stretched, lifting his leg of lamb arms above his head. He was covered from head to foot in coal dust. Amy's mouth gaped as she took in the enormous bulk of the man. He had to be at least six foot eight tall, and almost as wide.

'That's our stoker, Marek,' Luther said. 'He got out of Czechoslovakia just as the Nazis were going in. He doesn't speak at all. I'm not sure why.'

Amy checked her watch. 'Right, we'd better get to the platform. The train will be here soon.'

They walked to the open staircase where Amy came to a sudden halt. 'Rose, I'm so sorry, I didn't even stop to think how you were going to get across the bridge.'

'I'll give it a go,' Rose replied, looking up with trepidation at the steep flight of steps in front of her.

'I'll help if I can,' Luther said, offering a hand.

Suddenly a huge shape appeared in their midst. With a grunt, Marek swooped Rose up in his arms, then turned and carried her to the back of the train. Amy collected her crutches from the floor and hurried after the giant.

When he reached the final carriage, Marek lowered Rose gently to the floor leaving her sitting with her broken leg jutting out over the tracks, then, after jumping down, he scooped her up again and carried her across the two lines of track before depositing her on the opposite platform.

'Oh, well done!' Amy called from the other side. She turned to walk back to the steps, but stopped when she heard a loud grunt behind her.

Marek beckoned to Amy, then pointed to the other side of the track.

Amy shook her head, but the man was insistent. Taking the crutches from her, he hurried across the rails, laid them down at the side of the still-sitting Rose, then stomped back across to Amy.

'In for a penny,' Amy said, and sat down on the edge of the track wall.

Marek stuck one hand under her legs, the other under her armpit and lifted her like she weighed no more than a packet of sugar.

Wriggling her in his arms, Marek, placed one hand on her right buttock while the other cradled her left breast.

'Ooh, I say,' Amy gasped as the man's huge hand squeezed at it.

Deposited safely on the opposite platform, Amy shook her head as she thought about what had just transpired, then lifting her hand, she waved thanks to Marek as he stomped back across the railway line.

Looking down at her coat, Amy brushed at the black, perfectly formed hand mark on her breast, then tried to look over the shoulder at her backside to see if she had a matching one.

Rose pulled a face and pointed to her own chest that sported an identical hand print.

'Blimey!' Amy exclaimed. 'He wasn't quite the knight in shining armour we girls imagine, was he?'

As she helped Rose to her feet, a booming voice sounded across the station, announcing that the Spinton train had been delayed and was now running fifteen minutes late.

'That's a bit of luck,' said Amy thoughtfully. 'We've got time for a cup of tea.'

The station café had a few empty tables and Amy sat Rose by the window overlooking the platform, before walking to the counter to order tea.

A waitress wearing a white blouse and black pinafore, carried their tray over to them.

Amy poured the tea into the thick China cups, then added milk before giving her own drink a stir with a teaspoon.

'Why so sad?' she asked as Rose put her cup back onto the saucer and stared into the swirling brown liquid.

'Oh, it's just that... well, I really am grateful to everyone for what they've done for me... but I was just thinking about tomorrow. I haven't got any presents for Stephen and Harriet, whatever will they think of me?'

Amy reached out and patted Rose's hand. 'Believe me, my dear, they'll just be happy to have you with them.'

'I know, but I would like to have given them something, even if it was just a token gift.'

'There's a W.H. Smith's over there,' Amy said as she sipped her tea. 'Drink up, let's go and see what we can find.'

The shop was little more than a kiosk but it did have a good selection of newspapers and magazines.

Amy spotted the latest edition of her favourite movie periodical, Spotlight, and snatched it from the shelf. 'That'll save me having to try and find it in the shops on Boxing Day,' she said with a grin.

On the back wall were three shelves full of books. Rose tipped her head to the side as she scanned the spines, pulling out copies of Anna Sewell's, Black Beauty and Robert Lewis Stephenson's Treasure Island.

She held them up to Amy. 'They're two bob each, is that all right? I'll repay when I get back to work. I can send a postal order.'

'Don't worry about that. I think you've made perfect choices. The kids will love those books. Now, would you like to pick a magazine?'

Rose shook her head. 'I don't read a lot. I don't know where the kids get it from if I'm honest because Terry has never picked up a book in his life.'

Amy pulled out her purse and walked to the counter.

'Would you like me to wrap the books?' asked the girl on the counter who had been listening to their conversation.

'You've got wrapping paper? How on earth did you get hold of that? It's like gold dust,' Amy said with wide eyes.

'We have some left over from last year,' replied the young woman as she set about wrapping the books in gaily coloured paper.

'I, erm... don't suppose you could sell me a few sheets, could you?' Amy asked with a shy smile.

The girl looked past Amy and out across the platform.

'Go on then. I doubt I'll be needing much more of it this year. I can let you have four sheets for a shilling. How's that?'

Amy nodded eagerly and the woman handed over four sheets of shiny, coloured paper that had been folded into eight-inch squares.

After paying for her purchases, Amy opened her case and put the wrapped books and the paper inside. Shoving the magazine under her arm as she turned away, she spotted a red telephone box and led Rose over to it.

'I really ought to report in,' she said, pulling out her purse again. As she opened it to fish out a few coins she hesitated. 'Or, shall we give them a big Christmas surprise? We're only half an hour away now.'

Rose grinned. 'Let's do that.'

Amy slipped her purse back into her pocket and the two women walked slowly back to their platform. Five minutes later, the Spinton train pulled into the station.

Chapter 34

Godfrey
Tuesday 24th December

The radio spluttered, then died completely as Godfrey drove further along the ancient road. At times the trees thinned out so that he could see around some of the many curves and bends that made travelling at more than five miles an hour, impossible. After a while the wind picked up, blowing snow from the drifts at the sides of the track across his windscreen. He pulled in as close to the side of the road as he dared when the snow became heavier and the wipers could no longer cope with the intense flurries that were thrown at them.

After half an hour, the storm eased and Godfrey put the car into gear and pulled away again, cursing his decision to try this route when the smooth, tarmacked highway might well have been cleared by now.

He thought about turning around and driving back to the main road but there just wasn't enough space on the track to enable him to perform a three, or many more, point turn.

Sighing, he drove on.

After twenty minutes or so, the trees began to thin out and the track appeared to be a little wider, but not wanting to risk getting stuck in a ditch, Godfrey kept the car trundling along in second gear in the centre of the path. He ducked down and peered through the windscreen into the tree tops when a shaft of moonlight suddenly hit the bonnet of the car. Feeling that he might be nearing the end of the track, Godfrey patted the steering wheel and urged the Humber on.

At the next clearing he slowed to a crawl as he saw what appeared to be a small figure sitting on a fallen tree trunk. Pulling alongside, he wound down his window to see for certain if his eyes had been deceiving him. Putting his foot on the brakes more firmly than he intended, the car skidded to a juddering halt.

Godfrey applied the handbrake, then opened the door and slid out of the car.

'Are you all right? Can I give you a lift somewhere?' he asked as he approached the hunched over figure.

'Are you going to London?' a small, hopeful voice asked.

'No, I've just come from there,' Godfrey replied, realising to his horror that he was addressing a child, and a young one at that.

'Come on, son. You can't stay out here tonight; you'll freeze to death.'

The boy shook the snow from his hair as he looked up.

'STEPHEN? What in the name of God are you doing out here?'

'I'm going to find Mum,' Stephen replied as he began to shiver uncontrollably.

'You'll never get to London in this lot, Stephen,' Godfrey said, crouching down.

'How far is it?' the boy asked, stubbornly.

'From here? It's about fifty miles,' Godfrey replied.

'How far have I come?'

'From the farm? Possibly four or five miles, though I'm not absolutely certain where we are.'

Stephen's head fell to his chest. 'Fifty... it will take me days.' His body suddenly wracked with sobs. 'I'm so tired.'

Godfrey sat down on the fallen trunk and put his arm around the child.

'You've done very well to get this far, young man. I don't think I could have done it.'

Stephen looked up through wet eyes.

'It's not enough though, is it?'

Godfrey pulled him close and held him for a few minutes without speaking, then he got to his feet and pushed out his hand towards the boy.

'Come on, son. Let's get you out of this weather.'

'But that means I gave up,' Stephen complained.

'Not at all, you can always try again another day... When the weather isn't so foul.'

'Mum needs me now though; she's hurt and all on her own.'

Godfrey pushed his hand closer to the boy.

'Come on, Stephen, I've got a lovely heater in the Humber. Let's discuss it in the warmth of the car, eh?'

Stephen wiped his eyes with the back of his sodden, gloved hand, looked up the track and then at the car with its dark bonnet glistening with melted snow.

'If I don't go now, Mum will be all alone for Christmas.'

'She's got friends in London, Stephen, she'll be all right and I believe young Amy is on the case. I'm sure she'll find her, she's a clever girl. I'd bet a year's pay that your mum won't be alone for Christmas.' He waved his hand in the direction of the car. 'Look, I'll tell you what. If you haven't heard from your mum or Amy by tomorrow. I'll drive you down on Boxing Day and you can look for her yourself. How would that be?'

Stephen thought about it for a moment, then got to his feet.

'You promise?'

Godfrey closed two outstretched fingers and pulled his hand up to his brow to salute the young boy.

'Scouts honour,' he replied.

Stephen nodded, accepting the ritual salute and shuffled around to the side of the car. Godfrey opened the door and sliding his briefcase onto the floor, helped Stephen settle in the passenger seat. Looking up into the leaden skies, he whispered, 'Thank you, God,' then returned to the driver's side.

'Alice and Harriet must be worried sick,' he said as he slipped the car into gear and eased off the hand brake.

Stephen looked up at Godfrey with an earnest look on his face.

'I didn't mean to make them worry. I just had to try.'

Godfrey nodded. 'I understand completely. You know, when I was about your age, I decided I wanted to run away to sea.'

'Did you? How far did you get?'

'I made it all the way to the edge of town, then I went back home again. I wasn't as brave as you.'

'I'm not really brave. It was quite scary out there on my own.'

'It must have been.' Godfrey reached forwards and turned the heater on full. 'There, are you beginning to warm up now?'

Stephen nodded as the radio buzzed and whined, then found the station again.

'Ah, at last. We must be nearing civilisation,' Godfrey said as he concentrated on the narrowing gap on the road ahead.

Chapter 35

Alice
Tuesday 24th December

The party mood was subdued to say the least. My workforce and their families stood around in little groups making small talk, recycling the town's gossip or discussing the progress of the war. Even the arrival of the ceremonial silver tray containing the bonus laden pay packets couldn't lift the gloomy atmosphere.

The workers' kids, usually so boisterous, stood together in front of the Christmas tree, sipping bottles of pop in virtual silence, each seemingly lost in their own thoughts. One of their own was missing and each one of them knew instinctively that given the same circumstances, it could easily have been them, alone and probably lost in the foul weather.

When the phone rang, all conversation stopped and I rushed through to the front room, but when I picked up the receiver, I received an apology from the operator who had inadvertently connected a caller to the wrong number.

Desperately disappointed and feeling as low as I could ever remember feeling, I walked slowly back to the kitchen, shaking my head as I stepped around John Postlethwaite's silent accordion.

Miriam, determined to keep up the traditions of the party, came in from the parlour carrying a huge bowl of punch. Any other year, this event would have been greeted with a big cheer, but tonight, it only raised a few smiles and a couple of acknowledging nods.

I tried to drag my thoughts away from the missing boy, but this only led to more angst as my mind focussed on Amy, who was also out there somewhere in the snow, in a strange city with no friends to turn to. *She must be in trouble or she'd have telephoned by now,* I thought.

It was almost time to make my annual, rousing speech, to thank the lads for their hard work over the year and to wish them strength and happiness in the year to come, but I couldn't bring myself to do it. I doubted my voice would have held out.

Miriam squeezed my hand and gave me a sad smile.

'Keep going, lovely. It will all work out.'

As if she had summoned up the Happiness Fairy, the back door was flung open and Godfrey stepped into the kitchen ushering a clearly embarrassed Stephen in front of him. The cheer that went up could have come straight from Wembley Stadium when the winning goal in the cup final had been scored. The wives cried, the men cheered and I hurled myself across the kitchen towards him, my eyes bright with tears of unbridled joy, my face a mask of relief.

'Stephen. Oh, Stephen,' I croaked, unsure whether to hold, or scold him.

'Where have you been, you silly boy?' I said, my voice breaking but my heart bursting with love. I began to shower his head in kisses, but he flinched and ducked out of the way.

'I'm sorry, Aunty Alice,' he said eventually. 'I thought I could help Mum.'

Harriet, who had been standing silently with the other kids, stepped towards her brother and after giving him a weak smile, hung her head and looked at her feet.

'I'm sorry, Stephen, I had to tell them. I did try to keep your secret.'

Stephen reached out and touched her shoulder, softly. 'That's all right, I understand,' he said.

Miriam, her face as wet as her dishcloth, scurried across the kitchen, crouched down and began to undo his coat. Pulling off his sodden gloves, she eased him out of the overcoat and passed it to me.

'Come on, young man, I've got warm clothes for you to change into. I've had them hanging in front of the fire all afternoon.' Looking up to the heavens, she took the clean clothes from the fireguard and ushered him into the bathroom to get changed.

The party mood changed in an instant. Where there had been gloom there was now laughter, where there had been dismal conversation, there was now happy chatter. I took Godfrey's arm and led him into the front room as John Postlethwaite's accordion burst into life.

After telephoning the police to tell them to call off the search and closing my eyes to send up a silent prayer of thanks, I turned around with leaking eyes and held my arms out to my lawyer lover.

'Godfrey, thank goodness you found him. Where was he? I looked everywhere.'

'He was on the Old London Road; I'm not surprised you couldn't find him.'

'The Old London Road? How on earth did he find that? Half of the locals don't know of its existence.'

'I don't know how he found it, but it was logical I suppose. He must have thought that, as the name suggested, it would lead him all the way to London. He'd only gone a few miles. I found him sitting on a fallen tree.'

'But what were you doing on that road? I've only been on it once in my entire life, it's only a farm track, really.'

Godfrey shrugged. 'Pure luck, Alice. There was a bad crash on the A2 as I was on the outskirts of Gillingham, I was told that it would be a long wait until the road was cleared, so I looked at the map for an alternative route. That was the only other way. It was pure luck. I still can't quite believe I found him sitting there.'

I kissed him on the lips and looked up into his eyes. 'It was fate, Godfrey. You were meant to find him.'

Godfrey shook his head slowly. 'Luck, fate, whatever it was. I consider myself blessed.'

He wrapped his arms around my back and pulled me towards him. 'It's so lovely to see you, Alice.'

I lay my head on his chest and wrapped my own arms around his waist. 'Likewise, I'm sure.'

After a couple of minutes, he pulled away, then pushed a few strands of hair away from my face.

'Have you heard from Amy at all?'

I shook my head. 'No, not a word, I'm worried about her to be honest, Godfrey.'

'I wouldn't worry too much, Alice. You know Amy better than I do, but we both know that she's a very resourceful girl. She'll be all right.'

'Her mum and dad must be frantic,' I replied. 'I'll have to go up to see them in a while, they'll be wondering if I've heard any news.'

Godfrey checked his watch. 'I'd give her a little while yet, Alice. There is still a chance she made the train, even if Rose wasn't with her.'

'Poor Rose,' I said quietly.

'I did go around to her house again earlier. I was bang on time and I waited a good twenty minutes but there was no sign of her. An old lady told me she was still in hospital so there didn't seem much point in hanging around. I had no idea where Amy was.'

I kissed him again. 'You did your best, Godfrey.'

He nodded quickly, then suddenly patted the pocket of his coat.

'I had almost forgotten in all the excitement,' he said, pulling out a thin, black velvet box. 'Happy Christmas, Alice. I hope you like it.'

'Ooh, my first Christmas present.' I hesitated. 'Do you think I should open it with the rest of them in the morning.'

'No, I don't,' Godfrey said, sternly. 'I might be selfish, but this is my moment. I want to be here when you open it.'

I eased the lid of the box open and gasped as I saw the delicate, gold necklace. 'Is that a sapphire?' I said, as I lifted it carefully out of the box.

'I hope so,' he said, happily. 'Turn round.'

A did as I was asked and Godfrey fastened the clasp of the necklace. Stepping to the side, I looked into the wall mirror, my hand on my chest as I admired the glittering jewellery.

'There are some earrings to match it in the bottom of the box,' Godfrey said. 'They came as a set.'

I turned back to him, hugged him and planted a kiss on his lips.

'My turn,' I said, opening the tall cupboard and pulling my newspaper wrapped photograph from the top shelf.

'Happy Christmas, Godfrey. I really wasn't sure what to get you, so I decided on this.'

Godfrey tore the newspaper from the frame of the picture. His eyes lit up as he looked down at my gift.

'My God, Alice. You look... well, it's stunning. It could be hanging on a Hollywood Mogul's office wall.'

'Thank you, kind sir,' I said with a courtesy. 'It did come out rather well, didn't it?'

'Rather well? It's incredible... your... I mean... it looks... like you aren't...'

'I was wearing a dress, I assure you,' I said, slapping his wrist. 'What is it with the male of the species? First, Stephen, then Amy's dad, now you.'

'I wasn't... I mean, I didn't think...'

'I was wearing a mermaid dress, that was about half a size too small for my... what did Amy say... my Matronly figure. That's why my bust is pushed up so much. It was literally bursting out of the dress.'

'Matronly?' Godfrey laughed. 'You're hardly matronly. You're beautiful... Perfect. I wouldn't have you any other way. The vast majority of women would give anything to have your figure.' He took another long look at the photo. 'Stunning,' he repeated.

'I thought you deserved a better picture than that little grainy thing you have by your bed,' I said, taking another look at it myself.

'I'll treasure this, Alice. Thank you.'

'Do you want to leave it here until Friday?' I asked. 'I mean, I wouldn't like your wife to find it.'

'I'll keep it in my case. I pack and unpack it myself; it will be as safe as houses in there. I'll put it on top of my wardrobe... Just think, you'll be with me in my bedroom over Christmas.'

I felt a sudden pang of guilt.

'I'm not sure your bedroom is the best place to keep it, Godfrey. She is your wife after all, you should be concentrating on her when you're lying in bed.'

'There's a lot you don't know, Alice,' Godfrey replied, 'but I'm not going to go into it now. Maybe when I pick you up on Friday night for our meal.'

I smiled, thinly. 'I do get a fit of the guilts now and then, I have to admit.'

Godfrey smiled reassuringly back at me. 'Alice, I swear to you, my relationship at home isn't what you think it is.'

I turned away. 'Isn't that what most married men say when they embark on an affair?'

He put a soft hand on my shoulder. 'I'm not most men, Alice. I wouldn't lie to you.'

I turned back and gave him a hug. 'I know, Godfrey, I know.'

He kissed my forehead then checked his watch. 'Having said all of that, I think it's time I went. The kids will be up for another couple of hours so I'll be able to spend some time with them before Santa arrives.'

I unlocked the front door and opened it to let him out.

'Have a lovely Christmas, Godfrey.'

He turned on the bottom step and lifted his hat. 'You too, Alice. Seeing you, and finding Stephen, of course, has made mine a happier one already.'

I tipped my head to one side and listened to the silence of the night. The snow had begun to fall again, but it was light, the magical sort of snow you liked to stand outside in as a child and imagine you had just spotted Santa's sleigh high up in the sky.

'Listen, can you hear that?' I asked.

Godfrey looked puzzled. 'I can't hear a thing,' he said.

'Exactly,' I replied, my face lighting up. 'No bombers. They're always here by now. Either the weather is too bad for them, or Old Adolph is giving us a night off.'

'I think it's the latter,' Godfrey said, with a smile. 'Although the blitz hadn't begun last year there were still a fair number of bombs falling. We didn't see one from Christmas Eve through to Boxing Day though. I think we have some sort of unwritten agreement. Remember in the First World War when the two armies stopped and played football in No Man's Land?'

I nodded slowly, revelling in the silence.

He doffed his hat again and climbed into the car. Suddenly I was lit up from the knees down as the slatted headlights burst into life. Godfrey turned the car around and I waved until his rear lights were a dot in the snowy distance.

Chapter 36

When I returned to the party the place was in uproar. Stephen had been reunited with his friends and they had set up an impromptu game of armies. There were kids hiding under tables and buried under the pile of coats in the corner of the kitchen. One lad, a sniper, I assumed, lay under the Christmas tree, firing off bullets at random.

The girls were almost as riotous, haring around the kitchen, dodging in and out between the adults as they engaged in a loud game of tag.

I checked the big clock on the wall. *The last train should be in by now, weather permitting.* I crossed my fingers and hoped for the best. Stephen's homecoming had given me a little more strength and a smidgeon of hope.

Clapping my hands, I shouted out above the din.

'Right, you lot.'

There was instant silence. The rowdy games were stopped, children's faces looked up at me from under the pile of coats.

'Listen to this,' I said, marching over to the back door. I threw it open and held my arms apart, like a magician waiting for a round of applause.

'What, Missis?' Barney asked with a puzzled look on his face.

I pointed out into the snowy night and cupped the other hand to my ear.

'No bombers!' I cried.

Barney came to the step and looked up into the sky. 'It's true,' he called. 'It's all quiet out there.'

'Godfrey is sure they're giving us all a few days off for Christmas,' I said, grinning from ear to ear. 'So... I think we ought to move this party outside to where it belongs. Who's in agreement?'

Thirty voices shouted back their reply and suddenly I was swept up in a tsunami of bodies as they rushed to get outside.

'Barney,' I shouted over the din. 'Light the brazier.'

'But what about the Blackout, Missis?' he asked.

I looked up at the sky. 'The only things up there are snow clouds. Who's going to notice?'

'The ARP might,' John Postlethwaite answered.

I pointed in the general direction of the town. 'Can you see anything through the snowflakes? I can barely see the barn.'

John followed the direction of my pointing finger. 'True enough,' he said.

'Right, everyone, if we hear so much as the rumble of a single aircraft, we douse the brazier and go straight back inside. Okay?'

There were nods and murmurs of agreement, the next second, kids were haring about all over the yard as they resumed their games, this time by torchlight, using snowballs for hand grenades.

Barney brought out our battered old brazier from the shed, dropped in a few handfuls of firewood, then splashing a dash of petrol onto the timber from a green Jerry can and making sure there was no one standing too close, he struck a match and dropped it onto the fuel-soaked wood. A flame erupted immediately to the wild cheers of the party goers.

'Now it feels like Christmas,' shouted Ethel Brown, George's wife.

George himself began to dance a jig as John began to squeeze at his accordion.

'Who's for more punch?' Miriam shouted, carrying a tray of drinks down the back step.

'Martha's dressed and ready,' she said as she held out the tray to a rush of takers.

I stepped back into the kitchen and picked Martha up from the playpen. Miriam had dressed her in her red winter coat, her warm leggings and a woolly hat and mittens.

'Piggies!' she shouted as I held her high in the air, realising not for the first time, how lucky I was to have such a character in my life. For some reason, our relationship wasn't as good as it could have been, but I was more determined than ever to work on that.

'Piggies are bye byes,' I said. 'We can see them in the morning. Now, who wants to go outside to see the snow?'

I carried Martha outside and walked carefully down the back steps, Martha laughing at the antics of the workforce and their families as they danced, sang and hugged each other.

Just after eight-thirty, John stopped playing and the crowd ceased their frolicking, knowing what was coming.

'Time for some carols,' he said, striking up the first notes of We Three Kings.

All the adults sang along, Barney's deep, gravelly voice lending a bass note to the higher pitch of the women.

After a rendition of Hark the Herald Angels Sing, John stopped playing and looked across to me. 'Your turn, Missis. The usual, is it?'

I grimaced, but knowing I was never going to be allowed to get away without singing, I gave in and nodded to John, who immediately began to play the opening chords of my favourite carol, In the Bleak Mid-Winter. I smiled into Martha's chubby little toddler face as I cleared my throat to sing.

I finished to a rapturous round of applause. I knew I wasn't the world's greatest singer but I also knew that by taking part, it cemented the bond between me as an employer and my workers' families. Tonight, as ever, I was one of them.

'Now then, children. It's your turn,' John announced to a chorus of boos from the kids.

'We can't sing, we're hopeless,' said little Freddy Hotchkiss, an eight-year-old with the cheekiest grin you ever saw on a child's face.

'Well, someone's got to sing next,' John said, looking at them askance.

'Harriet can sing,' Mary Lane said, pointing to Harriet who was attempting to hide behind Barney's wife. 'She sang at the school assembly last Friday.'

There was a quick round of applause and Harriet was eased through the crowd. She stood in front of the bottom step and looked at me for support. I smiled and crouched in front of her.

'We'd love to hear Harriet sing, wouldn't we, Martha?'

Martha nodded eagerly and Harriet rolled her eyes to the snow-filled sky.

'All right then,' she sighed.

'What are you going to sing, little one?' John asked, playing a few warm up notes.

'I sang Silent Night at school,' she said with more confidence in her voice than earlier.

'All right, are you ready... after two... One, two...'

'Silent Night, Holy Night,' Harriet's crystal-clear voice rang out across the farmyard, and as the snowflakes fizzed, popped and crackled into the brazier, she gave us three full verses of the famous old carol before coming to a stuttering halt. The applause was something to behold. Harriet hung her head and looked around the yard from beneath her eyelids.

'Next!' John shouted.

'It's Stephen's turn now,' Harriet said, staring her belligerent brother down. 'Come on, I did it, it's your go.'

Stephen looked at me hoping to be given clemency, but I just shrugged and smiled at him encouragingly. Usually, he would have put up a fight if he was asked to do something he didn't fancy doing, but that night, he gave in without a single word of complaint. Whether he was feeling guilty about his exploits or whether he thought he owed his sister a favour, I don't know. What I do know was that he sang beautifully.

'I can do, O Little Town of Bethlehem,' he said, looking at John for the cue to start.

'O Little town of Bethlehem
How still we see Thee lie
Above Thy deep and dreamless sleep
The silent stars go by
Yet in the dark streets shi... iii...neth
The everlasting light...

And then, from over by the gate, came the sound of a woman's voice. Crystal clear and pitch perfect.

...The hopes and fears of all the years
Are met in Thee tonight.'

All eyes turned towards the gate as Amy pulled the release catch back and Rose swung herself through the gap and into the yard.

'MUM!' two voices shouted in unison as Stephen and Harriet hurled themselves across the snow, almost knocking her over in the process. Rose bent over them, arms around their shoulders as she smothered their heads in kisses.

'Oh, my babies,' she whimpered. Floods of tears fell from her eyes. 'My babies.'

There wasn't a dry eye in the place. Even my tough as boots workforce wiped away tears from their grizzled faces. The women looked at each other then back to the joyous scenes and openly wept.

Amy stepped into the yard, closing the gate behind her. Godfrey stayed where he was on the other side of the fence, smiling as the scene unfolded in front of him. 'Godfrey's Taxis at your service,' he said with a doff of his hat. 'Now, unless there is anyone else to pick up. I'll be off.'

I waved to Godfrey, then stepped quickly across to where Amy was standing, holding her little case in her hand as she looked directly towards me.

'Well, that was a bit of a faff,' she said.

After I had prised the limpet-like children away from their mother, I introduced myself.

'It's lovely to meet you at last, Rose. We've all been so worried about you.'

Rose looked at me and tried to smile, but the tears took over instead and she just couldn't speak. Harriet rushed back to her mother's side and looked up at her anxiously.

'It's all right, Rose,' I said, giving her a gentle hug. 'Come inside, you must be absolutely shattered.'

I helped her up the steps to the kitchen and sat her down at the big table.

Miriam, the miracle worker, appeared from nowhere, placing a plate of sandwiches and a mug of hot tea in front of her.

'Unless you'd like something a bit stronger?' she said.

Rose shook her head. 'I'm not a drinker, the tea will be perfect.'

Stephen arrived at the table carrying a low stool onto which he had placed a soft cushion. Judging the distance carefully, he put it on the floor and watched anxiously as Rose lifted her plaster covered leg and placed her foot carefully on top.

Harriet stroked the plaster while looking up at her mother. 'Your poor leg... does it hurt?'

'Not really, not any more. I'm feeling so much better now that I've found you two again.'

Leaving the three of them alone to catch up, I sauntered across the kitchen to where Amy was standing, drinking a glass of punch.

'You're back then,' I said casually, as though she had just returned from the shops.

Amy nodded and finished off the drink. 'Ooh, that reached the spot, I've been dreaming about that since Gillingham.'

'I take it you couldn't find a working telephone,' I chided.

'They're not the easiest thing to find down there,' she replied. 'Though I will admit, I nearly rang you from Gillingham station, but Rose and I decided that as we were so close to home, we'd leave it and surprise you instead.'

'Well, you certainly succeeded in that,' I said, trying to keep a stern look on my face.

'You know, me, I'm full of surprises.'

I bit my lip, then lurched forwards towards her, throwing my arms around her neck and almost knocking the punch glass out of her hand.

'Oh, Amy, you clever, clever girl,' I said.

Amy gave me a big hug and we were silent for a few moments, just happy to be close to each other.

'It was touch and go at the end, Alice. I had almost given up hope.'

I pulled away. 'I want to hear all about it,' I said.

'Tomorrow,' Amy replied. 'I'd better get home now; Mum and Dad will wonder where I've got to. Mum will be convinced I've been kidnapped by the enemy; you know how she is.'

I nodded. 'Of course you must go home. Shall I walk up with you?'

She shook her head. 'No, dear heart, I want to get in before midnight and if I get gossiping with you at the gate, we'd still be there in the early hours.'

I placed the palms of my hands on her face and grinned at her. 'It's so lovely to see you. I was beginning to think we might not be together this Christmas.'

'You should know better than that, Alice. I'd have walked all the way back from London just to get my Christmas present from you. I ran out of bath salts earlier in the week.'

'How do you know I bought you bath salts? I might have got you something different this year.'

Amy looked at me seriously. 'You'd better not have. I'm relying on you.'

I looked at her quizzically as I noticed the black hand print on her breast. 'There's a story to be told there too.'

Amy rolled her eyes. 'Don't even ask,' she replied turning around to show me the identical mark on her backside. 'He was a knight in rusty armour. Let's just leave it at that.'

She picked up her case and flicked her head towards the front room. 'I'll go out that way, I want to give you something.'

In the front room, Amy opened her case and pulled out the two, gaily wrapped books.

'The blue is for Stephen and the gold one is for Harriet. They're from Rose, I bought them with your money... there's very little left of that, I'm sorry... Anyway, Rose lost all the presents she had bought in the bombing. She's got nothing but the clothes she's standing up in and she was really upset about not having anything to give them for Christmas.'

She pulled out her purse and handed me a pound note, one ten-shilling note and a handful of change.

'That's it... sorry.'

'It wouldn't have bothered me in the slightest if you'd used all of it up, Amy. That's what it was there for.'

'Well, I did spend some of it on... No! You'll see tomorrow, but I'll pay you back for my share when I give you yours.'

I looked at her quizzically.

'You'll see,' she said with a giggle. 'Meanwhile, here's your share of this.'

Amy pulled out two sheets of the rare as hen's teeth wrapping paper out of her case.

'Oh, my goodness,' I said, holding them to my chest as though they were precious heirlooms. 'How on earth did you manage to get hold of this?'

'I have my ways,' Amy replied. 'Oh, nice sparklies, by the way,' she said, pointing at my neck. 'Godfrey got his present in early I take it. I bet he was wowed by yours.'

'He was,' I said, touching my necklace. 'He thought I was naked in the picture too.'

Amy sighed. 'Men, eh?'

I opened the door for her and she stepped out onto the front yard before turning around to face me.

I looked lovingly down the steps at my best friend, but found myself unable to speak. My eyes glistened as I looked at her. I could feel a huge lump rising in my throat and I knew my voice would break if I spoke.

Amy must have been feeling the same way, because she lifted her head and looked me directly in the eyes, then nodding a curt nod, she turned away and walked towards the lane.

Chapter 37

I took off my necklace and laid it on the velvet cushion in its box and put it on top of the safe, then, after checking my hair in the mirror, I picked up a cardboard box that contained the packs of sweets I'd had made up for the children, and walked back through to the kitchen to say goodnight to my lads and their families.

'Who wants sweets?' I called out of the back door as Barney tipped over the brazier and kicked snow over the still glowing embers.

The kids lined up impatiently, smallest to tallest, and stepped forward one at a time to receive their little bag of sweets and a shiny sixpence. The money would almost certainly be handed over to their parents, to be replaced by a copper penny if they were lucky, but for now, I could tell by their little faces that they felt as rich as Croesus.

I opened the gate and shook the lads' hands as they left, giving their wives a peck on the cheek, spending a little extra time with the three wives whose husbands had left the security of their farm jobs to pull on a uniform and fight for their country on foreign soil. Earlier, I had handed them wage packets with their annual bonus as I was determined to do every year until the boys came home.

Back inside, I found that Miriam had already cleared the table, she waved to me from the sink where she washed bowls while keeping a watchful eye on Rose and the kids.

Rose was sat at the end of the table, her foot still raised on the stool. Stephen and Harriet had pulled seats up as close as they could get. Harriet, just content to sit quietly next to her mother while Stephen waffled on about anything that happened to come into his mind.

I dipped a glass into the punch bowl before Miriam could empty it down the sink, pulled up a chair and sat down a couple of feet away from Rose.

'How are you feeling now, Rose?' I asked as I stretched my hand out towards her.

Rose took it gently in her own. 'I'm fine now, thank you. Tired, but happy.'

She squeezed my hand then looked at her kids and back to me.

'I was worried, I must admit. The kids have been with you so long, I was a little concerned that they might have forgotten me... saw you as their new mum, if you see what I mean.'

My face softened. 'They'll never forget you, Rose. The word 'mum' is seldom off their lips. No one could ever take your place. I wouldn't even try to.'

'I know that now,' Rose said, quietly. 'I did get a bit down at times, especially when I was alone at night.'

'I understand completely,' I replied, 'but I hope the welcome you received from the kids put your mind at rest.'

Rose put an arm around the shoulders of her children and smiled. 'Oh, I've dreamed of that moment for months.'

'And, what perfect timing,' I said. 'When you sang the hopes and fears line of the carol, it summed up everything that we've been feeling here all week. Tonight, our hopes were fulfilled and our fears put right behind us.'

Miriam joined us at the table and we chatted about how the kids were doing at school for a while. Eventually, bored with the topic, Stephen and Harriet left the table, picked up their comics and sat in the big armchairs on either side of the fire.

'Do you think I could have a quick wash before bed?' Rose asked.

'Of course, you can have a bath if you... sorry, you'd struggle with that wouldn't you.'

Rose laughed. 'Can you imagine me lying in the tub in front of the fire with my leg in the air?'

'Oh, we're posh, here,' I said. 'We had a bathroom installed a year or so back.' I pointed to the big Ascot heater on the wall. 'We even have hot water on tap.'

'A bath would be heavenly,' Rose said, 'but I'll settle for a strip wash.' She looked from me to Miriam. 'I don't suppose you have a dress, or some trousers and a jumper I could borrow until I can get this lot washed.' She looked down at her dress, then lifted her arm and sniffed. 'Oh my God, I hope the soap has a strong scent. I probably need Carbolic.'

Miriam got to her feet and hurried upstairs. When she returned, she was carrying a pair of flannelette knickers and a warm, winter dress.

'This should fit you, Rose, you look to be about my size. The knickers are brand new, they've never been worn,' she added quickly.

'We'll take you up to Woolworths to get some new underwear on Boxing Day,' I promised. 'We can drop into Stan's nearly new shop too, there are always some nice second-hand clothes in there. That should keep you going until you get on your feet again.'

Rose shook her head. 'You're both so kind,' she said huskily.

When Rose had washed and changed, Miriam dropped her dirty clothes into the washing basket in the parlour before stepping back into the kitchen.

'All right, you two,' she addressed the children. 'Come on, time for bed. Santa won't come until you're fast asleep.'

Rose struggled to her feet. 'Do you think I could see them to bed tonight?'

'Oh, Rose, you don't have to ask. Let me give you a hand up the stairs,' I said, getting quickly to my feet.

'Don't forget to hang your stockings up,' Miriam called as the excited kids rushed up the stairs. 'They're lying on the bottom of your beds.'

Miriam had stashed the two heavily darned silk stockings in her mending basket weeks before.

I gave them fifteen minutes before I climbed the stairs. Rose was turning out the light as she came out of the kid's bedroom.

'Where am I sleeping, Alice? I'm so tired I could sleep on a clothes line.'

I led her along the passage until we got to Miriam's room.

'You're in here tonight,' I said. 'You should be comfy enough; Miriam has a double bed.'

'I couldn't take her bed; she's done so much for me already.'

'It's all right,' I replied. 'She's bunking up with me, it won't be the first time.'

'But...'

'We've almost finished clearing out the spare bedroom. It should have been ready for you but it all got a bit hectic today. There's a nice bed in there and it won't need airing. I had a lodger until a few weeks ago. A police detective, believe it or not.'

'If you're sure. I really don't want to make life difficult.'

I opened the door and showed her inside. 'I'll bring you a glass of water when I come up to collect the kid's stockings. Do you mind if we fill them downstairs? You're more than welcome to do it if you'd rather.'

'No, please, I'm so tired.'

I stepped into the room and switched on Miriam's bedside lamp.

'Just shout if you need anything... oh, there's a pot under the bed here.' I knelt down and pulled out the porcelain chamber pot. 'I'll leave it at the end of the bed for you. That'll save you trying to get up and down the stairs in the night.'

After closing Miriam's door behind me, I stole into the kid's room without turning on the light and retrieved the two stockings from the ends of their beds. Tiptoeing out of the room, I smiled to myself as I remembered the Christmas mornings when, as a child, I had woken up to find a full stocking on the end of my bed, the first clue that Santa had paid a visit during the night.

Back in the kitchen Miriam and I sipped milky Ovaltine as we stuffed the stockings full of Christmas goodies.

Right at the bottom of the stocking, in the toe section, we left two bun pennies, a threepenny bit and a sixpence, on top of those we added a handful of mixed nuts, almonds, hazel and brazils, the latter had been particularly hard to get hold of this year. On top of those we pushed in an orange and an apple, then a small pack of cards, Snap for Harriet, Old Maid for Stephen. On top of those we stuffed in the latest edition of the Dandy and Beano comics, then right at the top, three cowboy figures and three Indian braves for Stephen and two doll's dresses that Harriet had spotted in the box at Stan's Emporium.

Satisfied with our efforts, I smiled at Miriam and flicked my head towards the door. 'Why should I have all the fun?'

A delighted Miriam, picked up the stockings and crept across the kitchen floor as though it was the floor of the kid's bedroom. Only two minutes later, her head appeared around the door. Her face dripping with tears. She beckoned me with her fingers and I got to my feet and followed her up the stairs. 'In there,' she whispered, pointing towards her own bedroom door.

I eased open the door and stuck my head inside. By the light of the landing behind me, I could see Rose, lying on her back in the centre of the bed, on either side, snuggled up close and with a loving mother's arm around each of them, were Harriet and Stephen. My heart almost burst with happiness.

Miriam nudged me and passed me a stocking, then flicked her head towards the bedroom. I eased the door open a little further and crept into the room, hanging the top of the stocking over a bed post. Turning around, I repeated the process with the other stocking, before backing out and closing the door quietly behind me.

I returned to the kitchen still wiping my eyes and walked directly to the cupboard under the stairs. Pulling the key from my pocket, I unlocked the door and began to pass the Christmas presents to Miriam.

When the cupboard was empty of gifts, I suddenly remembered the books and wrapping paper that Amy had handed to me, and after retrieving them from the front room, I made rough gift tags for the books and wrote Stephen and Harriet's names on them. Then picking up the gift that I'd bought for Rose, I carefully cut a strip of the precious wrapping paper and made a neat package. When Miriam came in from the bathroom, I handed the astonished woman a sheet of gold and yellow paper and picked up Amy's bath salts, already knowing that I had, once again, chosen the perfect gift for her.

Just before heading off to bed, I walked through to the parlour and carried the big wooden clothes horse through to the kitchen. Placing it strategically so that no one would be able to see what was hiding behind it, I draped a thick blanket over it, wrote a quick note on a scrap of paper and pinned it to the woollen bedcover. Then, taking one last look around the kitchen, I switched out the light and made my way to bed.

Chapter 38

Alice
Wednesday 25th December

I was up at my usual time on Christmas Day, determined to get the pigs cleaned and fed before the kids woke up. The snow storm had blown over and as I stepped out of the back door I was treated to a beautiful, pale blue, winter sky.

Whistling as I worked, I got the job done in record time and I returned to the kitchen just as Miriam was pulling the big iron skillet from the rack.

'Breakfast? Or shall we have it later with the others?'

'Let's have a mid-morning breakfast,' I said. 'Mind you, I wouldn't mind a bacon sandwich to keep me going.'

Miriam dropped a knob of lard into the pan and added four thick rashers of bacon. After pouring boiling water into the tea pot, she put the lid on and placed it in the centre of the table.

Half an hour later, my rumbling stomach had been calmed and I got up from the table, opened the door to the stairs, stuck my head around the corner and listened.

'SANTA'S BEEN!' Stephen's voice echoed around the landing.

I held two thumbs up to Miriam and began to climb the stairs. Tapping on the already open door, I peeped inside. 'There's tea in the pot, Rose,' I said.

'Come in, Alice, please come in.'

Rose was sitting up in the centre of the bed grinning like the Cheshire Cat as Stephen and Harriet explored the contents of their stockings.

'Tea would be lovely,' she said, finally managing to drag her eyes away from the children.

'I'll bring you a cup up,' I said.

Twenty-five minutes later, I helped Rose negotiate the last couple of steps as Stephen and Harriet stood impatiently behind.

As she swung herself into the kitchen on her crutches the children immediately filled the gap she had left, then with whoops of joy, they rushed across to the Christmas tree, Stephen sliding the last few feet on his stomach.

'Miriam, Alice, Harriet...' he shouted as he pushed the newspaper wrapped parcels out of the way.

'Whoa, there,' I said, chuckling to myself. I grabbed hold of his feet and slid him out from under the tree. 'One for each person please, then you can open some of yours.'

Stephen grinned his cheeky grin and I ruffled his hair. 'Okay, pass them around, Santa must have put all yours at the back.'

Stephen picked up Miriam's first parcel and handed it to her. 'For Miriam, from Alice,' he read.

'Ooh, I wonder what this is,' Miriam pressed at the large, soft parcel.

'Rose...? Oh, that's you, Mum.'

'Me? I didn't expect to get anything.'

'Santa doesn't forget anyone,' Harriet said, watching her mother with an excited face as she eased the newspaper from her gift.

'Oh, that's so lovely,' she said with a broken voice. 'Pirates... my pirates. Whose idea was the parrot?' She looked at the kids with glistening eyes and ran her hand softly over the glass. 'I'll treasure this,' she said quietly.

'Here's one for Aunty Alice... from... MIRIAM!' Stephen yelled.

'Shhh, you'll wake the neighbours,' I said.

'But they live half a mile away,' Stephen replied.

'Exactly my point,' I said, tearing open my gift which turned out to be a knitted hat and scarf. 'Bless you, Miriam.' I smiled across the room. 'Open yours then.'

Miriam tore the package open and pulled out a powder blue dressing gown. 'Oh, my... this is the one I was looking at in town, how did you know?'

I tapped the side of my nose and winked at Stephen who had been my informant.

'Harriet... from Miriam and Alice.'

Harriet snatched the parcel from her brother's hands and tore it open.

'A DOLL, A NEW DOLL!' she squealed.

Stephen looked at me expectantly and I nodded my head. Pulling out a few more packages, he selected a curiously shaped parcel and ripped it open. Inside was a cowboy set, including a hat, a gun-belt with a holster, a silver pistol and a shiny sheriff's star.

Pinning the star to his pyjama jacket, he stuck the hat on his head, pulled out the gun and fired it into the air.

'There are some caps in there too,' Miriam said, 'but they're only to be used outside. They're much too loud for indoors.'

Martha was standing in her playpen pointing at the gifts under the tree. 'Santa,' she said.

Sorting through the parcels, I found one of the gifts I had bought for her, then lifting her out of the pen, I sat her on the kitchen floor and helped her open her present.

'Piggy!' she cried, grabbing at the toy.

I blew out a sigh of relief as she got to her feet and began to drag the pink-painted wooden dog around the kitchen making grunting noises. Her imagination matched mine, it seemed.

When I had returned Martha and her new pet pig to her pen, I walked back to my seat by the table to be solemnly presented with a gift by Harriet as Stephen passed a small, thin package to Miriam.

'We made them at school for you,' she said, proudly.

I removed the triple wrapped parcel carefully. Inside was a sheet of cardboard with a winter scene painted onto it. At the bottom was a two-inch square, 1941 calendar.

'Do you like it?' Harriet asked, seriously.

'I absolutely love it,' I replied, giving her a hug. 'This will take pride of place on the wall next to my desk.' I gave her a big smile and glanced at Miriam who was hugging Stephen's last breath out of him.

After opening a parcel each from Amy, which contained three sets of doll's clothes for Harriet and a pirate's eye patch and cutlass for Stephen, the kids pulled out one of the remaining three parcels from under the tree.

'Here's another one for Mum,' Harriet called after returning to the tree.

'For me? I really wasn't expecting...'

'Open it, Mum, it's from Aunty Alice and Aunty Miriam.'

Rose eased the packaging from her gift and unfolded the paper to find a bottle of Rose water and a tube of scented hand cream.

'We weren't sure what to get you,' I said, apologetically.

'It's a lovely thought,' Rose said with a smile, 'but I don't have anything to give you.'

I put my arm around her shoulder and kissed her cheek. 'Your presence is enough,' I whispered. 'Please, don't fret.'

Rose nodded and wiped her eyes on her sleeve.

'Martha, from Amy.'

I carried Amy's gift and three other presents for my toddler across to the playpen and helped my excited daughter to open them. Building blocks from Amy, picture books from Miriam and a brown, fluffy Teddy bear from me.

'Stephen... and Harriet,' Stephen pulled two more parcels from beneath the tree. 'From Aunty Alice.'

He passed the gold-coloured package to his sister, then tore open his own parcel.

'Treasure Island,' he said, reading from the cover of the book. 'PIRATES! Thanks, Aunty Alice.'

Harriet gently removed the gaily coloured wrapping from her parcel, turning it over in her hands, she stroked the beautifully drawn horse on the book cover, then looked up to me with a grin. 'Thank you, Aunty Alice. I've been trying to get this out of the library for ages.'

Rose looked towards me and lifted her hands palms up, obviously puzzled. 'I thought that I was...'

I shook my head and put my finger to my lips. 'Shh.'

Getting up from my seat, I strode to the back of the room where the blanket-covered clothes horse had remained unnoticed.

'What's this doing here?' I said with a look of puzzlement on my face.

Stephen and Harriet moved across to my side.

'There's something pinned onto it. What does it say?'

Stephen tore the scrap of paper from the blanket.

'To Stephen and Harriet. Love, Mum and Dad,' he read.

'Why did you buy us a blanket?' Harriet said with a laugh.

'Oh, I don't think you should be concentrating on the blanket, but what's behind it,' I said.

I took hold of the blanket and whipped it aside like a magician revealing a vase of flowers. Behind the timber frame of the clothes horse sat a wooden fort complete with Cavalry soldiers on the battlements and half a dozen, headdress clad Red Indian warriors aiming their arrows towards them. At the side of the fort was a large, three-foot tall, white-painted dolls house, opened at the front, displaying a plethora of fully furnished rooms.

The kids didn't make a sound as their jaws dropped open, then Stephen finally found his voice.

'But... but they were sold. We saw them in the shop with a sold sign on them.'

'Mum and Dad bought them to be picked up by Santa,' I replied, winking at Rose who was about to burst into tears yet again.

'Thank you,' she mouthed. 'Thank you.'

Chapter 39

Amy arrived at ten-thirty; her arms full of beautifully wrapped presents. Dropping them onto the table she gave everyone a hug while wishing us all a happy Christmas.

'Oh my, you have done well,' she said to Stephen and Harriet.

'Thank you for the doll's clothes,' Harriet said.

'And, thank you for the pirate set,' Stephen added, waving the cutlass at her.

Amy stepped over to the playpen where Martha was stacking up the brightly coloured wooden blocks that she had bought her.

'Clever girl,' she said, as Martha swung her arm, knocking her wobbly tower over.

Miriam pushed a cup of tea towards Amy as she took off her coat and hung it on the back door.

'Right,' she said, picking up one of her parcels. 'Santa appears to have left these at my house by mistake.' She handed a present to Miriam. 'This is for you, my darling, happy Christmas.'

Miriam smiled broadly and tore open the soft package.

'OH MY!' she said, lifting up a pair of silk Cami knickers and a soft white slip. She held them to her face and cooed.

'That'll make your John's eyes water,' Amy said with a wink.

'He won't see me in these... not until I've got a ring on my finger.'

Miriam had been engaged in an on-off romance with our local builder, John for over a year but the widower had yet to propose, despite Miriam's many hints.

'This one's for you,' Amy said, smiling at Rose.

'For me?'

Amy nodded quickly and handed her a soft, gift-wrapped package.

Rose carefully opened the present and held up her own pair of knickers and a silk slip.

'I made these myself. I thought they'd come in handy, things being as they are,' Amy said with a grin.

'You made these?' Rose looked at the beautifully sewn garments. 'They're better than shop bought.'

'Parachute silk,' Amy replied. 'Only the best for my friends.'

'And now, for my best friend ever.' Amy turned to me, wrapped her arms around my neck and whispered, 'Merry Christmas,' in my ear before handing me my gift.

I took my time opening it, much to Amy's annoyance.

'Yours took a bit longer, due to your matronly hips,' she said, her eyes bright.

I pulled out my silk knickers and slip, then noticed something else in the pack.

'NYLONS! My God, Amy, where on earth did you get these from?'

'London,' Amy said with a nonchalant air. 'You can buy anything there if you know where to look.'

'But... Oh, I'm not going to delve any further.' I hugged her again. 'You've used a lot of silk on us, Amy, do you have anything left over for yourself?'

'Scraps,' said Amy. 'I gave my set to Rose as I didn't have time to buy her anything else.'

'Oh, no, please, I've been so lucky already, please... you have them.,' Rose said, offering the garments to Amy.

'Not likely,' Amy said. 'Don't worry about me, I'll just have to tap up Jimmy the rope man again.' She narrowed her eyes as she looked across the room at Miriam. 'I'm going to have to ask him for enough silk to make a wedding dress and a Christening gown as it is, what difference will one extra panel make?'

As Amy sipped her tea, I handed her the two remaining gifts from beneath the tree. She shook them and opened Miriam's first.

'Oh, look at these,' she said, holding up a beautifully knitted hat, scarf and mittens set. 'Thank you, my darling.'

'You'll never guess what's in that one,' I said, pointing to my gift.

Amy shook it, then prodded at it before pulling open the wrapping.

'Well, I never,' she said, lifting up the huge jar of her favourite bath salts and unscrewing the lid to take a sniff. 'I know what I'm going to be doing tonight.'

At twelve-thirty, Amy pulled on her coat and left the house, promising to return at tea time.

'We're going to Aunty Madge's for Christmas dinner. She's a miser, so our plates will have hardly any food on them. Make sure you save some turkey sandwiches for me.'

That afternoon, after clearing the dinner plates from the table, I sat in my armchair by the fire with Miriam sitting opposite, for once, not clicking her needles.

I looked around the kitchen. The kids were playing with their big presents as Rose sat quietly at the table watching them with a look of pure love on her face. Martha was asleep in her pen, her chubby little arm wrapped around her pull-along pig.

I checked the big clock on the wall. Amy would be back in an hour or so. I was dying to hear about her adventures in London, but most of all, I wanted her company. When she arrived, we'd start the Christmas evening ritual by carrying my record player from the front room before clearing the decks and spending the next couple of hours dancing to my small, but wonderful record collection.

I sighed happily as I sipped at my glass of port. It had been a stressful week but everything had turned out right in the end. Raising my glass, I silently wished Godfrey a happy Christmas, then, after putting the port on the wide chair arm, I reached down and stroked Tess, my gorgeous Border Collie pup. Hearing something scratching at the back door, I got up to investigate. I opened the door with a puzzled look on my face and found my old feral cat, Jemima, aka Slasher, sitting on the top step.

Jemima was a champion ratter and shunned people, preferring to live in the barn with the chickens. She was fourteen years old and no one but me was ever allowed to pat her. I had rescued her as a tiny kitten when my father had found her in the barn.

'Hello, Jemima,' I said, reaching down to pat her head.

She purred as I ran my hand down her back, then, to my amazement, she slipped through the door and sauntered across the kitchen to the rug in front of the fire. Tess watched her warily, she had had one or two confrontations with her out in the yard.

‘Slasher?’ Miriam said, her mouth dropping open. She had never wandered into the house before.

Jemima flopped down on the rug and began to clean herself. I shrugged, pulled a chunk of turkey from the carcass and laid it down next to my old pet.

‘Merry Christmas, Jemima,’ I said, stroking her again, delighted that she had finally decided to become part of the family.

I returned to my chair and picked up my glass of port as, for some reason I couldn’t fathom, the words of Tiny Tim from the Dicken’s Christmas Carol novel, came into my head.

‘God bless us, every one,’ I said.

The End

Thank you for reading Hopes and Fears, I hope you enjoyed it. I would like to take this opportunity to wish all of my readers a very Merry Christmas and a happy and prosperous New Year.

T. A. Belshaw

If you enjoyed Hopes and Fears you might also like the Unspoken trilogy which features many of the characters found in this book. Signed copies of all my novels are available on request.

Email: author@trevorbelshaw.com or find me on Facebook.

Unspoken

A heart-warming, dramatic family saga. Unspoken is a tale of secrets, love, betrayal and revenge.

Unspoken means something that cannot be uttered aloud. Unspoken is the dark secret a woman must keep, for life.

Alice is fast approaching her one hundredth birthday and she is dying. Her strange, graphic dreams of ghostly figures trying to pull her into a tunnel of blinding light are becoming more and more vivid and terrifying. Alice knows she only has a short time left and is desperate to unburden herself of a dark secret, one she has lived with for eighty years.

Jessica, a journalist, is her great granddaughter and a mirror image of a young Alice. They share dreadful luck in the types of men that come into their lives.

Alice decides to share her terrible secret with Jessica and sends her to the attic to retrieve a set of handwritten notebooks detailing her young life during the late 1930s. Following the death of her invalid mother and her father's decline into depression and alcoholism, she is forced, at 18 to take control of the farm. On her birthday, she meets

Frank, a man with a drink problem and a violent temper. When Frank's abusive behaviour steps up a level. Alice seeks solace in the arms of her smooth, 'gangster lawyer' Godfrey, and when Frank discovers the couple together, he vows to get his revenge.
Unspoken. A tale that spans two eras and binds two women, born eighty years apart.

An emotional read that had me hooked very quickly. The characters are written well & I had quite an affection for Alice and felt for the hard life she had led. A great start to the series.

Dee Groocock

I'd highly recommend this book to anyone looking for a heart-warming story full of grit, humour and a great deal of love. No hesitation in giving it a well-deserved 5-star rating.

Joy Wood. Author.

This is a super family saga with well-drawn characters who will stay with me for a long time.

Teresa B.

The Legacy

Where there's a will there's a rift.

The Legacy continues the story of Jessica Griffiths and her fractious relationship with her grandmother, Martha, her gambling addicted father and her narcissistic ex, Calvin who refuses to accept that their relationship is over.
Jessica an aspiring novelist, is writing a book based on her great grandmother's hand written memoirs. Still grieving for Alice, she receives a telephone call that will change her life, and her relationship with her family, forever.
During the process she meets Bradley, a handsome young lawyer. Calvin, meanwhile, believes he can work his way back into Jess's life by fair means or foul.
When Martha, the matriarch, complains that she hasn't been treated fairly, she puts pressure on her granddaughter to 'do the right thing.' Meanwhile, Jessica's father returns with the loan sharks on his tail.
As Jessica prays that the 'man curse' which has plagued the women in her family for generations, has finally been vanquished, she meets the beautiful, calculating, Leonora, a woman with a secret and a fondness for mischief.

Superbly written from the author, and very much look forward to more to come.
Booklover Bev

I did not want to put this book down.
P. M. Millward

I went through every emotion as the story unfolded.
M. Meredith

The Reckoning

Unspoken. Part Three

After a fractious few months trying to appease her dysfunctional family, Jessica Griffiths realises that her great grandmother Alice's legacy has become a millstone around her neck.

With her feisty elderly relatives cruising around the South China Sea she is hoping for a less stressful time, but when Leonora, the meddling ex-wife of her lawyer boyfriend begins to plot and with her own ex, Calvin unable to accept that their relationship is over, she begins to feel the pressure mounting again.

Into the mix walks Josh, the handsome young café owner. Jess is drawn to him immediately. Will he be the one to finally break the Mollison man curse?

Jessica discovers new family secrets as she continues to read through Alice's wartime diaries but more shocks await as Martha hands over her own disturbing memoirs.

With the cruise ship in trouble and problems nearer to home, Jess finds herself at the centre of another family maelstrom.
Feeling desperately alone and with the weight of the world on her shoulders, can she weather the storm with her family and sanity intact?

I read this book in three sessions and didn't want it to end.

Pollyfloss

The writing flows so easily making the stories effortless to read.

Jane Porter

Amazing writer, can't wait for his next book.
Carol Broadbent

Murder at the Mill

A Gripping New Cosy Crime Series with a light hearted touch.

January 1939 and the residents of the snow-covered streets of a small Kentish town awake to horrific news.
When young Amy Rowlings meets Detective Sergeant Bodkin at the scene of a burglary on the way to work at The Mill one snowy January morning, she is blissfully unaware of how much her life is about to change.
She is drawn into the murky world of murder when the body of Edward Handsley is found lying on the floor of the clothing factory.
Edward, the son of factory owner George is a libertine, philanderer, and a young man with a lot of enemies, many of them female.
Twenty-one-year-old Amy is a vivacious, quick-witted collector of imported American music, a movie buff and an avid reader of crime fiction. A girl who can spot whodunnit long before the film star detective gets an inkling.
Bodkin is new to the area and accepts Amy's offer to provide local knowledge but she soon becomes an invaluable source of information. When Adam Smethwick is arrested for the murder, Amy, a family friend, is convinced of his innocence and sets out to prove that the detective has arrested the wrong man.
Amy befriends Justine, the young French fiancé of the elderly George, and soon discovers that it was not all sweetness and light in the Handsley family home.

Meanwhile, back at the factory, Amy is sure that the foreman, Mr Pilling, has something to hide.
As the investigation proceeds, Amy finds that her burgeoning relationship with Bodkin is pushed to the limits as the detective becomes even more convinced that he has arrested the right man and while Bodkin relies heavily on the facts as they are presented, Amy has a more nuanced approach to solving the crime, born out of her beloved Agatha Christie books and the crimes she has witnessed in the movies.

It was good to meet characters from the family saga Unspoken, yet this book can be read independently. Five stars out of five.

Beverley Lucas

Amy is a fun, caring and funny character who will stop at nothing to solve the crime!

Paula Guy

Sit back and enjoy as Amy joins forces with Bodkin and they piece together a plot with many twists and turns. As in real life, there are many secrets to unfold.

Little Bird

Printed in Great Britain
by Amazon

67996293R00159